David Laing

Early Scottish metrical Tales

David Laing

Early Scottish metrical Tales

ISBN/EAN: 9783337024833

Printed in Europe, USA, Canada, Australia, Japan

Cover: Foto ©Andreas Hilbeck / pixelio.de

More available books at **www.hansebooks.com**

EARLY SCOTTISH
METRICAL TALES

EDITED, WITH INTRODUCTIONS

BY

DAVID LAING, LL.D.,

Editor of " The Ancient Popular Poetry of Scotland," etc., etc.

NEW EDITION

LONDON: HAMILTON, ADAMS & CO
GLASGOW: THOMAS D. MORISON
1889

PUBLISHERS' NOTE.

IN issuing a new edition of this interesting work, the publishers have only to remark that it is printed verbatim from the edition issued by the distinguished editor. In every instance the original spelling is adhered to. Careful attention and effect has also been given to the considerable list of *errata* detailed at the end of the original edition.

CONTENTS.

THE PREFACE.

THE Metrical Tales and Romance Poems peculiar to this Country, are very inconsiderable in number, when compared with those which belong to the Sister-Kingdom. But from various allusions to be found to the number and popularity of such compositions in Scotland, at an early period, it is evident that this portion of our Ancient Literature, in its transmission to modern times, must have suffered in a more than common degree. Nor indeed was it to be conceived, at the time " *Quhen gude Makars rang weill into Scotlànd,*" that our native Minstrels should have been behind their neighbours, either for invention, or facility of composition, in thus contributing to the amusement of their countrymen. In proof of the general esteem in which these works of fiction were held, it may here be sufficient to mention what has been incidentally recorded of two of the most renowned of the Scotish Monarchs.

When the followers of Robert the Bruce, in his retreat to the Isle of Rachrin, at the close of the year 1306, had to be ferried over Lochlomond in a boat, which held but three persons at a time, that " gude King," is said, by his venerable biographer, to have amused them for " a night and a day," by reading portions of the Romance of Ferumbrace.[1] After giving a brief detail of that part of

---

[1] This is evidently the Romance of Fierabras, but it must have been a different and earlier translation from the French, than that quoted by Mr. Ellis in his abstract of the story. (*Metrical Romances*, vol. ii. p. 369, &c.)

the narrative, which relates how Roland and his companions, the *dousiperes* of France, with only one attendant, manfully held out the Tower of Egrymor, when besieged by the Soudan of Babylon, and a whole host of Sarazens, the Archdeacon of Aberdeen declares—

> The gud King apon this máner
> Comfort thaim that war him ner ;
> And maid thaim gamyn and solace,
> Till that his folk all passyt was.[2]

From the same authority we learn, that on other occasions, Robert the Bruce was wont to "comfort" his adherents in their difficulties by relating to them

> Auld storyis of men that wer
> Set in tyll hard assayis ser.

The other instance alluded to, is of James the First of Scotland, who, according to the contemporaneous narrative of the very tragical fate of that accomplished Prince, spent the night previous to his assassination, *yn* REDYNG OF ROMANS, *yn syngyng and pypynge, yn harpyng, and yn other honest solaces of grete pleasance and disport.*

Were direct evidence, therefore, wanting, we might be warranted to infer that compositions which afforded delight, and were familiar to our Kings, would neither be unknown nor disregarded by their subjects. But deeply as we cannot but regret the loss which the early Literature of Scotland has sustained in the almost total destruction of these tales of romantick and legendary fiction,—it is a subject of inquiry, which might lead to a discussion disproportionate to the size and contents of this volume. One circumstance, however, may be mentioned, to shew that these compositions were not

---

[2] Barbour's Bruce, book ii. line 858-962. Dr. Jamieson's 4to. edit. 1820.

uncommon *in a written state*, at a remote period; although, with the exception of charters, hardly any MSS. (and not one in verse,) written in Scotland, are known to be extant of an older date than the middle of the Fifteenth Century:—Sir James Douglas of Dalkeith, the ancestor of the Earls of Morton, in his Last Will and Testament, dated in the year 1390, bequeaths to his son and heir, " OMNES LIBROS MEOS TAM STATUTORUM REGNI SCOCIE QUAM ROMANCIE." [3]

IN the present volume, a few Metrical Tales, from copies of a comparatively recent date, are collected, together with some Scotish poems, which appear to have enjoyed more than a common degree of popularity. That most of these existed in copies of a much earlier time, will be seen from the respective notices which are subjoined. The chief object in submitting this little collection to the Publick is, the hope that it may be the means of bringing some of these productions to light, in a more antique garb.[4] But whether or not the appearance of this volume shall contribute in any way to a more careful and extended research after such Remains, the Editor flatters himself that he performs an acceptable service in rendering attainable some few of these ‘delectable’ compositions, which even in their present state, (modernized and corrupted as most of them confessedly are,) will nevertheless be allowed to possess no ordinary charms

[3] Original deed, in the possession of the Earl of Morton.
[4] This little collection may be considered as forming a supplement to a volume printed about three years ago, under the title of *Select Pieces of the Ancient Popular Poetry of Scotland.* In the view of republishing this work, the Editor may here take the opportunity to solicit information on the subject, entertaining the hopes, that it is still possible to retrieve many more of these ANCIENT RELICKS from unmerited neglect and oblivion.

for those who are gratified with the simple and unaffected strains which gave delight to our ancestors.   To such as feel any interest in the revival of the literary productions of remoter ages, the Editor may use the words of an old English writer, and say,

> " Accept my paynes, allow me thankes,
>   If I deserue the same,
> If not, yet lette not meaning well
>   Be payde with checke and blame.
> For I am he that buylde the bowre,
>   I hewe the hardened stone ;
> And thou art owner of the house,
>   The paine is mine alone.
> I burne the bee, I hold the hyue,
>   The Sommer toyle is myne ;
> And all bicause when Winter commes
>   The honie may be thine." [5]

EDINBURGH :
JUNE, MDCCCXXV.

I.

THE HISTORY OF SIR GRAY-STEILL.

THIS is the Romance of *Eger and Grime,* which Bishop Percy says, "is a well invented tale of Chivalry, scarce inferior to any of Ariosto's ; " [6] and of which Mr. George Ellis has given an extended analysis.[7]   That it was extremely popular in Scotland for a length of time, will

   [5] " Tragical Tales, &e., by George Turbervile.   Imprinted at London, by Abell Ieffs, 1587."   8vo. bl. l. sign. Biii.
   [6] Reliques of Ancient English Poetry, 4th edit. vol. iii. p. xxxviii.
   [7] Specimens of English Metrical Romances, vol. iii. p. 308 to 357.

appear from various allusions which it may here be proper to specify. Indeed, this Romance would seem, along with the poems of Sir David Lyndsay, and the histories of Robert the Bruce, and of Sir William Wallace, to have formed the standard productions of the vernacular literature of the country. The author of *The Scots Hudibras,* originally printed at London, 1681, under the title of a *Mock Poem, or the Whigg's Supplication,* in describing Ralph's Library, says,

> And there lyes books, and here lyes ballads,
> As Davie Lindsay, and GRAY-STEEL,
> Squire Meldrum, Bevis, and Adam Bell ;
> There Bruce and Wallace.—

To this effect, John Taylor, " the Water Poet," a noted character in the reign of Charles I., speaks of *Sir Degre, Sir Grime, and Sir Gray Steele,* as having the same popularity in Scotland, that the Heroes of other romances enjoyed in their respective countries—"*filling,* (as he quaintly says) *whole volumes, with the ayrie imaginations of their unknowne and unmatchable worths.*"[8] We might readily believe, therefore, that this Romance had been often printed, if we were otherwise ignorant of the fact,— and yet, it is remarkable enough, that every ancient copy should have hitherto eluded the most active and unremitting research.

The earliest printed edition of which we can find any special notice, is one presumed to be from the press of Thomas Bassandyne, who is celebrated in our typographical annals as the first Printer of the Sacred Scriptures in Scotland. In an Inventory of his goods and stock in

---

[8] Argument to the verses in Praise of the Great O'Toole, originally printed 1623, 8vo., and included in Taylor's Works, 1634, folio, sign. Bb. 2.

trade, inserted in his "Testament Testamentar," which is dated 18th October, 1577, amongst a variety of other works, the following *item* occurs:

"IIIᶜ GRAY STEILLIS," valued at the "pece VIᵈ.— Summa £VII. X. O."—It is not the sum total of these three hundred copies which should deprive the writer of this notice, from *one* of the said *Gray-Steillis*, were he so fortunate as meet with it. But, alas! what has become of them?

This edition is evidently the one referred to in a poetical tract of that age, which says,—

> Even of GRAY STEILL, quha list to luke,
> *Thair is set fwrth* A MEIKLE BUKE.[9]

It may be inferred that there were many subsequent editions, as we find *Gray Steill* enumerated amongst the books for which Robert Smyth, Printer in Edinburgh,

---

[9] The poem quoted, is entitled "A Memorial of the life and death "of two vvorthye Christians, Robert Campbel of the Kinyeancleugh, "and his Wife Elizabeth Campbel. In English Meter. Edinbvrgh, "printed by Robert Wal-de-graue, Printer to the King's Majestie. "1595." sm. 8vo.

The author, John Davidson, (who was then a preacher in Edinburgh, and afterwards a minister at Salt Preston), says, in the dedication, that it was written 21 years before, that is, in 1574. The following lines form the commencement of the poem:

> " Sen Poets in all times before,
> Set all their care, and endéuore
> Of worthie persons for to write ;
> Whan euer thay saw them delite,
> In wisdome, justice, or manheid,
> Or any other vertuous deid : . . .
> As of those Campions most strong
> The Trojanes, and the Greeks among
> Did Homer write, and Seneca,
> Virgil, Ouid and many ma :

Renowmed Romanes to rehearse
Wants not their worthies put in verse :
So, we finde deeds of vassalage
Set foorth by Poets in all age,
Euen of Gray-Steill, wha list to luke,
Their is set foorth a meikle buke,
Yea, for to make it did them gude,
Of that rank Rouer Robene Hude :
Of Robene Hude and little Johne,
With sik like Outlaws many one
As Clim of the Clewgh and Cliddislie,
Because of their fine archerie :
Sen men I say than," &c.

obtained in 1599 a grant, under the Privy Seal, of the privilege and license of printing; which grant was successively confirmed to the sons and heirs of Smyth, in 1602; to Thomas Finlayson, in 1606; and to his son and successor, Walter Finlayson, in 1628.

But the only printed copy the Editor has yet been able to meet with, is one under this title :

THE

HISTORY

OF

Sir EGER,

Sir GRAHAME,

AND

Sir GRAY-STEEL.

Newly Corrected and amended.

Printed in the Year 1711.

This edition (in 12mo, pp. 84.) was printed at Aberdeen,

by James Nicol, Printer to the Town and University.[10]
The original is in the possession of Francis Douce, Esq.,
being the identical copy made use of by Mr. Ellis, whose
transcripts of this and other old Metrical Romances, are
now in the library at Abbotsford, having been presented
by Mr. Ellis's relations to Sir Walter Scott. The Editor's
best acknowledgements are due to his friend Mr. Douce,
for the kind manner in which he favoured him with the
loan of the volume for the purpose of re-publication; and
it is gratifying thus to bear testimony to the kindness
and liberality which this gentleman displays in facilitating
literary inquiries, and contributing to the revival and
preservation of (what Master Spenser has denominated)
thinges forgone.

We know, however, that the Romance of Gray Steill
was popular in Scotland, long previous to the date of any
of the editions which have been alluded to. *Syr Egeir
and Sir Gryme* is mentioned in the *Complaynt of Scotland,*
1549, in the number of such "stories" and "tayles" as
were common to the people. Sir David Lyndsay, in his
History of Squire Meldrum, written about the same time,
says of his hero,

> I wate he faucht that day als weill
> As did Schir Gryme aganis Gray Steill[11]

And again, in the Interlude of *The Auld Man and his
Wife,* Lyndsay introduces one of the characters, as a
braggart, saying,

---

[10] The place of printing, and the Printer's name, do not appear on
the original title-page; but bound in the same volume, is an edition
of Squire Meldrum, and of Bevis of Southampton, which mention
these particulars, and all the three are most unquestionably from the
same press.

[11] Lyndsay's Works, by Chalmers, vol. ii. p. 296.

Now, is nocht this ane grit dispyte,
That nane with me will fecht, nor flyte !
War Golias, into this steid,
I dowt nocht to stryk off his head !—
This is the sword that slew GRAY STEILL
Nocht half a myle beyond Kinneill. [12]

A notice of a still earlier date will be found in the following entries in the Treasurer's Accounts for the year 1497,
at the time when our gallant Monarch, James IV. was
resident at Stirling.

"ITEM, the xvij day of Aprile giffyn to the King that he
"tynt [lost, in shooting] at the buttis in Strivelin,   vij^s."

"ITEM, that samyn day to twa fithelaris that SANG
"GRAY STEIL to the King—ix^s."

It would elsewhere appear that this Romance had been
set to some particular tune, to which it may have been
chaunted.   In a curious Manuscript volume, formerly in
the possession of Dr. Burney, entitled "*An Playing Booke
for the Lute*"—"*Noted and Collected*" at Aberdeen, by
Robert Gordon, in the year 1627, is the air of a "GRAY-
STEEL ;" and there is a satirical poem on the Marquis of
Argyle, printed in 1686, which is said "*to be composed in
Scottish rhyme,*" and is "appointed to be sung according
to the tune of OLD GRAY STEEL."

Besides these allusions, other evidence of the popularity
of this Romance might have been adduced from common
sayings, and proverbial expressions which are current to
this day, in various parts of the country, although all
knowledge of the hero and his exploits have long since
ceased to be remembered.

In the present copy of the Romance, as Mr. Ellis
remarks, "the Printer has evidently followed a very imperfect Manuscript, with which also he seems to have

---

[12] Bannatyne's Manuscript, fol. 167.

taken great liberties, and the story, as it now stands, is so obscurely told, that the catastrophe is quite unintelligible;"[13] and which, in Mr. Ellis's abstract, is supplied by conjecture. The reader indeed cannot fail to perceive, that in many places the sense is very obscure, and the transitions abrupt, all of which are to be attributed to the corruptions it has undergone. As an instance of this, it is observable that the name of the *actual* hero, Sir Gryme, is converted to Sir Grahame. Another copy, which possibly might have assisted in removing some of these defects, is contained in the Percy Manuscript; but both of them, it is more than probable, would be found to differ essentially from the original text, if by any chance some of the more ancient copies should ever be brought to light. Of that copy which is divided into fytts or cantos, and contains only 1473 lines, the Editor is enabled to give the following detailed notice, in the words of the learned and worthy Prelate to whom the MS. belonged.[14]

Account of the Romance Eger and Grime, communicated to Dr. Robert Anderson by Bishop Percy, Sept. 20th, 1800, for the information of Walter Scott, Esq.

" The old Metrical Romance, entitled Eger and Grime,
" occurs in page 124 of the old folio MS. referred to in the
" Reliques of Ancient English Poetry, in 3 vols. but was
" by oversight omitted in some copies of the list of
" Metrical Romances prefixed to vol. iii. page xxxviii.
" where it should be No. 12 ; yet it is one of the best of
" these ancient epic tales, and little inferior to any in
" Ariosto, &c. It is in six parts (or cantos) whereof,

---

[13] Ellis' Metrical Romances, vol. iii., p. 308.

[14] The substance of this notice is already before the Publick, in Dr. Leyden's introduction to *The Complaynt of Scotland*, 1801, p. 231.

Part I. contains 346 lines
    II. - - 190
    III. - - 185   N.B.—The unequal ex-
    IV. - - 196   tent of the different
    V. - - 364   books is remarkable.
    VI. - - 192

    Total 1473

"The copy in this old MS. is tolerably correct, yet
"somewhat modernized in the rhimes, as where it should
"be *hond* it is written *hand;* for the copyist grew so
"careless, that it is in this piece occurs the blunder men-
"tioned in the Advertisement to the 4th edition of the
"Reliques, p. xii. viz. *want and will* for *wanton will.*
"It thus begins, and is all in distichs :

It ffell some time in the land of Beame[15]
there dwelled a Lord within y^t realme
The greatest he was of renowne
except the K y^t ware the crowne
the called him to name Erle Bragas
he marryed a ladye was fayre of face
they had na child but a daughter younge
in the world was none soe fayre thing
They called y^t ladye Wingtanye   *Lege* Wing-
husband wold she never have none   tayne.
Neither for gold nor yett for good   *Lege* nane.
Nor ffor no highnesse of his blood
W^tout he wold with swords dint
Win every battle where he went
      [*I omit a few lines.*]
There was in that same time
a courteous K^t called Sr Grime
& of Carwicke Lo. was hee
he was a wise man & a wittye
Soe there was in the same place
a young K^t men called Egace

---

[15] "This is a fac-simile transcript as far as it goes."

But his name was Sr Eger
ffor he was but a poore bachlour—

" These two knights are represented as sworn friends,
" and perform many acts of chivalry for each other; and
" after many curious. adventures, Sir Eger marries Wing-
" tayne, the rich heiress of Earl Bragas."

THE notices which have been detailed may, perhaps,
suggest the enquiry whether or not the present Tale be
the one actually alluded to. It appears that the name of
Gray-Steill has been applied at various times to distinguished persons, between whom and the nominal hero of
the romance, it is not easy to discover any marked
peculiarity of resemblance. Thus, Hume of Godscroft, in
his history of the family of Douglas,[16] relates of Archibald
Douglas of Kilspindie, that James the Fifth of Scotland,
" when he was young, loved him singularly well for his
" ability of body, and was wont to call him his Gray-
" Steill." William, first Earl of Gowrie, is so denominated
in one of Logan's letters,[17] produced as a proof of that
alleged and mysterious conspiracy, which, in all probability, shall remain a question of doubtful interpretation.
Alexander, Earl of Eglintoune, was a third person who
obtained the name of Grey-Steill. Of this nobleman, the
only Gray-Steill preserved in picture, it has been deemed
not superfluous in this publication to give a portrait, taken
from a curiously illuminated parchment in the possession
of the present Earl of Eglintoune. This Indenture is

---

[16] Hume's Douglas and Angus, fol. edit. 1644, p. 262.

[17] The evident purport of these words was to confirm the notion,
that John, Earl of Gowrie, was actuated in that conspiracy, with the
desire to revenge his father's death, who was executed when his son
was a child of about six years of age. But these letters have all the
appearance of being gross fabrications.

adorned with portraits of Lords Eglintoune and Airds, armorial bearings, cyphers, flowers, birds, etc., all extremely well executed ; and, as it is rather of an extraordinary nature, being what our Shakespearian readers would term " Much Ado about Nothing," it is here subjoined for the satisfaction of the curious :—

" THIS Indenture made the seven and twentieth day of Februarie, in the yeire of our Lord one thousand six hundred and thirty, betwene the right honourable Sir Hugh Montgomery Knight, Lord Viscount Montgomery of the great Ardes on the one parte, and the right honourable Alexander Earle of Eglinton in the kingdom of Scotland on the other part, witnesseth that whereas the said Lord Viscount Montgomery being discended of the honourable howse of the Earles of Egleinton within the said kingdom of Scotland, is most willing that hee and his heires should at all tymes foreever hereafter acknowledg the respect and duty which they owe to the honour of the said howse, in consideration whereof, and for the naturall love and affection which hee the said Lord Viscount Montgomery hath to the said Alexander now Earle of Eglinton and his heires, the said Lord Viscount Montgomery for him and his heires doeth grant, covenant, and agree to and with the said Alexander Earle of Eglinton and his heires Earles of Eglinton, which shal be of the name and surname of Montgomery, that the heire and heires of the said Lord Viscount Montgomery shall, in perpetuall remembrance of that love and dutie, freely give and deliver one faire horse of the value of thirty pounds of lawfull money of and in England, or thereabouts, to the said Alexander Earle of Eglinton and his heires being of the surname of Montgomery, within the space of one yeare after the heire and heires of the said Lord Viscount Montgomery shall have sued forth his or their livery, and entered into their manners, lordships, lands and hereditaments within the Kingdoms of Ireland and Scotland; and the said Lord Viscount Montgomery for himselfe, his heires and assignes doeth covenant promise and agree to and with the said Alexander Earle of Eglinton and his heires Earles of Eglinton, by theis presents, that upon default of the delivery of the said horce of the said price of thirtie pounds by the heire or heires of the said Lord Viscount Montgomery made at the said tyme, contrary to the true intent and meaning of theis presents, that then it shall and may bee lawfull unto the said Alexander Earle of Eglinton and his heires Earles of Eglinton, being of the surname of Montgomery, to fine for the same, together with the sume of fifteene poundes ster. : of like money, nomine pene, for every such default to bee made by the heires of the said Lord Viscount Montgomery, having first given due advertisement and notice of theis presents unto the heire by whom the default shall happen to be committed as aforesaid : and the said Hugh Lord Viscount Montgomery doeth by theis presents covenant, promise and agree to and with the said Alexander Earle of Eglinton, that hee the said Lord Viscount Montgomery shall and will doe, make, acknowledge, finish, and execute all and every such other reasonable act or acts, thing and things, conveyance or assurance in the lawe, for the good and perfet assurance and surety for the delivery of the said horse of the price aforsaid according to the true meaning of theis presents, as by the said Alexander Earle of Eglinton shal be reasonably devised or required, see that the said Lord Viscount Montgomery bee not desired to travaile for the making or acknowledging of such assurance from his dwelling house. In witnes wherof the said partyes have hereunto interchangeablie putt their hands and seals the day and yeire first above written.

MONTGOMERIE.

Signed, sealed and delivered
in pres. of Montgomerie. G.
Montgomerie. Montgomerie
senior. R. Montgomerie Minister of Newtowne."

For the above information, and the accompanying etching of the said portrait, as well as for the elegant design which serves as the frontispiece to the volume, the Editor gratefully acknowledges his obligations to CHARLES KIRKPATRICK SHARPE, ESQ., whose ingenuity and skill have been so often and so successfully exerted in behoof of his friends. This gentleman, in reference to the present Romance of Gray-Steill, says, "if this be all that ever " was sung of him, it was no great compliment to bestow "his name on subsequent worthies. There might be " some reason as to Lord Gowrie's nick-name, for it is " plain that Gray-Steill was a sort of magician; and " Spottiswood says, that Gowrie 'was too curious, and " 'said to have consulted with wizards, &c.'[18]—but for " Lord Eglintoune, it is only known that he fought stoutly "for the Solemn League and Covenant, was never " vanquished by Sir Grime, and had no deeper dealings " with the Devil than the rest of his fellow Puritans."— " It is a curious trait of Gray-Steill, (Mr. Sharpe continues,) " that he cut off the little fingers of the Knights whom he " conquered—probably for some magical operation—as he " resided in 'the land of Doubt,'—perhaps he is a personi-

---

[18] How very absurd and unfounded was such a report, appears from the contemporary account of the Earl of Gowrie's Trial, May, 1584. (*Bannatyne Miscellany*, part 1st.)

" fication of Impiety :—the anger of the Lady when her
" Knight went home without his little finger is very
" amusing—considering into what hands he fell, she might
" have been thankful that he made not greater losses."

There is no occasion to lengthen out these notices of
this Romance,[19] except to observe, that it contains too
many indications of belonging to an early period, to leave
us to imagine it to be only a recent composition. The
allusions throughout to the spirit and usages of Chivalrous
times, would certainly have been less observable had it
been written at a time when these had gone by. Judging,
then, from peculiarities in the style, and from the structure
of the verse, we might not greatly err were we to assign
it to the period which produced the *Life and Acts of
Robert the Bruce*, that is, to the reign of Robert II. or the
close of the Fourteenth Century.

II.

THE TALES OF THE PRIESTS OF PEBLIS.

THE only printed edition of the Tales of the Priests of
Peblis, of which any trace appears, is that imprinted at
Edinburgh be Robert Charteris, in the year 1603, 4to.[20]

---

[19] It may be added, that at least one edition of Gray Steill was
printed in Ireland. In a "Catalogue of Books lately printed by and
" for Sam. Wilson and Ja. Magee in Belfast," at the end of an
edition of Colvill's Scots Hudibras, printed at Belfast, by and for
the said Samuel Wilson and James Magee, M.DCC.XLI. 18°. is
" The History of Sir *Eger*, Sir *Grahame*, and Sir Gray-Steel.—

[20] At the end is an advertisement, stating that the Printer had set
forth with the King's Majesties license "sundrie uther delectabill
" discourses,—sic as are *David Lindsayes Play ; Philotus ; and the
" Friers of Berwick and Bilbo.*" It has been asked, but in vain, if

From this edition, which is of very great rarity, these Tales were published by Mr. Pinkerton, in 1792,[21] and a considerable portion of them by the late Mr. Sibbald in 1801.[22] Mr. Pinkerton's volumes having become scarce and expensive, it was thought advisable to include these tales in this little collection; as meriting to be better known, and more accessible than at present they can be said to be.

The title of the original edition is as follows:

The thrie Tailes of the thrie Priests of Peblis.

Contayning many notabill examples and fentences and (that the paper fould not be voide) fupplyit with fundrie merie tailes very pleafant to the Reader and mair exactlie corrected than the former Impression.[23]

OVID.

Expectanda dies homini eft, dicique beatus
Ante obitum nemo fupremaque funera debit.

IMPRINTED AT EDINBURGH
be Robert Charteris 1603.

CVM PRIVILEGIO REGALI.

---

any one ever heard of *Bilbo*. The other "discourses" are better known.

[21] Scottish Poems, &c. 1792, vol. i. p. 1-49.

[22] Chronicle of Scottish Poetry, vol. ii.

[23] The *merie tailes*, mentioned in the above title page, as Mr. Pinkerton remarks, "are in prose, and printed in a small letter on "the margin: they are taken from George Peele's Tales, and are "omitted as the work of an English author, written a century after "the poem."

IN the singularly curious volume, *The Complaynt of Scotland*, 1549, there is an allusion to these tales. " *The* " *Priests of Peblis*, (says the author) speiris an questioun " in ane beuk that he compilit, quhy that burgis ayris " thryuis nocht to the thrid ayr," etc. From this passage we might also infer that " the beuk" had been but recently compiled. Mr. Pinkerton, however, observes, that the Tales " appear, from internal evidence, to have " been written before the year 1492, because the kingdom " of Grenada is mentioned as not yet Christian. Con- " jecture (he shrewdly adds) may well suppose, that they " were intended to chastise the weak government of " James III. slain in 1488." With regard to the Author, not the slightest hint is to be discovered ; and, therefore, it were idle to have recourse to such suppositions as those in which Mr. Sibbald indulged ;—who at length seemed to have settled the matter to his own conviction, by fix- ing their date between 1533 and 1540, and attributing them to John Rolland, the author of a metrical version of the *Sevin Sagis*, which passed through several editions ; and of a long dull moral poem, under the title of *The Court of Venus*, printed at Edinburgh in 1575, of which one copy alone is known to be preserved. In answer to all Mr. Sibbald's conjectures, it is enough to state, that a portion of these Tales, with the title, " *Heir begynnis the buke of thre prestis of Peblis how thai told thar Tales*," is contained in a MS. which appears to have been tran- scribed at least twenty years previous to the date he assigns for their composition, and probably before Rolland was born.

Mr. Pinkerton says, " It is hardly necessary to remark, " that these Tales of the Priests are more moral than " facetious, and that their chief merit consists in a *naif* " delineation of ancient manners." In like manner, the biographer of the Scotish Poets has said : " The three

" priests of Peebles, having met on St. Bride's day for the
" purpose of regaling themselves, agree, that each in his
" turn shall endeavour to entertain the rest by relating ·
" some story. They acquit themselves with sufficient
" propriety. The tales are of a moral tendency, but, at
" the same time, are free from the dullness which so fre-
" quently infests the perceptive compositions of our
" earlier poets." [24]

III.

ANE GODLIE DREAME.

THE author of this poem, in what appears to have been
the earliest impression, is said to be " M. M. *Gentlewoman
in Culross*,"—but in all the subsequent editions, she is
designated " Eliz. Melvil, *Lady Culros Yonger;*" and, in
a volume of poems, by Alexander Hume, printed at
Edinburgh by Robert Waldegrave, 1599, 4to, which is
dedicated to her, she is styled " the faithfvll and vertvovs
Ladie, Elizabeth Ma-vill, *Ladie Cumrie.*" To reconcile
these apparent discrepancies, it may be stated, that this
Lady was Elizabeth, daughter of Sir James Melvill of
of Halhill, the writer of a most interesting volume of
Memoirs of his Own Times; and that, by her marriage
with John Colvill, eldest son of Alexander, Commendator
of Culros, (who, during his father's life, had the designation
of Colvill of Wester-Cumrie,) she received the honorary
title, first of " Lady Cumrie," and subsequently of " Lady
Culros." She is supposed to have survived her husband,
who, in the year 1640, not long before his death, succeeded
to the peerage;[25] but who did not assume the title,

---

[24] Irving's Lives of the Scottish Poets, vol. i. p. 372.
[25] Samuel Colvill, the author of *The Whigg's Supplication*, or *The*

although the succession of the Lords Colvile of Culross was carried on by his immediate descendants.

An extract from the dedication of Alexander Hume's Poems to our fair Authoress may not be unsuitable, as commending her virtuous dispositions, as well as poetical talents, by one who is himself entitled to no inconsiderable distinction amongst the writers of his time. It is dated 16th of February, 1598. " Hauing (he says) composed in " my youth, a few songes in verse to the glorie of God, " seeing the custome of men is to dedicate their workes " to their fauorites and patrones : shall it not be lawfull " to me also, after the manner of men, to present vnto you " (a faithfull and beloued ladie) a part of my little labours ? " And sa meikle the rather, because I know ye delite in " poesie yourselfe, and as I vnfainedly confes, excelles " any of your sexe in that art, that euer I heard within " this nation. I have seene your compositiones so copious, " so pregnant, so spirituall, that I doubt not but it is the " gift of God in you. Finally, because so little a worke " as this is, requires a short epistle, I take my leaue, not " doubting but my good meaning shall be fauorablie " accepted. Continue (good ladie and sister) in that " godlie course which ye have begun : let nothing be " done vpon ostentation. Loue your husband : haue a " modest care of your familie, and let your cheefe care be

---

Scots Hudibras, is usually spoken of as her son ;—if so, he unquestionably did not inherit much of her pious and godly spirit, as his imitation of Butler may evince. The allusion which he makes to " Lady Culros's dream,"

> Which sundry drunken Asses flout,
> Not seeing the Jewel within the clout,—

is neither conceived nor expressed in a very decorous manner ; to say nothing of the words he has put in the mouth of " John Cockburn " in the Preface to the said poem.

" casten vpon the Lord Iesus, who will recompense vs at
" his comming."

The Reader will have an opportunity, from the Godly
Dream, to judge whether Hume has over-rated her
poetical talents. We might almost suppose the poem to
have suggested some passages in that inimitable work of
fiction, the Pilgrim's Progress, in which the author has
succeeded so admirably in sustaining his allegory, and in
giving life and character to his abstract personifications.
It is uncertain if any other of her verses are preserved,
except the following Sonnet,[26] addressed to Mr. John
Welch, in the year 1605, or 1606, when confined in the
Castle of Blackness, with some other Presbyterian minis-
ters, on the charge of High Treason,—but, in reality, for
thwarting King James in his notions of the Royal
prerogative.

> My dear Brother, with courage beare the crosse,
> Joy shall be joyned with all thy sorrow here ;
> High is thy hope ; disdain this earthly drosse !
> Once shall you see the wished day appear.
> Now it is dark, thy sky cannot be clear,
> After the clouds, it shall be calm anone,
> Wait on his will whose blood hath bought you dear,
> Extoll his name, tho' outward joys be gone.
> Look to the Lord, thou art not left alone,
> Since he is there, quhat pleasure canst thou take !—
> He is at hand, and hears thy heavy moan,
> End out thy faught, and suffer for his sake !
> A sight most bright thy soul shall shortly see,
> When store of glore thy rich reward shall be.

Mr. John Livingston, in his MS. account of " Eminent
" Professors in Scotland," mentions Lady Culross " as
" famous for her piety, and for her Dream anent her
" spiritual condition, which she put in verse, and was by

[26] Wodrow's MSS. (Advocates' Library,) 4to. vol. 29. Rob. iii. 6.

" others published ; " and he says, " of all that ever I saw,
" she was most unwearied in religious exercises ; and the
" more she attained in access to God, therein she hungered
" the more; " of which he adduces an instance that came
under his own observation, at Shots, in the year 1630.
There is no doubt that the Godly Dream was long popular
among the Scottish Presbyterians;—a circumstance which
might have obtained for it a more favourable regard than
it has yet experienced.   But when writers, who have
treated of the early Scottish Poets, are so ungallant as to
dismiss a poem of considerable beauty and imagination,
as either unworthy of a single passing remark, or as being
a " nonsensical religious rhapsody " which " should be
consigned to oblivion,"—surely this is to be considered
either as prejudice on their part, or the want of taste and
discernment, so essential in giving a just estimate of the
character and genius of our political writers.

Dr. Armstrong, in his Essays, has alluded to " the
Godly Dream," in such a manner, as if he recollected
having heard it sung by the peasants to some plaintive
air.   In referring to " Scottish tunes," as " feelingly ex-
" pressive of the passions," he says, " Who was it that
" threw out those dreadful wild expressions of distraction
" and melancholy in *Lady Culross's Dream?* an old composi-
" tion, now I am afraid lost, perhaps because it was almost
" too terrible for the ear." [27] Mr. Pinkerton thought otherwise. He observes, that " This composition is neither lost,
" nor is it too terrible for the ear. On the contrary, a
. " child might hear it repeated, in a winter night, without
" the smallest emotion. The dreadful and melancholy of
" this production are solely of the religious kind, and may

---

[27] Miscellanies, by John Armstrong, M.D. vol. ii. p. 234.

" have been deeply affecting to the enthusiastic at the
" period in which it was written." [28]

In proof of the estimation in which this poem was held,
a list of the various editions may be given.　The earliest
is that printed in the year 1603, consisting of ten leaves in
4to. bl. letter, the text of which has been chiefly adopted
in this republication.[29]　The following is a copy of the
title-page,—which, in the original, has a border, and the
wood-cut device of the Printer.

ANE GODLIE

DREAME, COMPLYIT IN

Scottish Meter be M.M. Gentel-

vvoman in Culros, at the re-
quiest of her freindes.

Introite per angustam portam, nam lata est
via quæ ducit ad interitum.

EDINBVRGH
PRINTED BE ROBERT
CHARTERIS. 1603.

The Scotish idiom and orthography have been very
much changed in all the subsequent impressions.[30]　After

---

[28] Select Scotish Ballads, vol. i. p. xxxvii.

[29] The stanzas are not numbered, and the Saxon letter *z* is made
use of instead of *y* consonant, as in this reprint.

[30] At the end of nearly all the editions of *The Godly Dream*, is a
poem added, which begins, *Away vain world, bewitcher of my heart,*
(likewise printed with the *air* in the Aberdeen Cantus), but which
more recently has been printed amongst the poems of Alexander
Montgomery, author of the Cherrie and the Slae.

the edition just described, comes, (2) "A Godly Dreame,
"compyled by Eliz. Melvil, Lady Culros, yonger, at the
"request of a friend.   Edinburgh, printed by Robert
"Charteris"—no date, 4to., bl. l. 10 leaves.   (3) The
same; "Edinburgh, printed by Robert Charteris, 1606,"
4to., 10 leaves.   (4) "Edinburgh, imprinted by Andro
"Hart, 1620," 8vo., 12 leaves.   (5) "Aberdene, printed
"by Edward Raban, *Laird of Letters,* 1644," 8vo., 12
leaves.[31]   The later editions are, (6) "Edinburgh, 1680,"
12mo.   (7) "Printed in the year 1686," 12mo.   (8)
"Printed in the year 1692," 18mo.   (9) "Edinburgh, 1698,"
18mo.   (10) "Edinburgh, 1737," 12mo.   There are no
doubt other editions which have escaped the Editor's notice.

IV.

HISTORY OF A LORD AND HIS THREE SONS.

THIS "delectable little history" is taken from a copy
which the Editor has, said to be "Newly corrected for the
"use of Schools," and printed in the year 1708; compared
with another three years earlier in date, in the possession
of Archibald Constable, Esq.   There were previous
editions to either of these: the copy of one, printed at
Edinburgh in the year 1692, was lately in the library of a
gentleman in Edinburgh, but the volume containing it,
unfortunately, has been lost or mislaid.

The reader will observe that several allusions are made
in this history, to what *the author says,* although no

---

[31] Mr. Beloe, who notices this edition in his Anecdotes of Literature, is mistaken in supposing it to be the *first* book printed in Aberdeen. Raban carried on the art of Printing in that City, from the year
1621, after his removal from St. Andrews, where he had been
established about two years.

author's name is mentioned. But there can be no difficulty in tracing its resemblance to the latter portion of the favourite story of Fortunatus, which has been naturalized in most languages, and was probably of a Scandinavian origin.[32] It was first made known to the English reader by Thomas Churchyard, a noted and very voluminous writer in the reign of Queen Elizabeth, who professes to have translated it from the Dutch,—probably the High-Dutch, or German. In some parts, however, the story approaches nearer to the tale of Jonathas, of which Browne, the English Pastoral Poet, has introduced, in his Shepherd's Pipe,[33] Occleve's beautiful version of the tale of *King Darius' Legacy to his three Sons,* from *the Gesta Romanorum.*[34]

From whatever source the anonymous writer may have derived his version of the History of a Lord and his Three Sons, it is quite evident that he has exhibited no great skill in his adaptation of this popular story " for the use " of Schools ; " but there are so few compositions of this kind known, as to make it worthy of preservation, notwithstanding of its slender claims in point of merit.

The following is the title-page of the edition above mentioned :[35]

---

[32] Illustrations of Northern Antiquities, Edin. 1814.

[33] Shepherd's Pipe, printed with some Poems, by George Wither. London, 1620, 8vo.

[34] Douce's Illustration of Shakespeare, vol. ii. p. 390. Warton's English Poetry, new edition, vol. i. p. 229.

[35] This edition is in 16mo. pp. 24. printed in a very small letter. The other copy, which is almost a literal reprint, retaining all the errors, and adding a few others, extends to pp. 36. The only difference in the title page is the last line that reads,

" *Edinburgh,* Re-printed in the year 1708."

A

DELECTABLE

LITTLE

H I S T O R Y

IN 'METRE:

---

*Of a Lord and his three Sons, containing his
Latter will and Legacy to them upon his
death-bed, and what befel them after his
death, especially the midmost & the youngest.*

---

*Revised, Corrected, and Amended for the use
of Schools.*

Omne tulit punctum qui miscuit utile dulci.

---

*He gotten has all Commendation
Who profite hath with pleasure mixt in one.*

Edinburgh, Printed in the Year 1705.

V.

THE RING OF THE ROY ROBERT.

THIS poem, which is mentioned in the Complaynt of
Scotland, 1549, appears to have received, at an early
period, more attention than easily can be accounted for
any other way than from national feeling, which may
have responded to the sentiments it expresses with regard
to the independency and sovereignty of Scotland. The
author, according to the Maitland MS. from which this
poem is now printed, was Dean David Steill, a Scottish
poet, who is supposed to have flourished about the close
of the fifteenth century.

The occasion to which the poem alludes is evidently what took place, on the renewal of hostilities between the two kingdoms, after the accession of Henry IV. According to our historians, that monarch, in the year 1400, previously to his invading Scotland, with a powerful army, sent a summons to King Robert III.[36] and all the prelates and nobility of Scotland, to meet him at Edinburgh, on the 23d of August, to do homage and swear fealty to him as Superior Lord of Scotland; which he affirmed all the former Kings of Scotland had done to his predecessors since the days of Brute the Trojan. To such an arrogant demand he is said to have received a no less contemptuous answer, from Prince David, Duke of Rothsay; upon which he marched forward; but ere long he returned to England, without having done any thing worthy of his mighty preparations.[37]

But this poem cannot be regarded as a contemporary effusion. The probability is, that it may have been one of " those writings" handed about in the reign of Henry VII. which occasioned a remonstrance to be made on the part of the English monarch. A declaration on this subject, by the learned and upright judge, Sir John Fortescue, in the form of a dialogue, " Vpon certayn wrytingis sent " oute of Scotteland, ayenst the Kingis title of his Roialme " of England,"—is still preserved in MS.;[38] although the character of the author is sufficient, we should have supposed, to render any of his works deserving of publication.

Bishop Nicolson,[39] who was the first to notice Sir

---

[36] In this copy an evident mistake occurs, in calling Robert " the *first King* of the good Stewart ;" which probably occasioned, in one of the old printed copies, the answer being attributed to Robert II.

[37] Henry's History, vol. v. p. 9. Rymer's Foedera, tom. viii. p. 1182-1186. Pinkerton's History, vol. i. p. 56.

[38] MS. Bibl. Reg. 17 D. xv.

[39] Scottish Historical Library, 1703, 8vo. p. 154.

Richard Maitland's MS., in mentioning this poem, adds, that it is there attributed to Dean David Steill. From this simple notice, Dr. George Mackenzie[40] framed an account of the author, and tells us that he lived in the reign of James First of Scotland; and speaks of this poem as containing "the life of King Robert III. wherein several things are recorded of moment."

The printed copies of this poem are considerably modernized and corrupted. One of these, printed as a broadside, about the year 1680, preserved in Pepys's library, has this title, "The reply and challenge of King "Robert the second, the first of the Steuarts, unto Henry "the fourth, King of England, unjustly challenging his "homage."—There is another edition printed at Edinburgh, 1700, 8°. pp. 8. which has been very recently reprinted. It is likewise included in Watson's Collection of Scots Poems, Part II. 1709.

VI.

KING ESTMERE.

THIS tale, the Editor has without due consideration inserted in this volume, as he has not been able to give it in any other form than as it appears in the Reliques of Ancient English Poetry.[41] Dr. Leyden suggested,[42] that it might probably be the same with the "Tale of the King of Estmureland's marriage to the King's daughter of Westmureland," mentioned in the Complaynt of Scotland, 1549. Mr. Ritson,[43] however, was inclined to identify

---

[40] Lives and Characters of Scottish Writers, vol. i. p. 450.
[41] Percy's Reliques, 4th Edit. vol. i. p. 62.
[42] Complaynt of Scotland. Introd. p. 226.
[43] Ancient English Metrical Romances, vol. iii. p. 226.

that Tale with the very ancient Romance of Kyng Horn, which he has published. However this may be, it would have been desirable to have met with a copy of this interesting legend, in its original state.—Bishop Percy, from whose volumes the present text is printed, tells us, that he has given it " from two copies, one of them, in his folio MS. but which contained great variations." The other copy, it is more than probable, was one of his own making, as the Editor, after many fruitless inquiries, cannot hear of the existence of any such, either printed or written. Indeed, it is confessed that he had taken " some liberties " with this tale ; and it would be curious, by comparing it with the folio MS. to see how much it owes to his exquisite skill and ingenuity.

This romantick tale is certainly of some antiquity. Bishop Percy says, " As in one of the copies, the King of " Spain is represented as a Pagan, this ballad should seem " to have been originally written while a part of that " kingdom was in the hands of the Saracens or Moors, " whose empire there was not fully extinguished before " the year 1491." There is no occasion to copy out the interesting illustrations of this tale from so popular a work as the Reliques—which prove that several of the circumstances described are strictly " conformable to the real manners of the barbarous ages."—

VII.

THE BATTLE OF HARLAW.

THE exact age of this historical song or poem has not been ascertained, and has given rise to some discussion, on which it is not necessary at present to enter at large. Lord Hailes suspected, " that it will be found to be as recent as the days of Queen Mary or James VI." Mr. Sibbald concurs in this opinion ; but, on the other hand, Mr. Ritson, Mr. Pinkerton, and Mr. Finlay, maintain, that " from its manner, it might have been written soon after the event."

That this poem is of considerable antiquity cannot be doubted, the " battle of Hayrlau," being named amongst the popular songs of the time, by the author of the Complaynt of Scotland, 1549 ; and it may be considered as the original of rather a numerous class of our historical ballads. No copy of an earlier date than that in Ramsay's Evergreen, 1724, is known ; but it certainly had been printed long before his time. An edition printed in the year 1668, was in the curious library of old Robert Myln.

VIII.

LICHTOUN'S DREME.

THIS very whimsical production, which contains some curious allusions, is now printed for the first time. It is contained in Bannatyne's MS. 1568, and is also preserved in Sir R. Maitland's MS. where it is anonymous. Of the author nothing is known, except that from the signature attached to it, he appears to have been of the Priesthood. The only other poem attributed to him is a religious poem, of six eight-line stanzas, beginning,

O mortall man remembir nycht and day,

the burden of each,—*Memento homo quod cinis es.*

In an old English Poem,[44] full " of mervells," like this Dream, at an entertainment which is described, we are told—

[44] MS. Advocates' Library, Jac. V. 7. 27.

The sowe sat on hye benke, and harpyd Robin Howd,
The fox fydylyd, the raton rybybyd, the larke noty with all,
The hombull bee hendyld the horne pype, for ham fyngers wer small.

IX.

THE MOURNING MAIDEN.

THIS beautiful poem, "*Still under the leyvis grene*," is mentioned in the Complaynt of Scotland, 1549, and was first printed from Sir R. Maitland's MS. by Mr. Pinkerton. He speaks of it " as a capital piece, being a kind of rival " of the Ephesian Matron, narrated with exquisite " simplicity and beauty"—and elsewhere, he says, that " this piece, for the age [in which] it was written, is almost " miraculous. The tender pathos is finely recommended " by an excellent cadence. An age that produced this " might produce almost any perfection in poetry." It was indeed written in the Augustan age of Scottish Poetry ; and after such a high enconium, there needs no apology for its republication.

There are several other poems still extant, of a similar kind, but for various reasons are less fit for publication. From one of these, which was lately discovered in a mutilated state, (with various other fragments in verse and prose, pasted together in the boards of an old book of little value,) a few stanzas may be here introduced. Some portions of this Lament are very pathetick, but unfortunately, from parts of the lines being cut away, it is not easy to guess at the exact words to supply all the deficiencies; although much has been done for it by a gentleman, to whom the Editor has already made his acknowledgments. The orthography of the original fragment, being very uncouth, is, in part, corrected.

"Fareweill, fare' weill, my yellow hair,
"That curlit cleir' into my neck !
"Alace !' that ever it grew sae fair,
"Or yet in' to ane snood was knet.

.   .   .   .

"Qu' har I was wont to dance and sing ;
"A' mang my marrows mak repair—
Now am I put furth of the ring,
For fadit is my yellow hair.

My kirtill wes of lincu'm green,'
Weill lacit with silk'en passments rair ;'
God gif I had never pridefull ' been,'
For fadit is my yellow hair.

God gif my hair had been als b'lak'
As euer wes my hart full of cair,
It wald not put me to sic lac,
For fadit my yellow hair.

Quhen I was young I had great sta'it,'
Weill cherishit baith with less and ma'ir,'
For shame now steill I off the gait,
For fadit is my yellow hair.

I wes our wanton of intent
"Of wardlie joys I tuke my share ;
But sin hes nocht but sorrow sent,"
And fadit is my yellow hair.

God gif the dait of luf wer gane,
That I micht die, and luf na mair !
To Jesu Christ, I mak my mane,
And fadit is my yellow hair.

Sen all this folly is by went,
Out of this warld I maun repair ;
I pray to God Omnipotent,
To tak me, sinner, full of cair !
                Finis.—Amen.

The admiration of' yellow hair was not peculiar to the

old Scotish poets, one of whom compares the tresses of
their ladies " to the wire of gold that has been fined."
According to the ingenious author of the Anatomy of
Melancholy, " a flexen haire, golden haire was ever iṇ
great account ; " and after naming those in ancient times,
(" gods and goddesses," as well as heroes,) whom the
poets have commended for their "yellow hair ;" [45] he adds,
" Which belike makes our Venetian ladies at this day to
" counterfeit yellow hair so much, great women to cal-
" amistrate and curle it up, to adorne their heads with
" spangles, pearles, and made flowres, and all courtiers to
" affect a pleasing grace in this kinde."[46]   In reference to
this custom of the Venetian ladies,[47] a quaint English
writer[48] exclaims :—" What a curious accommodation to
" those people had some fountain been that had a harm-
" lesse property to colour their haire according to their
" mindes,—such a one as the River Crathis, mentioned
" by Plinie, whose nature was to make Haire yellow,
" with efficacy Ovid attributes to another."

> Crathis, et hinc Sybaris nostris conterminus oris,
> Electro similes faciunt Auróque Capillos.

Among the other fragments, were two or three love
poems, in the style of Alexander Scott, or of his contem-

---

[45] Bishop Jeremy Taylor takes notice, that "Menander in the
Comedy brings in a man turning his wife from his house *because she
stain'd her hair yellow*, which was then the beauty." *Sermons, Lond.*
1653, folio, p. 242.   But the words imply that this practice was not
adopted by any modest woman.

> Νῦν δ' ἔξπ' ἀπ' οἴκων τῶνδε. τὴν γυναῖκα γὰς
> Τὴν σωφξον' οὐ δεῖ τας τξιχας ξανθὰς ποιεῖν.

Menandri Fragmenta 199. edit. 1709, p. 295.

[46] Burton's Anat. of Melanch. edit. 1632, fol. p. 469.

[47] See Coryate's Crudities, &c.   4to. Lond. 1611 fol. 260-1.
Lassel's Italy, &c.

[48] Bulwar's Artificiall Changeling, 1652.   4to. p. 65.

4

porary, Montgomery.   The one least mutilated is here inserted; the words within the inverted commas being supplied, as in the former instance, by Charles Sharpe, Esq.

> "QUHEN we to Ladies lufe inclyne,
>   Our guerdon still growis less and less,"
> Bot quha sould press to suffer pyne,
>   Or for thair plessor thoil distres ?
> Sen thai regard to treuth hes none ;
> Nor yit reward for lufe allone,
>   Bot pane expres !
>
> Bot pane expres ! I sé rycht nocht ;
>   The moir I serve the less sett by !
> The moir I luff the les in thocht !
>   The moir I weip the war am I !
> My hart is sett, but variance
> Quhair I can get no recompans,
>   This is the quhy !
>
> This is the quhy ! I plainʒie foir
>   My Lady, on your excellence ;
> Ye sould support my panis soir,
>   "That" woundis me, without offence ;
> "Quhen" every day I am bot deid,
> "Allace ! nor can I find remeid"
>   "Bot patience."
>
> But patience ! remeid is none,
>   This langsum liff I leid, allace !
> Subject I am to you allone,
>   As bond and thral to byid your grace :
> This gret annoye quha may resist ?
> Cupide convoy me as thow list,—
>   Hard is my case.
>
> Hard is my case ! without comfort,
>   Bot gif ye help, my Lady free,
> Quha sould me succour, or support,
>   Quha sould me saiff or yit supplee,
> But ye sueit hart and soverane ?
> Thairfor reward my liff agane,
>   Yit or I dee !

THE EPISTILL OF THE HERMEIT OF ALAREIT.

THIS Satirical poem has been preserved by Knox, in the
History of the Reformation, where, in reference to the
contempt into which the Gray Friers had fallen in conse-
quence of their depraved conduct, he says, "not only did
" the learnit espye and detect their abominable hypocrisy,
" but also men in quhom nane sick graces nor giftis were
" thocht to have been, began plainlie to point the same
" furth to the people, as this ryme made by Alexander,
" Earl of Glencairne, yet alive, can witness."

Alexander Cunningham, Earl of Glencairn, early distinguished himself in promoting a reformation from the
errors of Popery ; and he continued a firm and zealous
supporter of the Protestant faith.

Alareit, or Laureit, is evidently the Chapel built in
honour of " our Lady of Loretto," in the village of Mussel-
burgh,[49] where troops of young men and women went in
pilgrimage ; but, there is reason to suspect, for other pur-
poses than those of penance or religion.

XI.

ROSWALL AND LILLIAN.

THE " pleasant history " of Roswall and Lillian, was the
last of the Metrical Romances that retained their popularity in Scotland ; and not many years have elapsed
since it was not unusual to hear it chanted in the streets
of Edinburgh.   Since that time, it has been familiar to

---

[49] See Notes to Poems, by Alexander Scott, 1568, 8vo.

the Publick, from an analysis by one of the most accomplished Editors of early poetical literature, Mr. G. Ellis.

Of this " history," which is not known to be extant in manuscript, the earliest printed edition discovered, is one in the year 1663, in small 8vo, of 14 leaves, printed in black letter, as it would appear, for the ancient fraternity of *flying stationers.*   The only copy of this edition known, is that which was purchased at the Roxburghe Sale, for the Advocates' Library.   Another edition was printed in the year 1679, as appears from the MS. Catalogue of that curious collector, Robert Mylne, whose books were disposed of by auction after his death, which took place in the year 1749, at the patriarchal age of 104.

The title of the edition 1663, (of which there is a paginary reprint,) is given on the opposite page.

The number of editions of a more recent date must have been considerable, as the Editor has seen not less than eight printed in the course of the last Century at Edinburgh, Glasgow, Newcastle, and Belfast.   Very considerable discrepancies occur in comparing these different copies; and the Editor has not scrupled to insert various emendations on their authority.   The lines, in the earliest edition, which amount to 846, in some of the others, are curtailed to less than half the number.

Mr. George Ellis, remarks, that " the style of this " Romance, has perhaps been modernized, and the tale " seems to have been awkwardly and carelessly abridged, " unless we suppose it to have been printed from a " mutilated and imperfect manuscript.   There is, I think, " no internal evidence to justify our ascribing its original " to an earlier period than the middle of the 16th century." This observation, however, is not so applicable to the older copies, in which the story has evidently suffered less than the language.   The copy in the possession of Mr. Douce, described by Mr. Ellis as the only one he had

A PLEASANT

HISTORY

OF

Roſwall and *Lillian.*

DECLARING

The occasion of *Roſwall* his removing
from his Native Kingdom, to the
Kingdom of *Bealm,* and what befell
him in his journey from his Steward :
The entertainment he met with from
an aged Wife : His Education at
School ; With his fortunate admission
to be servant to *Lillian* the Kings only
Daughter, with whom ſhe fell deeply
in love. The reward of the three Lords
by whom he attained the honour of the
three dayes Juſting before the Marriage
of the Steward, who was knowen to be
a Traitor and therefore justly executed ;
with the renewed wished-for Marriage
betwixt *Roswall* and *Lillian :* His
thankfull remembrance of his friends ;
the number of his children, and their
good fortune, all worthy reading.

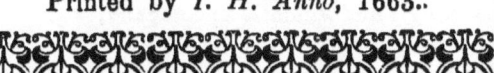

EDINBURGH,
Printed by *I. H. Anno,* 1663..

seen, is by no means of the age he conceived. It is
evidently printed at Newcastle, so late as the year 1775;
and contains only 426 lines.

XII.

POEM BY GLASSINBERRY.

THE name of Glassinberry is now, for the first time,
introduced into the List of early Scottish Poets. As his
history is altogether unknown, we can only conjecture
that he flourished in the reign of James the Second of
Scotland. The poem here printed, is preserved in " Gray's
Manuscript,"—a little diminutive volume, chiefly of
historical pieces, written towards the close of the 15th
Century,[50] which is now in the Advocates' Library.
Another copy of this poem, (without any author's name,)
is contained in a MS. volume in the Archiepiscopal
Library, at Lambeth.[51] Two or three anonymous poems,
contained in Gray's MS. might, from a similarity of style
and measure, be, with some propriety, assigned to the
same author.

A stanza or two from one of these poems may be here
subjoined. The subject is the transitory nature of the
present life, illustrated by various examples; amongst
which we have the " Nine Worthies," brought forward to
shew *This warld is very vanité.*

> MONY pape ar passit by,
> Patriarkis, prelatis, and preistis,
> Kingis and knichtis in company,
> Uncountit curiously up I kest ;

---

[50] See Father Innes's Critical Essay, vol. ii. p. 627-632.
[51] It is contained in the Volume, No. 853, of Mr. Todd's Catalogue
of the Lambeth MSS.

Women and mony wilsom wy,
As wynd and wattir ar gane west :
Fish, and foule, and froit of tree
On feild is nane formit na fest ;
Riches adew ! sen all is drest
That thai may nocht this dule indré !
Sen nocht has leif that heir ma lest
This world is but a vanité !

Quhar is Plato that clerk of price,
That of all poetis had no peir ?
Or yit Catoun wit his clergis ?
Or Aristotill that clerk so clere ?
Tullious that wele wauld tis ?
To tell his trety wer full teyr !
Or Virgil that wes war and wis,
And wist all wardly werk but wer ?
Is nane sa dowtit na sa dere,
Than but redemyng all mon dee !
Therfor I hauld, quha evir it heir,
This warld is verray vanité.

Ane uthir exampill suth to say
In summeris day full oft is sene
Thir emotis in ane hillok ay
Rinnand oute before thin ene ;
With litill weit thai wit away,
Sa worthis of ws all I wene !
May nane indur ouer his enday,
Bot all ouer drivis, as dew bedene,
That on the bery bidis bene,
And with a blast away willbe,
Quhile girse ar gray, quhile ar thai grene,
This warld is verray vanité !

The following lines, written on the margin of one of the leaves of this MS. in the name of "Aristoteles Magnus," may remind the reader of some verses usually attributed to the author of Hudibras.

GYF thou cummis to the flude,
And the wawis[52] be woude,
   Huse, and hald thé still ;
Thou may cum ane uther day,
Quhen wynd and wawis ar away
   Than ma thou waid at will.

XIII.

SIR JOHN BARLEYCORN.

THIS version of a very popular ballad, is given from a
common stall-copy, printed in the year 1781, with a few
corrections, on the authority of two others of a later date.
One of these occurs in the Collection of Popular Ballads,
by Mr. Jamieson, who is inclined to think it is derived
from an English ballad on the same subject, which he
has printed from a black-letter copy, preserved in Pepys's
Library.

Burns has given us an altered version of Sir John
Barleycorn, founded on the present ballad, and although
his good taste led him to preserve all that freshness of
description, which constitutes its principal charm, he cannot be said to have greatly improved it.   But the more
ancient appellation of our hero, was Allan-a-Maut; and
various songs or ballads in his praise are still in circulation.
The following stanzas, copied from Bannatyne's MS. 1568,
may be added to those already published.   They are by
an anonymous writer, who, not unaptly, designates himself
one of " Allan's soldiers."

QUHA hes gud malt, and makis ill drynk,
   Wa mot be hir werd !—
I pray to God scho rott and stynk
   Sevin yheir abou thé erd ;

---

[52] Wawis—for " waves."

About heir beir na bell to clynk,
  Nor clerk sing, lewid nor lerd ;[53]
Bot quytt to hell that scho may sink
  The tap-tré quhill scho steird ;
    This beis my prayer
    Fro that man slayar
Quhill Christ in Hevin sall heird !

Quha brewis, and giwis me of the best,
  · Sa it be stark and staill,
[Baith] quhyt and cleir, weill to degest,
  In Hevin meit hir that Aill !
Lang mot scho leif, lang mot scho lest,
  In lyking, and gude saill ;
In hevin or erd that wyfe be blest
  With out barrett or baill :
    Quhen scho is deid
    With outtin pleid,
Scho pass to Hevin all haill.

QUOD ALLANIS SUBDERT.

---

[53] Learned nor unlearned.

THE HISTORY

OF SIR EGER, SIR GRAHAME,

AND SIR GRAY STEILL.

THE HISTORY
OF SIR EGER, SIR GRAHAME,
AND SIR GRAY-STEEL.

INTO the kinrick of Bealm,
  There winn'd a lord of that realm ;
He was the greatest of renown,
Except the king that wore the crown ;
His name was earle Diges,
And his lady dame Biges ;
And his daughter Winliane,
Husband would she never have nane,
Neither for gold, nor yet for good,
Nor yet for highness of his blood,   10
But only he, that through swords dint,
That ever wan, and never tint.
Als there was men in that kinrick,
Many one, but very few sik,
They fought far off her for to fang,
And she was maiden wonder lang.
  Her father had a noble rout
Of bold knights, strong and stout ;
But in that court there was a knight
An hardy man, both good and wight,   20
They called him Sir Eger,
And he was but a batcheler :
His eldest brother was livand,
And brooked all his father's land ;
Yet he was courteously taught,
And he sought battells far, and fought

And conquered the honour,
With weapons and with armour,
Both in battels and in fight :
While on a time that she him heght,   30
And she granted him her good will ;
Her father assented soon theretill :
Her friends were fain that she would
Once in her heart it for to hold,
That she would have to her a pier,
A barron or a batchelier.
   There was into that earles train,
A young knight that heght Sir Grahame ;
Sir Eger and he,
They were of one companie :   40
They were not brethren born,
But they were brethren sworn ;
They were not of one blood,
But they were fellows very good ;
They had a chamber them alone,
Better loved never none.
   While that upon a time Sir Eger,
For to win honour mare,
And he went forth, him alone,
And all vanquished came he home,   50
In his chamber, upon a night,
Wounded sore and evil dight ;
His knife was tint, his sheath was tane,
His scabert by his thigh was gane :
He had mo wounds, with sword and knife,
Than ever man that had his life ;
A truncheon of his spear he bare
To lean him on ; he had no mare :
On his bed side, he sate him down,
He groaned sore, and fell in sown.   60
   Sir *Grahame* agast, and wightly raise,

And goes to him, and said, " Alace !
I for thy sorrow am full wo,
That I was then so far thee fro,
When that thou stood in such distress,
And I at home in merriness :
When we departed at yond gate,
Thou was full blyth, and light of late ;
Very deliver of thy weed,
To prove thy man-hood on a steed ;   70
And thou art now both gool and green,
Into thy walk where thou hast been :
What ever he was that gave thee sailyie,
It was not little that made thee failyie."
  " I am wounded and hurt full sore,
And tint my man-hood for evermore :
Lost the lady, for she is gone !
Other knights have stayed at home,
Keeped their man-hood fair and clean,
Will brook her now before mine een."   80
  Then said Sir Grahame to Sir Eger,
" Ye grieve you more than mister were,
Is none seemly in his weed,
To prove his man-hood on a steed ?
In battel though he be destroyed,
Why should his man-hood be reproved ?
Or yet his ladies love to tine ? "
  Sir Eger said, " let be Sir Grahame,
I rode adventures for to see,
Bodden as a man should be ;   90
Likelier armour than I had
Was no Christian man in clade :
Weapons and steed thereto,
A bodie like right well to do.
I saw no man, so God me reed,
But one knight upon a steed :

Hand for hand together we ran,
But company of any man;
He forcely pricked me again,
Defouled my self, my steed hath slain :   100
I met a man into my fare,
Forbade me that I should come there,
But if I sicker were and traist,
Of courage keen and mights maist,
Neither of heart nor yet of hand,
Nothing feeble nor yet dreadand;
And armed well in sicker weed,
Weapons, for they will stand in stead;
Of mine horse he held him payd,
He bade me if I were affrayd :   110
Counsell'd me I came not than
Within repairing of that man,
I should be ready and not to light,
To byde the coming of that knight,
For then there should no leasure be
But either to fight or else to flie.
    " I took my leave, and forth I fure,
Beside a mount upon a moor :
Then I perceived by my sight,
That he had teached me full right,   120
And understood which was the land ;
A forrest lay on every hand,
A river that was deep and wide,
I found no entress at a side,
Unto a foord, and over I rode,
Unto the other side, but bode ;
And I had but a short while ridden
Into the land that was forbidden,
When I heard moving in the street,
As it had been of horses feet :   130
My steed before me had good sight,

Cast up his head, and worthed light;
He crapt together, and would have run,
I hearkened where that din should come;
I looked a little me before,
I saw a knight ride on a sore,
With red shield, and red spear,
And all of red shined his gear :
He rode upon a sturdy steed,
He let him come with all his speed :   140
Our horse together rushed keen,
Alace, that meeting I may mean !
For through birnie, and through blasoun,
Through octoun, and through habergeon,
Out through my gear both less and mare,
And through my body he me bare :
Yet still upon my sadle I sate,
And on his breast my spear I brake;
His spear again to him he drew,
He mist myself, my steed he slew ;   150
Then lighted I deliverlie,
But not so soon, ready was he
Ere ever I might my good sword weild,
Again he strake me in the shield ;
Through force of him, and of his steed,
He bare me down, and over me yeed :
And then on foot I started soon,
And thought as I had lately done,
For to revenge my steeds bane,
The great defoul myself had tane ;   160
And even as he by me out drew,
I mist himself, his steed I slew :
To counter on foot he was full thra,
His good spear I stroke in twa :
He drew a sword, a worthie weapon,
The first dint on me could happen ;

5

For through ventil and pensil he share,
Into my shoulder five inch and mare.
Then I him hit upon the crown,
A cantil of his helm dang down;   170
And for that strake I would not let,
Another upon him soon I set,
Upon his breast with a fell braid,
At the ground I thought he had been laid :
Also I thought well he had gotten,
But at that strake my sword was broken.
I drew a knife, I had none other,
The which I got it from my brother :
Another of steel, soon hath he tane,
In hands we are together gane.   180
Upon his belt with all my pith,
I strake him, while he groaned with,
While I got blood through all his gear ;
And he me stroke in the visier,
And wounded me into the face,
Mine een was sav'd, such was my grace ;
I stroke him upward in the head,
And in the helmet my blade I leav'd,
And with mine heft behind the hand,
I strake him while that I might stand ;   190
While there came blood through the steel,
He wants some teeth I wote right well.
But what through blood, and proper stress,
My mights waxed less and less.
He had a knife of fine steel,
He strake fast, it lasted right well ;
Mine habergeon of Millain wark,
Lasted me no more than my sark :
Nor mine actoun of Millain fine,
First was my fathers, and then mine ;   200
Mine harness helped me not a resh,

It stinted never but in my flesh.
When I was blinded with the blood,
And all was gone should do me good ;
When blood me blinded, then in soun
Betwixt his hands I fell down ;
And there a while in sown I lay.
  " When I o'rcame he was away ;
My little finger I mist me fra :
And when I looked there I sa,   210
A slain knight, beside me lay,
His little finger was away ;
And thereby might I right well see,
The knight met both with him and me.
  " Beside me ran a river strand,
And there I crap on feet and hand,
And from mine eyes I washt the blood,
And drank while that I thought it good :
When I had cooled me, up I raise,
And looked about in every place :   220
My steed lay sticked, a little me fro,
And his lay stricken the back in two.
My weapons still there they lay,
My knife, my sword, none was away ;
But all was broken and none was hail,
And with mine hands, I could them wail.
A truncheon of mine own spear ;
Me thought it heavy for to bear :
Of a sadled horse I got a sight,
He was right wean, but he was wight ;   230
He had gone bridled days nine,
For fault of food was like to tine :
Heavily in the sadle I strade,
And all the day on him I rade.
  " When day was gone, and come was night,
Of a castle I got a sight :

A little from a noble town,
At an harber, I lighted down,
The fairest bow'r I saw me by,
That ever I saw since born was I.   240
I lean'd me on my sadle to rest,
Bethinking me what was the best;
For I had need some me to mend,
And I was loath for to be kend:
I had been but a short time there,
When that a woman, sweet and fair,
Came walking from the harber green,
And at the bower she would have been;
She stinted when she could me see,
A lady seemed she to be;   250
And in scarlet she was clade,
And all the weed that she on had,
In red gold could it birn,
And rich pearles set therein.
It seem'd to me by her parrage,
She was a lady of great linage:
And though that I had bled my blood,
Yet still upon my feet I stood;
And she descried me full right,
And hailsed me then as a knight.   260
Right as a knight she hailsed me,
And I her in the same degree.
  " Sir, she said, by mine intent,
Ye have need of better easement;
And here beside there is an hall,
A little space under the wall:
Therein is many cruel knight,
And leeches that are true of plight,
That ever man came in mister till;
Thereto the kindest lord at will: 270
Since I'm the first that with you met,

I would you were the better bet."
    " Then said I to the lady fair,
I would not be in such repair ;
But I require you, if ye might,
Of privie guesting for one night ;
And a maiden me for to keep,
While I were eased with a sleep ;
And some ease for mine hackney.
She said, I shall find if I may.   280
    " Then into her bow'r she me led,
It was great joy to see her bed :
She set me down, and I was fain ;
And lustily turn'd she again
To her maidens, she had but two,
And both she caus'd from her to go ;
The one, mine hackney to his stead,
And at his liking could him feed ;
The other, went with counsel soon,
As she her bade, so hath she done :   290
Baked fowles she brought again,
Spice and wine, bread of main ;
A laver they have gotten soon,
Warm water into it was done,
And, in a silver basen,
Her own hands washed mine een :
And when she saw mine hands bare,
Then waxt mine anger for the mare,
My glove was hail, my finger was tint,
She might well know it was no dint.   300
For Gray Steel he was of such pride,
And his word waxed ay so wide,
Of what countrey that he was commin,
She might wit well I was o'rcommin.
    " She perceived that I thought shame :
She asked not what was my name,

Or of what countrey I was come,
Into what place, or in what room,
Or of what countrey that I were,
But eased me in all manner.   310
Such drink, then, as she gave me there,
Saw I never in my fare !
That so much could me restore,
For I was vanquisht all before ;
More weak and weary might no man be,
And dry'd for blood, as any tree.
Her drinks they brought me soon in state
That I might speak, and answer make.
She and her maids, those ladys three,
Of all my gear they spoiled me :   320
Both of mine habrek, and mine actoun,
Washed me syn, and laid me down ;
'With' her own hands, white as the milk,
She stopped my wounds full of silk ;
And syne laid me into a bed,
That was with silken sheets spred.
    " Then to the lady could I say,
No longer than against the day,
It is not my will for to lend,
For I would that no man me kend ;   330
But I may ever more conteen,
Into such state as I have been,
It were good time to me to boun,
Of the gentrice that ye have done.
    " Sir, then she said, against your will,
I cannot treat you to bide still,
But if it likes you to tarry,
Shall no man know your privity,
Nor yet myself, I shal not fraine,
And though I wist, I could it lain.   340
Ly still and sleep with God's blessing,

I shall you waken then in due time.
   " Her self, nor yet her maidens two,
That night into no bed would go :
A plastron on her knee she laid,
And thereon love justly she plaid ;
Thereto her maidens sweetly sang.
This lady sighed oft amang,
What countenance ever she made,
Some heavy thing in heart she had.   350
Spice they had, and noble wine,
And ever took when they had time,
And sundry times at me they sought
If that I would, or yarned ought :
And thus they put the night near by.
Then soon after great din heard I :
Of bonny birds in a herbeir,
That of love sang, with voice so clear,
With diverse notes ;—against the day,
She came to me without delay,   360
And brought me drink into an horn,
And since the day that I was born,
Such a good drink I never got ;
When I had drunk, she could me hap,
Within a day she came again,
Of all my gear she made me plain.
The drink that she gave me was green,
Into my wounds it might be seen ;
The blood was fled when it was there,
And all was sound, before was sair.   370
The bloody tents away she drew,
And tented me again with new :
The tents that in my wounds yeed,
Trust ye well, they were no threed :
They were neither lake nor line ;
Of silk they were, both good and fine :

The mistenting of my wounds,
Cost that lady twenty pounds.
Withoutten spice, salves or gries,
And other things that did me ease.   380
My linnen cloaths were washed clean,
The blood in them might not be seen;
A sark of silk, that was full dear,
She put on me, which I have here;
And syne put on mine own abone,
And all my cloathing she hath undone;
And all my armour less and mare,
She would not let me leave ought there:
Of mine habreke I had great dreed,
It should me hurt and cause me bleed.   390
The sorest wound that grieved me,
I wist not where that it might be,
But it was as sicker and sound,
As never weapon had wrought me wound.
    "Then, to the lady fair, said I,
Either I am in fantasy,
Or else ye are the fairest May,
That ever I saw before this day;
All that ever hath wrought me wo.
She said, would God that it were so!   400
But I know, by your buskening,
That ye have something in studying;
For your love, sir, I think it be:
But trust ye well and certainly,
As soon as love makes you agast,
Your ointments will you nothing last;
Your wounds they will both glow and gell,
Sow full sore, and be full ill;
But ye have mends, that ye may mean,
Unto your love where ye have been;   410
And bid her do as I have done,

And they will soft and sober soon.
My ring, my beeds forth I dreugh,
Of most fine gold and good enough;·
She would not take them of me lang,
But on her bed down them I flang:
Her maidens brought me forth a scail,
Of fine main bread, and fowls haill,
With bottles full of finest wine,
And thereupon I lived syne.   420
Oft have I sleeped in my fare,
But short sleeps I think they were;
Evil reposed, weak and faint,
But sickness made me never grant:
Nor soreness found I never a pyle,
While I came here within a myle:
Then all my wounds did open ónce,
As knife had gone through flesh and bones;
I fell down dead as any stone:
When I o'rcàme, mine horse was gone,   430
A bed then I would had rather,
Than my weight of gold and silver.
    " Now have I told you less and mare,
Of all that hapned in my fare: .
How I did suffer all thè pain,
And how the lady sent me hame."
Sir Grahame, a sober man and meek,
Whatever he thinks, little will speak:
Then said he to Sir Eger:
" It forethinks me that ye were there: 440
I bade you always hold you well,
And namely from that man Gray-Steel,
For he is called uncanuand,
And spoken of in many land:
Many have proved him for to sla,
And all failed, and did not sa:

And now its best to make good chear,
And I am glade to have you here.
From the lady we will not lane,
That ye are now come home again;   450
That ye were in a far countrie,
And vexed with a fell minyie."
    Sir Eger wist not, nor yet Sir Grahame,
Where the lady was all the time:
The bour wherein the lady was,
Was from the hall a little space:
Upon her love she had great thought,
She lay waking, and sleeped nought,
And at the window had great sight;
When she perceived there was a light,   460
And longed sore to speak with him;
She trowed right well that he was come.
A scarlet mantle hath she tane,
And to the chamber is she gane;
She heard them with a privy din,
She stood right still, and stood within,
Under the wall she stood so still,
Heard the manner that it was ill;
She had no more things for to frame,
But to her chamber past again.   470
So privily she is not gone,
But they perceived that there was one;
They were rede, and discovered:
Sir Grahame about his bed reiked,
And both the windows opened plain,
And saw the lady pass again;
With the light he looked farre to,
Perceived well that it was she.
Sir Eger says, " Who makes that din?"
He said, " My spaneyard would be in."   480
Sir Grahame ceased not, nor would blin,

While that he got a man therein,
That right well, with all wounds could deal,
And was right happy for to heal :
And yet, ere day, the word was gone,
That Sir Eger was coming home,
And had mo wounds with sword and knife,
Than ever man that had his life ;
Riches may make him no remead,
There is no life for him, but dead.   490
The Earle into his chamber went,
The Countess, and her maidens gent,
And they beheld him so deadly :
He spake not, whatever they say,
Nor no language to them he had,
But Sir Grahame all the answer made.
He said, " Yestreen when he came home,
His tongue was not all from him gone ;
He hath me told right all the case,
And how that matter happned was :   500
A swadrick in a wilderness,
Where that never is near a place,
He wist nothing into his fare,
That their linage it was all there.ʏ
And they wist all of his coming,
Thought to slay him, and take his thing ;
They rose, and have against him gone,
They were ten, and he was but one :
Not one, but his own steed and he,
And yet he thought not for to flee :   510
With stout heart, and hardie alswa,
The field he took against all tha :
This may be wit that he was bold,
He slew seven ere he flee would.
On horse, as he out through them yeed,
He slew them two, and they his steed :

Ere his good spear was broken in two,
Of them he slew well six and mo :
And six into the field he slew ;
The rest they fled, and they withdrew :   520
And with that he was wounded so,
That scarcely he might ride or go.
An horse of theirs then by him stood,
Like to his own, but not so good ;
Syne, on that, he is coming home,
And it right seven days is gone ;
And though the deed he sought on him,
It is well sped to all his kin.
And for that worship he went there,
It will be told for evermare.   530
    The Countess mourns for Sir Eger ;
Her maidens mourned, and made great care ;
Sir Pallias, his own brother,
Made more sorrow than any other :
Sir Grahame was nothing of his kin,
But he was als right for him,
As any sister, or as brother,
Eme, or yet ant, or any other :
But it was more than days three,
Or his own love came him to see :   540
And when she came, she was but drie,
To him she made small courtesie.
When she came to the chamber within,
Little company made to him ;
Sir Eger might not one word speak,
Sir Grahame before the bed could sit ;
And to Sir Grahame said she then :
" Sir, how doth your sore wounded man,
Or how hath he sped in his fare ? "
Said, " Not so well as mister were :   550
So it hapned as you may see,

Not one forethinks so much as ye."
The lady said, " So have I feel,
I might have thol'd he had done well,
And better sped in his journey."
Sir Eger asked where he lay.
Then meekly said the lady free,
To Sir Eger, "Now, how do ye?
I rede you be of counsel clean,
Ye will not cose, Sir, as I ween.   560
I think your love be in no weer,
Therefere I rede you make good chear."
Sir Eger said, "My chear well is,
But even as I may with this,
As before when better hath been,
I will not mend suppose I mean."
Then said the Lady, "Certes, nay,
It mends not though ye do sway;
Fortune will not then from you wend,
Nor yet from me, though I should send: 570
But for follie to set at wit,
And so I must then do with it."
She no more tidings did refrain,
But bounded to her chamber again.
Then Sir Grahame stood before the door,
And held the Lady on the floor,
A little while, right by the hand:
Then by his fellow could he stand,
And said to him right courteouslie,
" Sir, this the Lady telleth me,   580
What makes her biding to delay,
And why she goes so soon away:
She was forbidden by the leech,
And also by her father's speech;
And the first night that ye came hame,
So great a sorrow hath she tane,

That she hath been as sick as ye:"
And thus his fellow comforts he.
   Eleven weeks, as I heard say,
Sir Eger there in leeching lay;   590
And seldom came the fair Lady;
But when she came, she was right dry.
Her drieness, and als her strange fare,
Sir Grahame then said to Sir Eger,
That she durst not otherwise do,
Nor yet in presence come him to:
And on this wise, as with Sir Grahame,
So with the Lady on a time,
On his foot with her would he gang,
Then to his fellow would amang;   600
And then told him a fern-year's tale,
And this, while thus he wrought all hale,
And to her ladies warrand well;
For he was red he should him spill,
And her will had been to him kend,
It should have letten him to mend,
But all was fained each a dale,
Yet, many said, he govern'd well.
   Then after that, upon a day,
He thought the lady to assay.   610
Then after mass to her he yeed,
Into a chamber where she stood,
And from her maidens hath her tane,
And to a counsel are they gane.
And first they spake of bourding,
And then they spake of earnest thing:
He said, "Lady, if ye would cover,
And of a thing that ye would sover,
Belonging both to you and me."
She said, "Say on, whatever it be."   620
"Yonder is your knight Sir Eger,

And he hath been in travel sair;
And hath met with a ferlie thing,
For fault of weapons and arming:
Armour they made me fresh and new,
And yet be false, and right untrue,
And that hath made him to beguile;
Give him the ware within a while,
And great skaith therethrow hath he tane,
But, certes, therein he hath no shame. 630
He is a man, that is well kend,
Hath doughtie hands him to defend,
I cannot treat him for to bide,
Fra time that he may gang or ride;
But he will pass his voyage right,
To seek for battel on the knight:
This hath he made me to you tell,
But ye may treat him here to dwell,
And comfort him in all manner,
But with your presence, and with chear. 640
Now sen it stands in such degree,
It 'longeth more to you than me:
Have ye not chosen him to your peer?
Your father it likes well, but weer!"—
The Lady mused, and stood still,
Then after made answer him till,
" Sir Grahame, ye wot this many day,
For him better I put away:
For I was of such nourishing,
I would have none for no kin thing; 650
Neither for riches, nor renown,
For lands breadth, nor provision;
But he, that wan with his hands two:
Sir Eger was call'd one of tho';
Called the best when he came hame,
How ever he wrought, such was his name:

In company such name he gat,
How ever he did, such was his hap.
I bade him let his journey be,
Make not this travel, all for me :   660
I said, such field he may come in,
Was as able to tyn or win.
I strake the nail upon the head,
All that he wan, ye may soon sead :
For trust ye me right well, Sir Grahame,
I wist the matter all sensyne :
For the first night that he came home,
I heard your words every each one ;
Under your chamber window stood,
And heard your carping ill and good.   670
I will not bid him for to bide,
Nor yet him counsel for to ride ;
Neither consent I will thereto :
Of his wedding I have no do."
Sir Grahame, he said, " I trow he will,
But little seeking make you till :
And he tells in his coming hame,
That he hath sped a better name,
That is far better of degree :
You love not him, will you love me ? "   680
This he did say into bourding,
But he was sorry for that thing :
Yet sadly in his heart he thought,
To help his fellow, if he moght ;
And down he sate into that place,
And then his dolour changed was :
For his fellow he was right mov'd,
Behind his back heard him reprov'd.
    The knight rase up, and went his way,
Sir Eger to Sir Grahame can say :   690
Then hath he said to Sir Eger,

" Me think that it then better were,
To seek yon knight, and him expell,
That you destroy'd in battel:
But I trow well, and by your tale,
That had your weapons holden hale,
He had been either tane or slain;
But sen it is against you gane,
For him we must go make some cast,
For to cause fight him at the last.   700
As with his hand, he had him led,
Though ye be sleeping in your bed,
And that is sooth, I shall you see,
We shall fight him where ever he be.
Ye rise up in your best full set,
And put you on your robes full meet,
And at your window stand or go;
Books of Romances shall ye read so,
The whole court will be full fain,
When they see you now up again: 710
The Earle himself will be full blyth,
For he thinks ye shall have to wife,
Yon young lady, his daughter gent,
But I cannot tell her intent:
Of women I can never traist,
I found them fickle and never fast:
Thus shall ye govern days nine.
Then shall ye rise, when ye think time,
And put upon you all your gear,
As ye would ride, in land of wear: 720
And take your leave at the knights all,
And at each one, both great and small,
And at the ladies, white as lake,
To your love no countenance make;
Be of few words, and stillarie,
Of countenance see ye be slee:

6

I force not though that ye so do,
And then turn you again me to.
My steed brought forth, and saddled well,
I bide no more, so have I fell,   730
Your coat armour then shall I take,
Your basnet, and your gloves of plate,
Your knife, your sword, I bid no mare;
And graith you right as you did aire,
Your brother's spear, your own was broken;
Then this gear when I have gotten,
In faith, I shall no longer bide,
Nor yet shall spur my steeds side;
And though the lady come and see,
Either me turn, or else to flee.   740
If I be in great jeopardie,
Stand ye, and look there after me;
She shall say on, to others than,
Sir Eger is no discomfite man:
Yet shall she say, and others ma,
A better journey will he ta."
Sir Eger turned, and said " Nay !
These seven months though here I ly,
Shall no man take that deed on hand,
While I myself may ride and stand.   750
I think you much, but not for that,
Ye ween I am put far aback;
And ye trust no comfort in me;
I shall revenge me, or else die."
Sir Grahame said to him that time,
" It is not all as you do mean,
And if ye ly seven months there,
Or yet but one, or little mare,
Some new tidings that ye will hear;
The Lady will get her a feer: 760
For Sir Olyas, I understand,

Will brook the lady and the land;
For since ye lay here, I have seen,
A privy message them between;
She hath heard all his whole intent,
And hath given him her consent:
For trust ye well," then said Sir Grahame,
" She knows the matter all sensyne :
Since the first night that ye came home,
She heard your words ever each one,   770
And by your chamber window stood,
And heard your carping, ill and good."
Sir Eger says, " If it be so,
Then wot I well I must forgo
Love-liking, and man-hood all clean."
The water rushed out of his een :
His head he shook, his hands he wrang,
And each hand on another dang:
Sir Grahame then said to him, " Let be,
Ye shall be helped hastily,   780
For here I vow to God of might,
That I shall ride and seek the knight,
Into what land that he in be,
I shall him slay, or else he me ;
And if I chance to win the field,
And get his helm, or yet his shield,
Or any mark of him to see,
The lady will think it be ye :
She will say soon, and to you seel,
That she is wood, and would you well."   790
They called to him Sir Pallias,
And told him all the very case,
They shew to him both all and some,
They kend full well that he would come,
The man that loves, and als is leel,
Is worthiest to keep counsell.

Then after that, upon a day,
Sir Grahame to Sir Eger can say,
"If I should meet with yon Gray-Steel,
I had need to be holden well: 800
And your emes sword, Sir Agam,
These seven winters can it ly:
The lady locks it in a chist,
She thinks it should not come in thrist;
Nor yet be born into the field,
While that her son be come to eeld:
Had we it now in borrowing,
It might make us some comforting:
We must now have it, ere we gang,
With other weapons good and strang."   810
Sir Grahame is to the lady gone,
And said, "Sir Eger is at home,
And hath a journey tane on hand,
With a great knight of a strange land,
And his own good sword hath he broken,
And he hath not another gotten:
And prays you for a noble brand,
And take the charters of his land."
"Now trust ye well, withoutten weer,
Sir Grahame," she said "it is right here,   820
Though ye be charg'd, I you assure,
It will not fail, but ay endure;
And shall stand you into good stead,
While that ye have Gray-Steel's head:
For the first time that it was wrought,
To the king's forrest it was brought,
And seven winters he it bare;
His life-time was but little mare.
Then he betaught it to the queen,
And to his son for to be given.   830
And with them dwelled then, Sir Grahame,

Was right instant at the making,
While he had made that noble brand,
For there may nothing it gainstand.
He may be sure to give a strake,
For it will never bow, nor break;
Teugh as the wax, when it was wrought,
Hard like the flint, and faileth nought,
It was never won by no strength,
Nor yet put back by its own length :   840
What flesh it ever hapneth in,
Either in lyre, or yet in skin,
Whether that were shank or arm,
It shall him do wonder great harm :
There is no fault in any thing,
But it was in misgoverning ;
For a man of evil guiding,
May tine a kinrick, and a king :
And I would not, for both our lands,
That it came in other men's hands."   850
 Sir Grahame is from the lady gane,
To Vaclaw, and his leave hath tane ;
And, ill-disposed with fainted chear,
Sir Eger hath put on his gear :
Within seven days and seven nights,
On this same wise dealt both the knights ;
While on the eight day of the prime,
"Sir Eger," saith now Sir Grahame,
"Wind up, Sir, and on your feet,
And see your gear be good and meet ;   860
Look that you arm you, and als clean,
As any time that ye have been,
And as warlick as ever ye would,
Ride this day a battel to hold :
Into the hall make you repair,
Of countenance see ye be fair,

Then turn again, and hold you still,
And let me do that which God will :
As for my work, I have no dread,
I trust in God, right well to speed."   870
Sir Eger sighed, and said, "Alace,"
Right well payed Sir Grahame he was,
And said, "I pray you, Sir, let be,
If ye will any help of me :
But with your tongue you may be wise,
The nearest gate, and where it lyes."
"I shall you tell, wonderful well,
That ye shall not go wrong a deal :
Ye know the way is for a while,
The valour more than thirty mile,   880
Ye shall be four days, and than,
That ye shall see no kind of man,
Nor nothing but the fowles flyand,
Wilderness and all wasted land :
A river shal ye find at hand,
That runneth strait as any strand ;
Though ye never so fast you speed,
Yet two days it shall you lead ;
And then shall you see come runnand,
An water on the other hand,   890
For those two do both run in one ;
A riding place there is not one.
Cross the water, the first foord strand,
And hold them both on your left hand ;
Then of your way you have no dread,
The salt water it will you lead :
And in the coast of that salt sand,
A great forrest is on your right hand ;
But yet the wilderness will last,
One day, ride ye never so fast :   900
Then come ye in the plainest land,

And an alley on every hand ;
A fair castle then shall ye see,
Halls and bowres of great plenty ;
Orchards, harbers, and a fair green,
In that other a lady sheen,
That in fairest may be a flower,
And clearest of all other colour ;
She's courteous, and kind of speech,
Ov'r all the rest she may be leech :   910
Great God, if I had with her bidden,
By this I might have gone or ridden :
My counsel she would have covered,
The which myself hath discovered.
Take ye a small token from me,
There may ye right well eased be ;
Her own sark it is best to bear,
And then somewhat else of your gear."
Sir Grahame he said, " that may be ill,
Any token to take her till ;   920
For I was loath, so God me sane,
For to be known till I came hame."
Sir Eger says, " It is no skaith,
That she have 'quaintance with us baith,
For she is full of all gentrice,
Into her heart hath no fancies :
Will ye behave you cunningly,
You may make her trow it is I.
She served me with candle-light ;
I came, and yeed, both in one night,   930
And make her trow that both is ane."
   Sir Grahame the sark hath with him tane,
And twenty pounds in it hath he,
Beeds of gold, and broches three ;
And this is over little ware,
If he were purvey'd into mare ;

But all without I may not be,
Some part now ye must leave with me.
Sir Grahame said, " How shall I know
The woman that I never saw ? "　　　　　940
" I tell to you it wondrous well,
Cannot go wrong, or miss a deal :
She is large of body and bone,
A fairer saw I never none ;
With brows bent, and thereto small,
A drawing voice she speaks withall :
Betwixt her een, and eke her neise,
There is the greatness of a piese,
A spot of red, the lave is white ;
There is none other that is her like :　　　　　950
And so her brows on a running,—
There is a gay ready tokening !
And the bower it stands east and west,
Thereon a weather-cock is prest ;
It may be gold, it may be glass,
I might not see whereof it was ;
It might be glass, it might be steel,
But it was bright, it shined well."
　Sir Eger past into the hall,
And took his leave at the knights all :　　　　　960
Syne to the Earle kneeled on his knee,
He said, " Sir Eger, now where shape ye ?."
He said, " I have meekle ado,
And little beeting gets thereto."
The Countess said, " I red you bide,
For neither have you hew nor hide ;
I see your countenance is good,
But ye are pale, and ye want blood ;
For by your hue it may be seen,
Into such state as ye have been,　　　　　970
Ye will not be this many day ;

Therefore, Sir knight, I will you pray,
For any haste ye have to fare,
Bide still a while, let blood grow mare."
" Mine hue," he said, " let that alane ;
But with yourself, in faith, madam,
I will not bide, so God me sane,
Farewell, while that I come again."
" He " louted, and could the Countess kiss :
The Earle then took her hand in his,　　　　　980
And at the lady, white as lake,
Right reverently could his leave take :
And his own love, she was therein,
Spake not to her, nor she to him :
For, Sir Grahame had to him told,
How he should to the lady hold,
Yet he would not, for great reprove.
From all the rest he took his leave ;
But that he had something to say,
Ere that the time he went away ;　　　　　990
But neither would he beck nor kneel,
Nor lowt, nor yet his head down heel ;
But said, " Lady, what will ye mare ? "—
" God keep you better than he did aire !
You have a finger to let you land,
Now I am red you leave an hand."—
Displeas'd was many lady bright,
She gave such answer to the knight :
And so himself, he thought great shame,
But answer to her made he nane.　　　　　1000
　Forth at the door he passed her fro,
And to his chamber could he go.
Pallias was true as the steel,
And keeped bidding wonder well,
And at the door receiv'd him in,
But none in after him might win.

Few words then was there them among;
There hand shook, said, "Tarry not long."
Sir Grahame was ready to the rade;
A squyre upon the calsay bade,   1010
And in his hand had holding,
A bold steed and well lasting,
Tyed right well with his girths two,
Pallias himself gave him mo;
About his breast he laid a band,
To make the sadle fast on stand:
Great buckle of iron to make it last;
It had great mister to be fast,
For he was red that young Sir Grahame
In his travell he should them tine.   1020
His spurrs he keeped not so well,
But his steed's sides he made them feel;
The steed rebounded from the spurrs,
And rushed rudely through the furze.
The Lady stood, and had good sight,
To see the passing of the knight;
She might see passing perfectly,
Whether he passed in chivalrie,
Or there was any fainying,
Or in his heart discomforting: 1030
She perceived even, as it was,
With stout heart, and great manliness,
His spear, his shield, his helm of steel,
His steed he governed right well,
And was as fresh as any lyon;
He and his horse rode off the town.
The Lady marvell'd greatumly,
Then he past into such degree:
Whatever she thought, nought she said,
But on the knight small strut she made;   1040
And to the chamber could she pass,

Where both the knights there biding was:
The doors were closed, and put to,
The lady chapped, and made undo:
He received in that young lady,
And hailsed her right courteously.
Then Pallias a cod can fang,
And in a chair he it down flang,
And made the lady preserving,
Of all easement, and down sitting: 1050
And she said, "Nay," and walked by,
To the bed where he wont to ly:
She thought to have him lying there,
But in the bed was not Sir Eger.

 The window closed to hide the light,
That she of him might get no sight;
The curtains they were all drawn in,
That on no wise they might be seen.
She drew the curtains and stood within,
And all amazed spake to him :   1060
Then meened to him his distress,
Heart or the head, whether it was?
And his sickness, less or mare ;
And then talked of Sir Eger:
And said to him, " Where have I been,
Where the knights passing I have seen !
And I do think, by my knowledge,
He was as like in his visage,
For to do well, and thereto speed,
As any journey that ever he yeed ;   1070
But he hath made a fair showing,
And in his heart great comforting."
So lovingly to him she spake ;
But soon after she fell a-back,
And said, " It was no mastery,
Where there comes against a party :

But when there is a knight for knight,
They must do more to try a right :
Knight for knight, and steed for steed,
Then to do well were all the need.   1080
There is no better company,
Nor one to meet allenerly.
This tale I tell by Sir Eger,
That he may in his travel aire,
Whereto should he seek aventures ?
In armies he hath tint his armours! "
" Not so, but he was overcome,
In bushment, lying waiting him ;
And all they brake at Sir Eger :
But them then he did not fear ;   1090
But right stoutly he did them byde,
And all that hapned in that tide :
Ere any of them to him wan,
There he slew an hie-kinned man :
When he is felled on the ground,
And through the shield hath got a wound,
A north-land knight full dughty,
Rescued him with company :
There was but he and other ten,
And they were twenty hie-kinned men :   1100
And then were twenty tane and slain,
Then Sir Eger rescued again :
They brought Sir Eger to the king,
With meekle mirth and magnifying :
They proffered him for his voyage,
The King's sister in marriage :
And he sighed, and would not have,
And followed always on the lave :
I say not, Lady, your tale to 'peach ;
But, if I could, I would you teach :   1110
There should no man then it unlove,

Say that it was his own reprove ; "
Pallias said to that Lady,
But fair words, and right tenderlie.
When he had said all that he would,
The knight said, with steven full bold :
" Sick that I am, and wonder sore,
And for my fellow moved more,
That now is past in such degree,
And I wite none, Lady, but ye :   1120
While I hear word of him again,
Whether he slayes or bees slain,
Have more of my collation hold."
The lady went where that she would :
But they bode in their chamber still,
At leasure, and at their own will.
  ¶ Now we will let them all alone,
Carp of Sir Grahame that forth is gone.
He countered in the west-land,
Beyond the fell, the water fand,   1130
And followed as he was bidden,
And to the forest he is ridden,
And passed it in days three,
That they said fifteen it should be ;
And then he saw a tokening,
A reek did rise, and a gladning :
He saw before him on the way,
A yeoman ride on an hacknay,
Entring in at the forrest side ;
He call'd on him, and bade him bide :   1140
The yeoman hover'd, and stood still,
And said, " Sir, what is your will ? "
He said, " Fellow, thou tell to me,
Who is the Lord of this countrie :
Whether that he is old or young,
Or who hath it in governing ? "

The yeoman said, " I understand
He is an Earle that ought this land :
They do call him Earle Gorius,
And hath none heir but Lillias."   1150
" Is she a widow, then ? " said he.
" She is a maiden, certainlie.
Sir Alistoun, that gentle knight,
She and he else hath their troth plight :
The Earle, that heght Sir Garrentine,
Was slain by Gray-Steel on a time ;
And for Sir Garrentine, his head,
Sir Alistoun had him at fead ;
And so he thought him to have won,
But sped as ill as others have done."   1160
The yeoman said, I understand
That ye are unknown in this land ;
The Earl is fair-calling and free,
And there ye may well-eased be :
There may ye have right good gaistning,
If that ye will make sojourning."
The knight he said all these words syne,
" How farre is't to the castle hyne ? "—
" But miles three, it is no mo,
With you I shall ride of them two."   1170
    The yeoman rode forth with the knight,
While of the castle he got sight ;
Syne took his leave, and from him rade,
The knight to him great thanks he made.
He wail'd an inne into the town,
Before the gate he lighted down ;
And there they came to him on hie,
Great gentlemen and squyarie ;
And from him they took his good steed,
And to his stable could him lead,   1180
To hecks full of corn and hay,

And other horse were led away :
The master houshold was therein,
And he betaught them unto him,
Both his good horse and his armour,
And all that fell to his honour.
And he from him took them on hand ;
And said, that he should them warrand,
And proffer'd him a squyarie,
To go with him in company.   1190
But he said, " Nay, he needed none,"
But raiked forth, his way is gone ;
And when he came the town without,
He looked then him round about,
Orchards, harbers, and alleys green :
The weather-cock stood fair and sheen,
The samin bower as he me told ;
He was of all his tokens bold,
He had gone right and nothing wrong,
Joyfull in heart was he among.   1200
He thought if he might get a sight
Of the lady both fair and bright,
He would think the better to speed,
In any journey where he yeed.
    He stood a while, such hap he had,
He saw the lady, and was glad,
Coming was with a damosell ;
He perceived wonder well,
It was the same lady he sought,
By all the tokens, and failed nought :   1210
He raiked to the fair lady,
And hailsed her right courteously,
And in his visage could he mean
As he before had done her seen.
But she did know him in nothing,
Neither did he her, but faining,

And he seemed a courteous knight,
Of any that came in her sight.
Reverently she made him state,
But quantance none other they wate :   1220
Then hastilie he could out draw,
His sark of silk ; and could it shaw,
And costlie jewels als, but miss.
" Sir," then she said, " so have you bliss !
How fares the knight that did send this ? "
He sayes, " Lady, I do not lane,
He that it bure, brought it again."
Then blythly on him could she look,
Courteously to him could she mute,
And swore by Jesus, Heaven's king,   1230
" I am right glad of your coming !
And certainly, by God's grace,
Have ye gotten out at this place?
Or any thing that could you bet?
I would think that it were right fit."
Then sayes he, " Here was a bet,
Which I think never to forget !
Wherefore to you I make living
Of my life, and no other thing."
Then courteously she spake to him,   1240
And to his gaistning bade him come.
He said, " Lady, my inne is tane,
And squyers with me are mo than ane ;
I bade the ostler certainlie,
To purvey both for them and me."
He would been glad, if that he might,
Have been out of the lady's sight,
For he was dreading for kenning ;
He would have been out of feeling :
He could not get away so soon
As mister was for to have done :   1250

His fellow's visage it was fair,
But he was hurt under the hair;
A courcher over it was drawn,
To let it for to be unknawn;   ·
An oyntment over the skin he drew,
To make the hide another hew;
He did work wisely in that case,
But in somethings he was rackless.
   Talking as she then by him stood,
For to see if his hands were good,   1260
She took the glove as she could stand,
And turned down over his hand:
Syne when she saw his hands bare,
And all his fingers standing there,
She perceived that it was not he,
And kindly carping she let be:
And dryly to him could she speak,
" Where is the knight that lay here sick ?"—
He said, " Lady, as ye may see."
Yet did she say, " That might well be,   1270
What fairlie was he though long home,
For here such leeching there was none!
There is no leech in all the land,
Can put a finger to an hand!
The finger that he left in wed,
That is another in its steed,
Both as fair, as whole and as clean,
As ever it was or yet has been !—
Ye should not, sir, in a strange land,
Mock, or yet be over bourdand;   1280
But, if ye will with bourding dail,
Right cleanly then ye should them wail:
Your bourding could I well consider,
But scorn and heeding goes together.
Yet never allowed will ye be,

Nor yet in no good company.
Sir, if that ye was hither sent,
And to scorn me in your intent,
Ye shall not be but scorn'd of me,
And ere ye pass off this countrie."   1290
    First she was both right mild and meek,
Kind and courteous for to speak;
Then waxt she angry, and so hate,
And all into another state:
The jewels that the knight had brought
The lady set them all at nought;
Down at his feet she let them fall,
And wrathfully turned her withall.
And to her chamber bowned her to gang:
The knight his hands in her's could fang.   1300
She shoot his hands, and bade, " Let go,"
But he to hold, she would not so:
" I pray you, lady, of your grace,
Your meekness, and your soberness,
Let not your will over-gang your wit,
While ye be advised with it,
Whether there be cause or none;
And that there be cause, I am to blame,
Hear me a point that I soall shaw,
There God in borrowes I draw,   1310
But I shall tell you all the ground,
The which, all sooth it shall be found."
What through prayer, and als through threat,
She stood and heard what the knight spake,
And then Sir Grahame his tale began,
And shew her forth the matter than:
" The knight that was here is my brother,
And I am elder than the other.
A journey I must take for him,
Whether that I must tine or wine;   1320

He hath a lusty love at home,
Love nor husband she would have none,
But he that ever in arms wan ;
And the first time that he begane,
That tint now, and that she wate,
And draws aback and makes debate ;
And he loves her in such degree,
Without her love he may not be.
But he will wed her to his wife,
Or tine his honour and his life.　　　　　　　　1330
And I would gladly, if I might,
Be acquainted with the same knight,
And see if he would be my brother,
Send him on wed for another ;
And will he not, by Heaven's king,
There shall men carp of our parting.
And so must I now honour win,
In any land that I come in.
Or ever in arms win the gree,
I have told you the verity."　　　　　　　　　1340
　　¶ The lady stood and her bethought,
For to reprove him would she nought ;
" This is a seemly knight to see,
And carps most courteously to me.
And I his tale for to impele,
I wot not but it may be lele,
Then it were great reproof to me ;
I shall allow it, however it be."
This was her thought into the time,
As she told after to Sir Grahame.　　　　　　1350
" Sir, then," she said, " I can well trow,
Your tale is good, and I allow,
For such points you-would not shaw,
Nor charge your manhood for to draw.
And ye shall bide all night with me ;

Will ye have twa, or will ye three :
I would ye hade your pith right well,
Ere that ye met with Sir Gray-Steel."
She caused a boy full soon him speed,
Where that the knight had left his steed ;   1360
A piece of gold with him she send,
The knight his cost for to amend ;
A royall supper there was dight,
To the lady and to the knight :
The meat and drink was not to spare,
All good easements then he had there.
Then after supper could she say,
To comfort him in his journey :
" If that ye will go to Gray-Steel,
I trow to God ye shall do well :   1370
And if that ye do win the gree,
It is but fortune, and not ye ;
And fra fortune against him rin,
There is no more defence in him.
And there is none other the whilk,
I trow to God ye be that ilk.
If ye have hap the knight to slay,
I trow to God ye shall do swa !
There is nothing in all this land,
That shall be holden from your hand ;   1380
And, namely, that belongs to me,
So that mine honour saved be.
He slew my brother, my father's heir,
Als mine own love, and that was mare !
And sensyne I was never aye
Into good likeing half a day."
And when she spake of her lemman,
The water over her cheeks soon ran.—
Sir Grahame beheld the lady free,
His heart wrought bold and held on hie,   1390

And trow'd if he might slay the knight,
Then might he win the lady bright.
   So spake the lady and Sir Grahame,
While that it was right good bed-time;
And thus they talked, and they spake,
Syne spices and the wine they take;
And to a bed then they him brought,
For to get sleep, if that he mought:
But he thought never night so lang.
While day come that the fowles sang,   1400
He was riseing and soon on steer;
The lady heard where she was near,
She caus'd two maidens bear him light,
And courteously did serve the knight
With baken meat, and spices hate,
To strength the knight in his estate.
Carved his meat, and to him share,
While he was full, and would no mare.
   When he was ready for to pass,
The lady said, that by him was,   1410
" Sir Grahame! ah knight of aventure!
In press, think on your paramour:
I will not bid you think on me,
Think on your love, wherever she be;
And on your friends that are at home,
And on your gasting ye have tane;
And here your supper shall be dight,—
I think ye shall be here all night.
Think not Gray-Steel, albeit he would,
Shall hinder you your tryst to hold."   1420
He said, " Lady, so God me reed,
And if ye would, he shall not speed!
I have more dread he will not come,
Than I have of his mother's son."—
" Then certes," said the lady fair,

" Trust ye right well he will be there !
Trust in the field he will be seen,
By ye have ridden over the green."
    She caus'd a boy out with him gang,
A wine bottle with him could fang.   1430
Unto the town then they both yeed,
Where that the knight had left his steed.
They found him in a good apply,
Both hay and corn and bread him by ;
The ostler he could thanking make,
And bade him more than he would take ;
The ostler saw him bown to fare,
Saddled his horse, and made him yare.
A spear that was both great and lang,
A squyer he brought it him to fang ;   1440
Women weeped sore for the knight,
When he passed out of their sight :
They trow'd that he would be in that steed,
Where many men had left their head.
    Ere it was mid-morn of the day,
He came where that the place did lay,
Which was called the land of Doubt ;
A forrest lying round about ;
In Roman stories who will read,
Two miles of length, and two of breadth ;   1450
He saw nothing into that steed,
But great felloun down deer and reed ;
He saw beside him, on an hight
A fair castle, with towers wight ;
A deep river, both long and brade,—
Was never one that over it rade,
That had not Sir Gray-Steel his leave,
That came again without repreave :
Sir Grahame he looked not to that,
But sought a foord, and that he gat.   1460

When he was on the other side,
Then fair and hulie could he ride:
He rode the two part of the land,
And nothing found he there steerand.
He lighted on his foot, and stood,
To ease his horse and do him good:
His spear he sticked, it was so lang,
His shield upon his sadle hang:
Syne drank of wine and made good chear,
Then thought he on the lady clear: 1470
And then he would no longer bide,
But near the castle can he ride:
For he was so red that the knight
Should not have come before the night;
But yet he needed not do so,
For Gray-Steel he had watches two:
The one of them could to him ride,
And said, "Upon yon field doth bide,
A ventrous knight upon a steed,
And he is biding you indeed;   1480
And hath over-ridden all the plain;
He hath now turned him again."
Gray-Steel then said, "Let him alone!
This half-a-year hath not gone one,
But either he shall fight or flee,
Or else a token leave with me."
The yeoman that the tidings brought,
Said, privily, "That would be nought:
Thereon now dare I lay my life,
Ere that he flee there shall be strife."   1490
They brought Gray-Steel then forth a steed,
Dressed him syne, and hither yeed.
    Sir Grahame was standing all alone,
Counsel to take he had not one:
He heard beside him at his hand,

As it were great horsemen ridand;
He wont there had been mo than one,
Looked, and saw but him alone !
A venturous knight full hardilie,
Came dressed soon and readily :　　　　　　1500
His gear was red as any blood,
His horse of that same hew he stood :
And fra Sir Grahame of him got sight,
He trowed well it was the knight,
Defoul'd his brother Sir Eger :
Then waxt he brim as any bare ;
His spear before him could he fang,
Suppose it was both great and lang ;
And called right fast at Sir Gray-Steel ;
Behind of it left never a deal,　　　　　　1510
And Gray-Steel called at Sir Grahame.
As wood lyons they wrought that time !
The horse together have they set ;
They missed not, but ever met.
Sir Grahame hath stricken his enemie
Through courch, and shield, right twenty ply,
Through habergeoun, and actoun under,
And cleave the shield all in asunder ;
And he got never such a strake,
Nor yet there might be few the make.　　　　1520
But he that did the dint lay on,
He left no vengeance to the son ;
For through the shield he did him bare,
Through vental, and through foreshare,
And so again through the actoun,
Through birnie, and through habergeoun !
The tees of the sadle down yeed,
Or else he had born down his steed ;
And als in two he clave his shield,
And bure him quite out of the field.　　　　1530

Wide open he lay on his back,
But soon upon his feet he gat,
And drew his sword, and thought to stand,
And then Gray-Steel came at his hand.
They might perceive then well Gray-Steel,
So by Sir Grahame right wonder well,
By his body, and by his red,
And by his countenance he made,
And by his course that he did run,
That lightly he might not be won.   1540
On horse he would no more sailyit,
On foot he thought not for to failyit:
He drew his sword, and to him ran,
Sir Grahame bure him off like a man;
And in old stories, he heard say,
That both in earnest and in play,
It were better who might it hint,
Get the first strake, nor the last dint.
Into his youth he learned had,
Most craftily to weild his blade: 1550
Of acward strokes he was right slee,
Of counter casts, both low and hie:
Sir Grahame thought not for all the haste,
The first strake in vain to waste;
An acward stroak with all his pith,
He strake him while he groaned with;
Such a great dint he hath him tane,
It prest the birnie through the bane:
The sword out through the mantle share,
Gray-Steel was wounded very sare;   1560
And such two stroaks in all his time,
Gat he never as gave Sir Grahame.
To failie he had little thought,
He sought revenge if that he mought;
And he hath quite him with another,

That might have been that straks brother :
He then, upon his shoulder bane,
Such a sore dint he hath him tane ;
The strake was of so great renown,
He failied force, and settled down :   1570
On that side he had lost his brand,
Had he not kept the other hand ;
Might Gray-Steel have had in that time,
And set another on Sir Grahame,
I trow he had not all that night,
Come again in the lady's sight.
They strake this wise an hour and mare,
But not so fast as they did aire :
An hour and mare, this wise they dang,
But never a word was them amang ;   1580
But their stiff swords, both bein and stout ;
While harness dang the edges out ;
Bodies they made both black and bla,
Like wood lyons so fought they twa !
What for fighting and blood he bled,
Gray-Steel was never so hard be-sted ;
And that perceived well Sir Grahame !
He hasted him in full good time,
And said, " Now yield thee now, Gray-Steel,
Or thou shalt never do so well."   1590
Then lightly said he, " Thou shalt lie,
For that man shall I never see."
Gray-Steel was grieved at that word ;
With both his hands he hint his sword,
And all the strength that he had lee'd,
He set upon Sir Grahame his head :
He came never in such a thrist,
At both his ears the blood out brist :
He staggered on his feet, and stood,
Grieved he was, and full of mood.   1600

Sir Grahame then with a noble brand,
He strake on him with both his hand;
Under the gorget got a girth,
And followed fast thereon with pith,
Quite thorow the throat soon did slide,
And made a wound both deep and wide:
So wight in world was never none!
But where two meets them alone,
And departs without company,
But one must win the victorie!   1610
Gray-Steel unto his death thus thrawes;
He walters, and the grass updrawes;
His armes about him could he cast,
He pulled herbes and roots fast:
A little while then lay he still,
Friends that him saw liked full ill
And blood into his armour bright,
For so he had full many dight.
 In world there is no bale nor bliss,
Or whatsoever that it is,   1620
But at the last it will overgang,
Suppose that many think it lang:
This tale I tell by Sir Gray-Steel,
That fortune long had led him well;
Now that he sembled with a knight,
That for his fellow came to fight.
Now hath Sir Grahame done this good deed,
He looked where he left his steed;
The steeds together have they run,
Fighting as they had first begun.   1630
Sir Grahame raik'd to them full right;
He took them by the bridles bright,
Stabled them soon, and made them stand;
The wine bottle he took in hand,
He set it to his head and drank,

And said, "The lady 'serveth thank,
For there was neither aile nor wine,
That came to me in so good time."
And then he came right soon again,
Where that the knight was lying slain;   1640
And then his right hand off he took,
Syne in a glove of plate it shook:
The helms he might not turse them baith,
But to choose he thought no skaith;
And so they might have gain'd him well,
The one was gold, the other steel,
The better helm then he it took;
The hand within the glove he shook;
The shields he knat together fast,
And over the sadle could them cast;   1650
Syne lap upon his fair red steed,
His own into his hand could lead,
And thereon he rade fair and hulie;
And from the castle came a skry:
Men did he see both gang and rin,
To horse and weapons that might win:
Ladys weeped right wonder sair,
Rave all their courches and their hair,
(Who oft times had been blyth and glad,)
Bloody steeds when he them made: 1660
For it was Gray-Steel his arming,
His death should be no challenging.
As then to them they spake right nought,
Few words they said, but many thought.
    It was well far within the night,
And yet, for all the haste he might,
Ere that he came into the steed,
Many one said the knight was dead!
A boy came ganging to the door,
Syne turned in upon the floor,   1670

And said, " This is the samine knight,
That rode away when day was light,
And the steed he rode on his red,
I trow that Sir Gray-Steel be dead!
For such tokens came never again,
But he was either tane or slain.
And soon they came to him again,
" Great gentle men and squyarie :
Then to the ostler said the host,
" Dress well the steeds, spare not for cost,   1680
Bed ye them well, and lay them soft ;
Give to them meat, that they want nought,
And what costs that ye do to tha,
I shall it double and mends ma."
They set a chair then to the knight,
And off they took his helm so bright :
The helm of gold it was so gay,
For it had been in hard assay,
And stalwart straikes on it was stricken ;
With great knowledge it was written.   1690
For doughtie hands made it to fail,
Had fourty straiks in it by tale.
An hundred straikes withoutten mo,
Was stricken in hardness also ;
And they were of so great degree,
That it was wonder for to see,
How any man might strick so fast,
On weapons dure, and ever last ;
Or lives could save that was then under :
Of that good knight they had great wonder!   1700
But other things he had in thought,
Whate'r he thought, he spake right nought ;
His journey was not brought to end,
And he was loath for to be kend.
He had rather his fellow at hame,

Had the worship and als the name.
   Then to the burgess can he say,
" Good sir, one thing I would you pray,
That ye would speed one thing by you."
The burgess said, " Will ye me trow,   1710
What ever it be you show me till,
It shall be done at your own will."
He said, " I harbered this last night,
With a good lord, the gentlest knight ;
This day at morn I from him yeed,
I heght if fortune with me stood,
That I should be this night again ;
And I would keep my tryst right fain !
Als I wot not but yon knights keen,
May stabled be where mine horse been ;   1720
And they will have some watch or spy,
Where that I bide, or where I ly :
If I do ly into plain land,
And there a castle at mine hand,
Where that I may received be,
And ought but good should happen me,
It were too great reprove and shame,
To be discovered by my name.
And I would fain be at the knight,
Or his daughter, the lady bright ;   1730
Of leeching craft she is right slee,
I have great need of one to me !
Into great peril am I nought,
But I am sore, and all forfought !
I pray you ye will with me gang,
Yon helm and sheild ye with you fang."
The helm and sheild he took him till,
And went the way before him still.
   When they came to the bower and door,
There was no light upon the floor :   1740

A folding boord was covered,
And with white cloths laid upon it:
Their supper dight, and to them brought,
The lady sat and ate right nought,
And neither would she eat or drink,
But ever on the knight did think;
Nor to her maidens would she speak,
But sat so sad as maiden meek.
A long while she sat in study;
And then she said right suddenly: 1750
" He that supper for is dight,
He lyes full cold I trow this night!
The streen to chamber I him led,
This night Gray-Steel has made his bed!
It is great loss that he was sent,
Upon Gray-Steel for to be spent;
For he was large of lyre and bone,
And nourishing he wanted none.
And I know well by his own tale,
That he hath wrought without counsel,   1760
His friends they may be right unfain,
When that the word is to them gane,
That such a tinsel they should tine;
For so would I if he were mine!
As of my brother or my kine,
Or any quaintance had of him;
Me sore forethinks that the good knight,
Persued ever in my sight."
    This did she say, and sighed sare,
And then sate still, and spake no mare: 1770
The knight heard all where that he stood,
And thought the lady meaned good.
Then to the burgess can he rown,
And bade him speak in fair fashioun:
The burgess call'd and to them spake,

The maiden answered, " Who is that ? "
Because he was no man of state,
She says, " What do ye here so late ? "
The burgess said, " I would be in."
The maiden said, " Ye may not win."   1780
We close the door before the night,
And opens not while day be light.
The kyes unto the boord are born,
We see them not till the next morn ;
If ye would ought, go gang about,
Or stand and shew your charge without :
To gang about there is no gate ;
But first in at the Castle yate,
Syne through a wicket there withall,
Ere any came to the maids hall."   1790
The burgess knew the gate full well,
And said, " Faith now, ye damsel,
Ere I should go so far about,
I will you tell my charge without :
If ye will not let me in,
Here is a token then from him,
Which was given the samen night,
The wine bottle she gave the knight ;
I will that she should understand,
I have it here into mine hand.   1800
A thing that she then to him spake,
But he and she none should have that ;
She said, ' Ye knight of aventure,
In press think on your paramour ! "
The lady said, " So have I feel,
I know the token wonder well,
And if he be at inn with thee,
And likes better than come to me,
Let him alone, with Christ's blissing,
For he shall have no send of mine."   1810

The knight was red he should her grieve,
And then he forethought without leave ;
That he should on such matter mean
· That they had spoken them between.
He thought, and the fairlie he said,
And of her gaisting thanking maid.
He said, "Lady, it was so late,
And I was not kend with the gate ;
And for doubt I should gang aside,
This made me for to have a guide."   1820
    Fra time she heard that he was there,
Better content she was not aire :
There was no keyes there him to let,
The door unclosed, wide open set ;
And he came in right blythlie,
She him received right thankfullie ;
With right blyth chear, and mouth laughand,
She took him in by the right hand,
And asked at him how he had farn ?—
"Well," did he say, "and sped my yarn :   1830
To the token I have been there,
The helm and sheild that he did bear,
And his red steed of great renown,
His gilt sadle is in the town :
Another thing to mend your cheer,
His right hand glove is sent you here :
Lady, perceive now, as ye stand,
That in the glove there is an hand."
Then took she it right courteously,
Syne gave it to the maiden by :   1840
The maiden hath perceived soon,
The glove was heavie, and not toom ;
And for to look she thought reason,
Opened the glove, the hand fell down ;
It dropped at the lady's foot,

The lady could upon it look;
She was joyfull for the knight's dead;
The hand was griesly for to sead:
She knew that hand, came from the glove,
Had slain her brother and her love.   1850
Such old malice made her to mean;
She waxed cold, and syne to teen;
Her hew it changed pale and wan.
The knight, he well perceived than,
That the lady was in distress,
And he thought ferly what it was:
He said, "Lady, why do ye so?
I thought this had been one of tho,
For ye desired for to see,
And ye heght some reward to me;   1860
And I have brought them in your sight,
Through grace of God, and of his might!
And ever I had mind of you,
The land of Doubt when I rode throw!
All that I heght have ye not dread."
"But, Sir," she said, "ye shall come speed.
It shall be holden, and well mare,
Ere that ye pass off this country fare;
Ye might have letten such go by;
What needs you to be so hasty?"—   1870
Then to the burgess can she speak;
She bade him wash, and go to meat.
The burgess said, "I will go home,
My menyie are biding each one."
They brought the burgess bread and wine;
When he had drunk, took his leave syne;
They closed the door soon at his back,
And off the knight his gear can take.
The lady was leech, and had skill,
And spared not, but laid him till,   1880

Both for the stang, and for the stound,
And also for his bloody wound ;
She handled him as tenderly,
As she had been his own lady :
With handling of the lady bright,
Swat sore so then the noble knight,
That she behoved to try his will :
" Ye have my truth, now there intill ;
And in the bower while I do bide,
For any thing that may betide,   1890
I shall be at your biding hail,
And govern me at your counsel ;
While ye be come to your estate,
Whereto will ye make now debate ?
For I heght you, this hinder night,
If ye had hap to slay the knight,
And force of fortune with you stood,
Then neither gold, nor yet should good,
Nor nobleness, nor yet treasures,
Or ought was mine, but it was yours.   1900
But a fair tale it may be shown,
Another in the heart be known !
Falset is ay a fained friend,
And cometh ay at the last end !
But I trust well to Heaven's King,
I loved you above all thing.
Doubtless I may not be put back,
And in lawtie there is no lack :
And, since I know your doughty deed,
How ye have put yourself in dreed,   1910
Through hardiness of heart and hand,
Ye hurt him so he might not stand.
The worst that ever rade or yeed,
Through your consel, may think to speed !
Your lawtie is above all other,

That ye had rather give your brother
All the worship, and als the name,
That lyes into his bed at hame."
The Lady said, "By Heaven's King!
Me marvels of your governing!   1920
That ye should pass off this countrie,
And make your 'quaintance but with me.
If ye do so into this land,
My friends they would do on each hand,
And fairly wonder greatumly,
For what ferlie it were, and why,
That ye should have my love so well,
Because your brother slew Gray-Steel!—
Yea, do my counsel ere ye go,
You shall acquaint you with some mo: 1930
My father is a man of might,
Gentle and free to every knight;
When that he was in his youth age,
He was a man of stout courage,
Forthy, and forward in the field;
But he is now bounden with eild,
That he may not in his own feer
Busk, nor yet ride in land of weer:
But he is wise, and gentle free,
A kinder shall ye never see!   1940
Fast and sicker of his tongue,
Both to the old, and eke the young:
Fra he hath known your worthy deed,—
How ye have put yourself in dreed,
How worthily that ye have won,
And ye but young, and new begun,
He will reward you, ere ye pass,
Of reason, what ye will him as:
Whether ye would have gold or land."—
The Knight said, "Nothing but your hand."   1950

" Yea, then," she says, " it may well be;
If it be so, so it likes me !
For he that hath my marriage,
Shall have my father's heritage;
An hundred pound he may well spend
Of pennie meal, each year to end;
Withoutten wards, or relesies,
Great lords hold of him all their chiefs;
Earles, and bishops, and als barrouns,
And many royal Borrow towns :   1960
Yea, and I shall have such gentrice !
And work all whole at my device,
Ye put upon you all your gear,
As ye should ride in fair of weer;
And in a chair ye set you down;
And my maidens, in their fashion,
Shall stand, and make you comforting;
And serve you both with spice and wine :
And be you blyth, and make good chear !
I will go bring my father here,   1970
And my dear mother, the Countess,
And shew to them of all the case;
To me and my mother, us two,
I shall not kyth you to no mo."
  Be that the Earle, into the hall
Had supped, and his knights all;
They went in royalty to sing:
The Earle bethought him on a thing,
How this young lord, Sir Garrentine,
In arms, that was both fresh and fine,   1980
Was brought to dead upon a bier !
Soon after that, within a half-year,
Sir Alistoun, that gentle knight,
Who should have had the lady bright;
And fra the time he caus'd her dy,

That was both might, and als manly :
For great man-hood, and als nurtour,
He might have been an emperour !
He had an host in governing,
But Gray-Steel had such chance given;   1990
In world was never none so good,
Had strength that yet against him stood.—
When that came to the Earle's thought,
He left his play, and held it nought,
And in the chamber walkt a space.—
In came the Lady, fair of face,
With laughing mouth, and lovesome chear:
He said, " Welcome, my daughter dear !
The comforter of all my care,
Sen he is dead that was my fare !   2000
Mine heart is bound, and also broken,
I am full wo while I be wroken ! "
The Lady said to him again,
" Sir, he that slayes, he will be slain !
Therefore be blyth, and make good chear,
For I am come with tydings here,
To comfort you, and make you glad,
That ye would passing fain have had !
A man may covet many a year,
That, may right hastily appear,   2010
And he may soon have all his will :
That felloun freek, that was so fell,
He lyes low, and is right cold,
That right redoubted was and bold;
And the right ablest in his gear,
That ever rade with shield and spear !
His helm of gold, that was so bright,
It stands at my bed-side this night;
And the hand liggs upon my bed,
That hath tane many wrongous wed."   2020

The Earl asked, "Who did the deed?"—
The Lady said, "So God me speed,
It is a quarter of a year,
Sen that time that a knight came here,
Right sore wounded with sword and knife,
Scantly was left in him his life:
Yet, I perceived, by his effeer,
He was a ventrous knight of weer;
And he had met with Sir Gray-Steel,
As many did, and he might feel: 2030
When I had seen that of the Knight,
I held him in my bower all night,
Dispoyled him of all his gear,
Then the most wound that did him dear,
My stones of vertue stemmed the blood;
I made him salves, both fine and good,
They softed him, and made him sleep,
And laid him down, and could him keep;
And in the dawning of the day,
He bowned him, and made his way.   2040
Fra that he would no longer bide,
Another salve to him I made,
That lasted him a day or two;
A sark of silk I gave him to:—
It is a quarter of a year,
Sen that time that the knight came here;
I heard him say, that came him fro,
That he might neither ride nor go."
The Earl said to the Lady bright,
"When heard ye tidings of the knight?"—   2050
"From him, the streen, there came another,
And he is the samine knight's brother,
Came raiking to me, where I stood,
And brought me tidings fair and good:
Then hastily he shew to me

Beads of gold, and broches three,
The sark that I gave to the knight,
And twenty pounds of pennies bright:
Then, he said gladly if I might,
I would be quainted with the knight.   2060
And courteously he asked tythance,
If that of him I had quantance.   .
And when I asked after the knight,
He said to me, by Mary bright,
He lyes at home into my bed,
Right as I were with sickness led,—
Kept in secret, and quietlie;
And I am come in this countrie,
To see if he will be my brother,
Send him one wed for another: 2070
And will he not, by Heaven's King,
There shall men carp of our meeting!
And I have credance of the knight,
And held him in my bower all night;
And in the dawning of the day,
He bowned him to his journey;
And right now is he come again,
And brought me word the knight is slain!
And that made me this time come here,
To comfort you, and make good chear!   2080
Now make your quantance with the knight,
For he will ride ere day be light."
     The Earle he would no longer stand,
But took the Countess by the hand;
The Lady was as white as swan,
Before them to the bowr is gane.
The Knight before the chimney stood,
With right blyth countenance and good;
He took his helm into his hand,
Hailsed the Earl right reverand: 2090

The Lady brought the shield to see,
The Earle then kneeled on his knee,
Thanking the God of Heaven's King,
And to the Knight attour all thing,—
" On you be worship and honour!
Of Fortune you have won the flower,
So doughtily as ye have sailyed,
And that many thereof have failyed ;
Therefore, to God, a gift I give
Everlasting! that, while I live,   2100
It shall be yours ought that is mine."
The Lady made the Knight a syne ;
The Knight kneeled full courteouslie,
And said, " Then, Lord, this young lady,
I will now ask her for my wage,
And have her into marriage."
The Countess said, " Methinks it right
To give the maiden to the knight,
For his worship, and his bounty,
Give him the maid for honestie."   2110
The Earl said, " If her own consent
Be to the knight with good intent,
Then needs not any mo witness."
None but the Earl and the Countess,
And two maidens, right mild of mood ;
Against their wills, but for their good.
The Earle, he would no longer stand,
But took his helm in his right hand :
Then he shewed it into the hall,
Into the court among them all ;   2120
And they did know it wonder well,
To be the helm of Sir Gray-Steel ;—
Keeped the forrest and the green,
And many times did it maintain.
A knight asked, " Who hath him slain ? "

The Earle he said to him again,
" A courteous knight hath won the field,
And brought the helm home, and the shield;
Hath left them with my daughter dear,
At her own fang, in her harbeir :   2130
And he is past in his own land,
And tane the glove, and the right hand."
They prayed all to Saint Gregory,
To send the knight good harberie.
 Then seven days that gentle Knight
Was lodged with the Lady bright;
And all easements he had there,
That might serve for his own welfare.
He warn'd the burgess on the morn,
Bade bring the two steeds him beforn,   2140
And have them ready ere the day,
He would make no longer delay :
But he would pass in his own land,
With helm, and glove, shield, and the hand.
He takes his leave, with lovesome chear,
Syne at the Lady fair and clear,—
" Farewell, my love, and my liking !
I leave mine heart in your keeping ! "
The Lady said, " Ye shall not tine,
If I have yours, ye shall have mine ! "   2150
 The burgess rade forth with the knight,
While he might see to ride full right,
Through all the countrey, but a guide,
And left him at the forrest side.
He spur'd the steeds, and did not spare,
And rade out fourty miles, and mare :
While that it drew toward the night,
The passage lay out over an hight;
He would not take the fell so late,
So far he came another gate.   2160

A burgess had been at the fare,
In merchandise selling his wair,
A yoeman riding at his back;
A little boy driving his pack;
The knight stood still, went not away:
The burgess was on an hacknay,
He hails'd the knight right reverently!
Then to the burgess thus spake he,
" Wish me, good friend, if that ye can,
Where that I may get any man,   2170
Where I may find both corn and hay,
And stables for my steeds till day;
And lodging for myself this night,
That I may have my steeds well dight;
For I have ridden fast and sare,
I dread the steeds they are the ware,
But they get meat, and noble stand."
The burgess said, "Here is at hand,
Will ye ride west, a little down
Under the fell, a little town.   2180
And ye may get both wine and aile,
And all kind 'of' wealth that ye can wail;
And service both of man and knave,
And all easements that ye would have:
It draws late, and near the night,
A stranger man may ride unright;
I will pass with you when ye ride,
Good sir, myself shall be your guide!
We shall not twin while it be late,
Then shall I put you in the gate."   2190
  The burgess is a man of might,
And he rade talking with the knight;
He perceived well by his feir,
He was a ventrous knight of weir;
And by his helm, and by his shield,

That he had fought and won the field;
He call'd the man that by him stood,
Go! hy thee home with all thy mood,
And see that there be ready dight,
A royal supper for the knight :   2200
This is a knight of aventour,
To me it were a great honour,
In company, sen we are met,
That I had him in my reset;
For we must now wit, ere we pass,
Into what countrey that he was;
Where he was born, and what degree,
Or, in what land that he would be."
   The yeoman sped him to the town,
And swyth he caus'd lay the pokes down;   2210
Call'd the good-wife in privilie :
" The good man pray'd you tenderlie,
To see that there be ready dight,
A royal supper for the knight :
His court is but in quietie,
A gentleman he seems to be."
The good-wife says, " It shall be done,
Go! speed you to the kitchin soon."
Of cookerie she was wonder slee,
And marked all as it should be;   2220
Good beef and mutton to be broo,
Dight spits, and then laid rosts too,
Both of wild fowles, and als of tame;
Of each good thing they wanted nane.
The burgess said, " I have sons fair,
Two are great clerks, and great of lare;
The eldest is a young merchand,
He is right fair, and weel farrand."
They bade the hall soon should be dight,
And a fair fire was burning bright,   2230

And then belyve they set up light,
To keep the coming of the knight.
  As they were entered in the town,
The burgess said, " In fair fashoun,
It shall not turn you to your skaith,
I have an inn may serve us baith,
Will ye vouchsafe to pass with me,
To take such a simple harberie!
We shall not twin, sir, all this night."
Greatumly thanked him the knight: 2240
The fairest inn in all the town,
Before the yate, they lighted down;
Two yeomen came out of the hall,
When that they heard the burgess call.
Each one of them hath tane a steed,
A boy syne to the hekney yeed;
Then to the burgess could he say,
" Good sir, while it be near the day,
Ye must these steeds both look and see,
And for to govern them and me."   2250
The burgess said, " It shall be done,
And bad they should be stabled soon.
Dight ye them well while it be day,
And bed them soft where they do lay:
Feed them right well with hay and corn,
Make them good chear untill the morn,
And ye shall have none other meeds,
But I shall quite you all your needs."
The clerks they came and bare in light,
Past to the hall before the knight,   2260
Took off his gear, and laid it by;
The eldest brother yeed on hy,
And brought in soon a stowp of wine,
With baken meat, and spices fine,
While that the supper it was dight;

The spice and wine then drank the knight,
For he had been in travel long ;
Then fell a talking them among :
Then, at the burgess could he speer,
" Whom off have ye your holding here ?   2270
Whether of earle, lord, or barroun,
Of bishop, or of king with crown ? "
" He is an earle that ought this town,
And holds it in possession."
The knight, he says, " Where wins his hold ? "
The burgess said, " As I have told,
Betwixt the forrest and the sea,
In Galias, that great countrie."
When he heard tell of Galias,
Then thought he on of Lilias,   2280
That was ay worthy, ware and wise ;
And joyned full of great gentrice.
Be that the supper even was dight,
Boords covered and set on light.
Then the goodwife made the good chear,
And said, " Ye are all welcome here :
I pray you take it as your own,
For of your quantance I am fain."
When they had eaten, they drew the cleas;
The clerks they stood and said the grace;   2290
Then brought they water to the knight;
While it was bed time of the night,
They carped, and drank of the wine,
They had him to a chamber syne.
Then said the knight to the burgess,
"I pray you, Sir, of your gentrice,
That ye will rise before the day,
And put me forward in the way :
If ever ye come where that I dwell,
I shall quite you of your travel ! "   2300

The burgess said, " So mot I thrive,
Although your charge were greater five,
I should be furthered in that I might."
Greatumly thanked him the knight.
He bade the yeoman he should not sleep,
For they had two steeds for to keep,
But to wake him before the day,
And put him forward in the way;
And laid the sheild upon the soar,
And then he rode the knight before;   2310
Himself lap on upon his own.
The worst of them might well have gaind
For king, or bishop, or baron;
For they were steeds of great renown.
The burgess rode on his hakney,
And rade before to guide the way.
Thus rade they but two miles or three,
Before it was day light to see;
And when the light of day was plain,
The burgess said, " I will again;   2320
Now may ye ride where ever ye will,
I pray God keep you from all ill."
The knight he said, " Farewell, adieu!
Trust ye right well, I shall be true."
   Sir Grahame, when he saw the West-land,
And great mountains on his right hand,
Both daes and raes down and red,
And harts, ay casting up their head;
Bucks that brayes, and harts that bells,
And hynds running into the fields;   2330
And he saw neither rich nor poor,
But moss, and ling, and bare wild mor.
So it was then four days and mare,
Ere he could win to Sir Eger,
Who lived into great distress,

Byding at home in longsomeness.
　Then came he home within the night,
And no man got of him a sight,
Nor young, nor old, into that place,
While that he came to the palace:　　　　　　2340
He past into the chamber than,
Sir Eger was right wonder fain;
For nothing was into that time,
Could be more welcome than Sir Grahame.
Pallias then, with little din,
He privily took the steeds in,
Ere any day was dawning light.
Then said Sir Grahame unto the knight,
" Now arm you soon in right effeir: "—
And he put on Sir Grahame his gear.　　　　　2350
Sir Grahame into the bed down lay,
Then to Pallias could he say,
" Into the hall go ye right swyth,
And see that if the Earl be blyth."
Then he is at his bidding gane,
He went full soon, and came again;—
And said, " The Earle was gone to meat,
With lords, and ladies that are sweet;
The Earle served us of his bread: "—
Sir Grahame says, " Now, it is my reid,　　　2360
That ye shall pass into the hall,
And show to them their tokens all,—
And though that fair young lady
Would come, and kiss you courteously,
Keep no kindness to her now,
And love her as she loveth you."
The knight he went, and would not cease,—
Laid down the jewels on the dais,
Hailst the Earle and the Countess,
And barrons, that full worthy was,　　　　　2370

And ladies, quyet as any faine:
Then courteously rose fair Winliane—
But he did hold his head on hight;
She kneel'd, and would have kist the knight;
She laid her hands about his hals.—
He said, "Lady, will I be false?
For I may no ladies' mouth kiss,
Untill I come where my lady is:
I am but a simple batcheler,
And may not be to you a peer;   2380
We may then choose, and let all go,
To win a friend, and tine a fo :—
I will not say all that I think,
As ye have brew'd, so shall ye drink."—
    And then she would no longer pine,
And to the chamber to Sir Grahame;
But she said, "My lord, Sir Eger,
Is none in world to me so dear,
At me he is grieved greatly,
And I wot not wherefore nor why :   2390
He was never christened with salt
That could on me set any fault,
In open, or in privitie,
But, that I tarryed cruellie,
And that, I was not in grief nor spite ;
But lawfully, I may that quite,
Whether he would in church or queer."
The Lady wept, and made ill chear.
Sir Grahame he said, "Let be, Madam,
For he tells in his coming hame,   2400
That he hath spyed a lady gent,
A brighter bride, with browes brent,
That is as great of kin and blood;
And als for riches, by the Rood,
She is of lordship, and of land;
9

For ought that I can understand,
She is the best for his behove ;
He sets but lightly of your love !
Your foolish words have made him turn ;
I think no marvel that ye mourn ;   2410
And either, come in reverence
Before the court, in his presence,
While he forgive you heartfully,
Or else leave off, and let him be,
And take him as your fellon fo,
Syne love another, and let him go."
Sir Eger came into that time,
And found the lady with Sir Grahame :
And he said forth right hastily,
The words that griev'd him greatumlie :   2420
" The swiftest hound that ever was made,
May run so far into a stade,
Will suffer, ere he come to lack,
A simple hound the game to take :
I say this by you now, Sir Grahame,
Ye were full wise to wite your time ;
And I have, for the Lady's love,
Suffered the shame and great reprove,
And been in journeys her to please,
And ye have bidden at home in ease,   2430
Will brook her now, and her ladies two,
Wherefore mine heart is wonder wo ;
And, when your marriage is made,
Then would you go into that stade ;
I pray you, for your courtesie,
That ye would ride in towns with me ;
A lady I shall show you than,
Is gaining for a greater man."
    The Lady waxed wo and pale,
When that she heard him tell that tale ;   2440

And that perceived wonder well,
Pallias, and her damesell.
They took the Lady, led her away—
Sir Grahame to Sir Eger could say:
"Sir! let be your light language,
Yon lady is of hie barnage,
And great of kin and heritage,
And all mastrie of her linage;
And lowlie she made you to treat,
And ye bear you again too great: 2450
Yet, I do counsel you to bow,
And love the Lady that loveth you."
The Knight lay still, and spake no more:
The Lady sighed, and sowned sore,
Into the bower, upon her bed;
Pallias, then, he him forth sped,
And said to him, "Yon Lady clear,
Is like to buy your love full dear:
She is in soun ay sen she went;
Ye have great sin if she be spent: 2460
Go, comfort her, for Christ his sake,
And mean that ye should be her make."
Sir Grahame he said, "Not all this night,
Come in shall he the Lady's sight;
For, when he was most in disease,
She would do nothing him to please.
Her words hath grieved him fare more,
Nor hurt, nor harm, nor any sore."
¶ Soon after that, upon a day,
Sir Grahame to Sir Eger could say,   2470
"Pass on the morn as ye were wont,
Unto the forrest for to hunt;
And if ye may get any bread,
Pallias he shall your hounds lead:
This hundred winters saw ye none,

From hunting, get such welcome home."
And in the dawning of the day,'
He bowned him in right array,
With twenty mo then I can tell,
And caught a kid before the fell.   2480
He sought the forrest far and near,
Brake at an hart, and slew a deer,
And a great hart with many tynd,
A dae, a buck, and so an hynd:—
But good Sir Grahame at home could bide,
Past to the Lady the samine tyd:
He said, " Right many works, Madam,
Do serve good thanks, and yet gets nane,
And so I do, both late and air,
Betwixt you now and Sir Eger: 2490
The streen he said, that he would ride,
And I have treated him to byde;
But neither can I tell how lang,
Nor yet how soon, that he will gang;
And either buy his love this day,
Or else, let him alone for ay:
Go, warn the ladys white as lake,
To make some work now for your sake,
And als, ye charge them of the town,
That they meet in procession;   2500
And fairlie, and in good fashion,
Then meet him at his lighting down,
And I shall come, and stand you by,
Give him my counsel tenderly;
And mend you all, if that I may,
What I can do, or yet can say."
    She met him at his lighting down,
Before the whole procession,
She kneeled low down upon her knee;—
Then said, Sir Grahame, full courteously,   2510

" This Lady, that is white as lake,
Hath made great work, Sir, for your sake,
And courteously forgive her clear,
This hundred winters saw ye neir ;
Nor shall ye see such procession,
Betwixt the castle and the town."
. Into his armes soon he her caught ;
And trow ye well that was soon fought :
For both their hearts they were so light,
As ever falcon was of flight.   2520
Then to the Prieur of the town,
A worthy man of great renown.
" Where ever I travel, air or late,
I wrought wisely, not as a blate :
For we will now no longer sin."—
The Earle, he called on Sir Grahame,
And other barrons great of might,—
" Pass on your way all with the knight,
And maidens with the lady bright."
Be it was twelve hours of the night,   2530
They married them in rich array ;
And for twelve days they made a cry—
They cryed a banquet for to stand,
With the great gentles of the land,
All would come to that seneyorie,
And knights to honour that lady ;
And all that liked, far and near,
To eat and drink, and make good chear ;
To comfort them, and make them glad,
Minstrels they play'd as they them bade.   2540
    ¶ Soon after that, upon a day,
Sir Grahame could to Sir Eger say,
" I thought I had a little thing
To purpose, if I might it bring,
We shall be fellowes as for ay."

Sir Eger said, " It shall be sway;
For here I vow to God of might,
I shall never come in that sight,
Nor ye too low, nor I too hie,
But ye shall be as good as me;   2550
Where ever ye eat, or where ye ly,
For all kind thing that ever may be;
And well arrayed in all kind of thing,
To make good service for a king."
Sir Grahame said, " I have made a band
To pass again into your land,
And I may not but perceiving;
Would ye say to your lady young,
That ye live here in lasting pain,
While ye go to yon land again."   2560
Soon after that, then, Sir Eger
Said to Winliane, the lady clear,
" Madame! I am under a vow,
My counsel I must take of you;
Me think I live in lasting pain,
While I go to yon land again."
Sir, then, she says, " There is no need
Ye put yourself in such a dread,
Send ye Sir Pallias, your brother,
Ye love him better than another;   2570
He shall have gold enough to spend,
And men of armes him to defend;
He is an hardie man and wight:
Sir Eger said, " He is too light,
He loves too well to sit at wine,
That man's travel is eith to tine.
But, if ye would that I should bide,
Go, treat Sir Grahame for me to ride:
If he will pass into that land,
And take my charge upon his hand."   2580

And she would bide no longer syne,
But sent a squire to Sir Grahame:
" My Lord hath made a sober band,
To pass again into yon land;
In the countrey he slew the knight,
But though a man be never so wight,
He should not pass in perils ay,—
And I should fain he bade away."
Sir Grahame then said, " Get me a knight,
And fifty squires both bold and wight,   2590
And I shall pass in that countrey,
And make him of all charges free."
They gave a knight, that heght Sir Hew,
An hardie man, both wise and true;
Then the fourth day they made them bown,
They took their leave, and left the town.
   Through the West-land full right they rade,
And at the burgess inn they bade,—
Before where they took herberie,
With all their court and company.   2600
He received them right reverendly;
But they knew not that it was he:
He said, " Sir burgess, where are ye bown?"
The burgess said, " Unto this town;
And als he said, I have an hall,
Both wine and ale to serve you all."
The knight, he said, " Ken ye not me:"
The burgess said, " So mot I die,
I saw you not before this night,
But that you seem a courteous knight."   2610
" Once I caus'd you travel right late,
And come your errand in my gate.
I shall it quite, and all your meeds,
And for the stabling of the steeds."
Then knew the burgess it was he,

And kneeled down upon his knee;
And swore by Jesus, Heaven's King,
" I am right glad of your coming,
With such a court and company,
And right so will my lady be."   2620
" See that you make this court good chear;
Let no man wit that we are here,
Not for a finger of mine hand,
That ever ye saw me in this land."
He past to his wife from the knight,
And bade her soon a supper dight:
He says, " There is come to this town,
A pretty court, and lighted down;
Of them there is but knights two,
And fifty squires, and no mo,   2630
A little boy upon a steed;
But in no country that I ride,
Saw I never in land or sea,
A more cleanlier companie:
In all Gallias, is not such ten,
As they be fiftie gentle-men.
The knight, that is their master-man,
In all the haste I may or can,
Bade me that I should come to you,
And tell, that ye might right well trow,   2640
That this is he, the samine knight,
That rode home by the day was light;
When that I stabled the steeds tway,
And then I guided him the way:
He says, That he will be your guest,
When he hath put his court to rest."
She said, " Speed thee with all thy meed,
To comfort them, and make them glad;
And chamber them as they should be."
    They brought the knight on privilie,   2650

Where he met with the lady clear:
He said, " My soveraign, and my dear,
How fare ye sen I went you fro ? "
" Well, Sir," she said, " Have ye done so ? "
And your two maidens, myld as mood ?
(They becked low, and by him stood,)
And if I live a year to end,
To your marriage I shall you mend,
And fourty pound shall be the least,
For your good will, and your request."   2660
They covered boords all of new,
Brought spiced meats of noble hew,
All dainties into dishes dight,
To the lady, and to the knight.

 Thus sate the lady and the knight,
While that ten hours was of the night,
Sitting at their collation :
Then to a chamber they are bown,
Whereas she made the knight to ly;
Here self went in a chamber by.   2670
And, on the morn, at service time,
The burgess came to see Sir Grahame ;
Said, " Graith you, Sir, and make you bown,
To go to service in the town !
The Earle is come unto service,
And all his houshold, more and less ;
The Countess, that is much of might,
And fair Lillias, the lady bright."
Sir Grahame met him upon the street,
And fiftie squyers upon their feet,   2680
Kneeling right low upon their knee,
Which was a seemly sight to see ;
Hailsed the Countess, then the clear,
And other ladies fair of feir.
So did Sir Hew, the gentle knight,

The Countess, and her maidens bright.
The ladies, that were white as lake,
Kissed the squyers all for his sake.
The Earle called upon a knight,
Bade see the dinner should be dight,   2690
For all his court and company,
For I will bring them all with me.
Then after service went to meat;
And as soon as the Earle was set,
And the Countess that is much of might,
Then sate Lillias, the lady bright;
I wot they marshal'd her full right,
Right with Sir Grahame, that noble knight;
Sir Hew upon the other side,
With him a lady of much pride.   2700
Thus they were altogether set,
Even at the board to eat their meat.
The Earle was served in his state,
With cup and piece of golden plate;
And all was silver, dish and spoon;
The emperor or pope of Rome,
Might have rung in such royaltie!
This same day, in their mangerie,
Then twentie days, the knight caus'd cry.
Into that land that he should ly,   2710
If any would in peace or weer,
To come in plain, and prove his gear,
They should find him there ready bown,
And fiftie squyers in the town;
Or yet a knight to bear a tale,
To just, if any would assail.
    ¶ Then wrote Sir Grahame to Sir Eger,
The burgess him the letter bare;
He bade him he would pass the fell,
And in no countrey he should dwell,   2720

Nor rest him in no kind of realm,
While he came in the land of Bealm.
Fra Sir Eger heard of Sir Grahame,
Was like a lord in such a fine ;
Soon in haste he caus'd be dight
An hundred men in armes full bright ;
And of them there was but knights two,
And landed men many of tho :
There was no yeomen men but ten,
For all the rest were landed men.   2730
The burgess, then, that was their guide,
For all the haste that he could ride,
It was late ere he lighted down ;
On the first night in his own town,
Rested them well while on the morn,
And fed their horse with bread and corn ;
And then upon another day,
Dyned ere they would pass away :
Through the ryot then that they made,
And the long time that they there bade ;   2740
That night they went to the Garrace,
And harber'd in another place,
Right late upon the water down,
Twelve myles it is by west the town.
The burgess he had an inne there,
And made them all right well to fare.
And by ten hours was of the day,
To Garrace town upon a way,
Sir Grahame was bowning to a play,
And all his men in good array,
With helm and shield, and spear in hand,
Upon a gentle steed steerand,
And fifty squyers bold and wight :
Then said the burgess to the knight,
" Yon are men, Sir, of your countrie,

Riding adventures for to see;
They govern them in good manner,
And have done, ay, sen they came here."
Sir Eger came into such fear,
And was so glittring in his gear;
Came ne'r none such in that realm,
As was the gentle-men of Bealm.
And fra Sir Eger got a sight
Of Lillias, the lady bright,
He lighted down, and left his steed,
And to her on his feet he yeed,
And hailsed her right reverently;
And he knew not that the Earle was by;
And that perceived well Sir Grahame.
To Sir Eger he past that time,   2770
" While I be quick, or yet be dead,
Either for friendship or for fead,
Our company shall be as true,
As first when we began of new."
Then sent he forth on every hand,
His messengers to warn the land,
That all should semble far and near,
Bishops, Abbots, both monk and frier;
There was, then, at his lighting down,
Four hundred in procession,   2780
That were men of religion,
Singing for him devotion.
    ¶ When he was dead, and laid in grave,
Sir Eger lov'd him by the lave,
And said, " In faith, so God me save,
I am too ill to be your knave,
And that was for thy doughty deed;
For when I was into most need,
With that great campion Gray-Steel,.
Both sore vanquisht, and wounded ill;   2790

He armed me, then, with such gear,
And caus'd me gang in fained fear,
To take my leave, into the hall,
Then past I forth before them all ;
And when he bade me keep mine̅ hand,
I had rather than all your land,
He might had fortune to long age,
For he was still and full outrage.
Your words they grieved me so sare,
They brought me in sorrow and care,   2800
Behoved me for to ly down :
But he was bold, and ready bown !
He past stoutly on aventour,
And wan me worship and honour,
And slew Gray-Steel for all his might ;
Syn privily, upon a night,
He brought me home both helm and hand,
Which wan me you, and all your land ;
Wherefore, it shall example be,
To all that shall come after me,   2810
Both poor and rich, I let you wit,
That I all company shall quite ;
It shall go with him to the eird,
That he hath won with knife and sword,
The honour he shall never tine,
He was so good in governing !
I make it known to good and ill,
It was Sir Grahame that slew Gray-Steel !"—
Then said Winliane, the lady, this,
" Then, he shall have away the prise,   2820
The worship it is with him gane ;
Now may I live in lasting pain !
I should never have made you band,
Ye should never have had mine hand,
And ye should never have been mine,

Had I kend it had been Sir Grahame!"
Thus, she was so set all to ill,
As wanton women change their will:
Amongst thousands, there is not one
Can govern them, but wit of none :—   2830
Into her hand she took a book,
And to God's mercy she her took,
And left the fair lordship of Bealm,
And thought to live upon her seam.
    ¶ Now, Sir Eger thought, upon a time,
Upon himself, and on Sir Grahame :
He bowned him, with shield and spear,
On God his foes to fight in weer.
To Rome he went the ready gate,
And was assalyed by the Pape ;   2840
Then to the Rhodes he took his way,
And there was captain years tway :
He discomfeit a set battel ;—
Thirty thousand were told by tale,
For twenty thousand dyed there.
A better man than Sir Eger,
Was not counted that day to live,
So good in fight, by other sive,
Then he discomfeit in years tway,—
    By that Winliane was laid in clay.   2850
He took his leave, and passed hame,
Lillias had husband tane ;
And they lived at so good concord ;
Of her lands she made him Lord,
And he made her Lady of his ;
A bishop made a band of bliss,
And wedded them both with a ring :
I pray to Jesus, Heaven's King
To grant them grace, and good to spend,
And love ay, while their latter end !   2860

THE THRIE TAILES

OF THE THRIE PRIESTS

OF PEBLIS.

THE PREFACE.

IN Peblis town sumtyme, as I heard tell,
   The formest day of Februare, befell
Thrie Priests went unto collatioun,
Into ane privie place of the said toun.
Quhair that they sat, richt soft and unfute sair;
They luifit not na rangald nor repair:
And, gif I sall the suith reckin and say,
I traist it was upon Sanct Bryd's day.
Quhair that they sat, full easily and soft;
With monie lowd lauchter upon loft.   10
And, wit ye weil, thir thrie they maid gude cheir;
To them thair was na dainteis than too deir:
With thrie fed capons on a speit with creische,
With monie uthir sindrie dyvers meis.
And them to serve they had nocht bot a boy;
Fra cumpanie thay keipit them sa coy,
Thay lufit nocht with ladry, nor with lown,
Nor with trumpours to travel throw the toun;
Both with themself quhat thay wald tel or crak;
Umquhyle sadlie; umquhyle jangle and jak;   20
Thus sat thir thrie besyde ane felloun fyre,
Quhil thair capons war roistit lim and lyro.
Befoir them was sone set a Roundel bricht,
And with ane clene claith, finelie dicht,
It was ouirset; and on it breid was laid.
The eldest than began the grace, and said,
And blissit the breid with Benedicite,
With Dominus, Amen, sa mote I the.

And be thay had drunken about a quarte,
Than speak ane thus, that Master was in Arte,   30
And to his name their callit Johne was he ;
And said, sen we are heir Priests thrie,
Syne wants nocht, be him that maid the mone,
Til us wee think ane tail sould cum in tune.
Than spake ane uther, to name hecht M. Archebald,
Now, be the hiest Hevin, quod he, I hald
To tel ane tail, methink, I sould not tyre,
To hald my fute out of this felloun fyre.
Than spak the thrid, to name hecht S. Williame,
To grit clargie I can not count nor clame ;   40
Nor yet I am not travellit, as ar ye,
In monie sundrie land beyond the see.
Thairfoir me think it nouther shame nor sin,
Ane of yow twa the first tail to begin.
Heir I protest, than spak maister Archebald,
Ane travellit Clark suppois I be cald,
Presumpteouslie I think not to presume,
As I that was never travellit bot to Rome.
To tel ane tail bot eirar I suppone,
The first tail tald mot be Maister Johne :   50
For he.hath bene in monie uncouth land,
In Portingale, and in Civile the grand ;
In five kinrikis of Spane al hes he bene ;
In foure christin, and ane heathin, I wene.
In Rome, Flanders, and in Venice toun ;
And other Lands sundrie up and doun.
And for that he spak first of ane tail,
Thairfoir to begin he sould not fail.
Then speiks maister Johne, Now be the Rude,
Me to begin ane tail sen ye conclude,   60
An I deny than had I sair offendit,
The thing begun the soner it is endit.

THE FIRST TAILE TALD BE MAISTER JOHNE.

A KING thair was sumtyme, and eik a Queene;
As monie in the land befoir had bene.
This king gart set ane plane parliament,
And for the Lords of his kinrik sent:
And, for the weilfair of his Realme and gyde,
The thrie Estaits concludit at that tyde.
The king gart cal to his palice al thrie,
The estaits ilkane in thair degrie.   70
The Bishops first, with Prelats and Abbotis,
With thair Clarks servants, and Varlottis:
Into ane hall, was large, richt hie, and hudge,
Thir Prelats all richt lustelie couth ludge.
Syne in ane hal, ful fair farrand,
He ludgit al the Lords of his Land.
Syne in ane Hal, was under that ful clene,
He harbourit al his burgessis, rich and bene.
Sa of thir thrie Estaits, al and sum,
In thir thrie Hals he gart the wysest cum.   80
And of thair mery cheir quhat mak I mair?
Thay fuir als weil as onie folk micht fair.
THE King himself come to this Burgessis bene;
And thir words to them carps I wene,
And says, Welcum burgessis, my beild and bliss!
Quhen ye fair weil I ma na mirths mis.
Quhen that your ships halds hail and sound,
In riches gudes and weilfair I abound.
Ye are the cause of my life, and my cheir,
Out of far Lands your Marchandice cums heir.   90
Bot ane thing is, for short, the cause quhy
Togidder heir yow gart cum have I.
To yow I have ane question to declair,
Quhy Burges bairns thryves not to the thrid air?
Bot casts away it that thair eldars wan.

Declair me now this questioun, gif ye can;
To yow I gif this questioun, al and sum,
For to declair againe the morne I cum.
VNTO his Lords than cumen is the king,
Dois gladlie al he said baith old and ying :   100
My lustie Lords, my Leiges, and my lyfe,
I am in sturt quhen that ye are in stryfe.
Quhen ye have peace, and quhen ye have pleasance,
Than I am glade, and derflie may I dance.
Ane heid dow not on bodie stand allane,
Forout memberis, to be of micht and mane;
For to uphald the bodie and the heid;
And sickerlie to gar it stand in steid.
Thairfoir, my Lords, and my Barrouns bald,
To me alhail ye are help and uphald.   110
And now I will ye wit, with diligence,
Quheirfoir that I gart cum sic confluence :
And quhy ye Lords of my Parliament,
I have gart cum, I will tell my intent.
Ane questioun I have, ye mon declair,
That in my minde is ever mair and mair;
Quhairfoir, and quhy, and quhat is the cais,
Sa worthie Lords war in myne elders dayis;
Sa full of fredome, worship, and honour,
Hardie in hart, to stand in everie stour.   120
And now in yow I find the hail contrair ?
Thairfoir this dout and questioun ye declair.
And it declair, under the hiest pane ;
The morne this tyme quhen that I cum agane.
THAN till his Clergie came this nobil king;
Welcum bishops, he said, with my blissing ;
Welcum my beidmen, my blesse, and al my beild :
To me ye ar baith Helmeit, Speir, and Scheild.
For right as Moyses stude upon the Mont,
Prayand to God of Hevin, as he was wont ;   130

And richt sa, be your devoit orisoun,
Myne enemies sould put to confusioun.
Ye ar the gainest gait, and gyde, to God;
Of al my Realme ye ar the rewl and rod.
If that ye dome think it sould be done;
Quhen that ye shrink, I have ane sunyie sone.
Thus be yow ay ane example men tais:
And as ye say than al and sundrie sayis:
It that ye think richt, or yit ressoun,
To that I can nor na man have chessoun.   140
And that ye think unressoun, or wrang,
Wee al and sundrie sings the samin sang.
Bot ane thing is I wald ye understude,
The cause into this place for to conclude,
Qubairfoir and quhy I gart yow hidder cum,
My Clargie, and my Clarks, al and sum;
To yow I have na uther tail, nor theame,
Exceptand to yow Bishops a probleame;
Quhilk is to me ane questioun and dout;
Out of my mind I wald you put it out.   150
That is to say, Qubairfoir and quhy
In auld times and days of ancestry,
Sa monie Bishops war, and men of kirk,
Sa grit wil had ay gude warkes to wirk.
And throw thair prayers, maid to God of micht,
The dum men spak; the blind men gat thair sicht;
The deif men heiring; the cruikit gat thair feit;
War naue in bail bot weill thay could them beit.
To seik folks, or into sairnes syne,
Til al thay wald be mendis, and medecyne.   160
And quhairfoir now in your tyme ye warie;
As thay did than quhairfoir sa may not ye;
Quhairfoir may not ye as thay did than?
Declair me now this questioun, gif ye can.

To the Burgessis.

VPON the morne, efter service and meet,
The King came in, and sat doun in his sait,
Into the hal, amang the Burges men ;
With him ane Clark, with ink, paper, and pen.
And bad them that thay sould, foroutin mair,
His questioun reid, assolye, and declair.   170
And the Burgessis, that this questioun weil knew,
Hes ordaned ane wyse man, and ane trew,
The questioun to reid foroutin fail.
And he stude up, and this began his tail.

The answeir to the first questioun.

EXCELLENT, hie, richt michty prince, and King !
Your hienes heir wald faine wit of this thing,
Quhy burges bairnis thryvis not to the thrid air ;
Can never thryve bot of al baggis is bair.
And ever mair that is for to say,
It that thair eldars wan thay cast away ?   180
This questioun declair ful weill I can :
Thay begin not quhair thair fathers began.
Bot, with ane heily hart, baith doft and derft,
Thay ay begin quhair that thair fathers left.
Of this mater largelie to speik mair,
Quhy that thay thryve not to the thrid air ;
Becaus thair fathers purelie can begin ;
With hap, and halfpenny, and a lambs skin.
And purelie run fra toun to toun on feit ;
And than richt oft wetshod, werie, and weit.   190
Quhilk at the last, of monie smals, couth mak
This bonie pedder ane gude fute pak,
At ilkane fair this chapman ay was fund ;
Quhil that his pak was wirth fourtie pund.
To beir his pak, quhen that he feillit force,

He bocht ful sone ane mekil stalwart hors.
And at the last so worthelie up wan,
He bocht ane cart to carie pot and pan ;
Baith Flanders coffers, with counters and kist ;
He wox ane grand rich man or anie wist.   200
And syne into the town, to sel and by,
He held a chop to sel his chaffery.
Than bocht he wol, and wyselie couth it wey.
And efter that sone saylit he the sey ;
Than come he hame a verie potent man ;
And spousit syne a michtie wyfe richt than.
He sailit ouer the sey sa oft and oft,
Quhil at the last ane semelie ship he coft.
And waxe sa ful of warldis welth and win ;
His hands he wish in ane silver basin.   210
Foroutin gold or silver into hurde,
Wirth thrie thousand pund was his copburde.
Riche was his gounis with uther garments gay ;
For sonday silk, for ilk day grene and gray.
His wyfe was cumlie cled in scarlet reid.
Scho had no dout of derth of ail nor breid.
And efter that, within a twentie yeir,
He sone gat up ane stelwart man, and steir.
And efter that this burges we of reid
Deit, as we mon do al indeid.   220
And fra he was deid than come his sone,
And enterit in the welth that he had wone.
He steppit not his steps in the streit,
To win this welth ; nor for it was he weit.
Quhen he wald sleip, he wantit not a wink
To win this welth : na for it sweit na swink.
Thairfoir that lichtlie cums wil lichtlie ga.
To win this welth he had na work, nor wa.
To win this gude he had not ane il houre ;
Quhy sould he have the sweit, had not the soure ? 230

Upon his fingers with riche rings on raw,
His mother not tholit the reik on him to blaw.
And wil not heir, for very shame and sin,
That ever his father sald ane sheip skin.
He wald him sayne with Benedicite
Quha spak of onie degrading of his degrie.
With twa men and ane varlot at his bak ;
And ane libberly ful lytil to lak.
With ane wald he baith wod and wraith
Quha at him speirit how sald he the claith ?   . 240
At hasard wald he derflie play at dyse ;
And to the taverne eith he was to tyse.
Thus wist he never of wa, bot ay of weil,
Quhil he had slielie slidden fra his seil ;
Syne to the court than can he mak repair,
And fallow him syne to ane Lords air.
He weips nocht for na warld's welth, nor win,
Quhil drink and dyce have pourit him to the pin.
He can not mak be craft to win ane eg ;
Quhat ferlie is thoch burges bairnes beg ?   250
And, Sir, this is the caus, as I declair,
Quhy burges bairnis thrives not to the thrid air.
Weil, quod the King, thow serves thy rewaird ;
For wyselie hes thow this questioun declaird.
Sir Clark, tak ink, with pen on paper wryte ;
And as he said thow dewlie put on dyte.

" *To the Lordis.*"

THAN to his Lords cum is this nobil king,
Desyrand for to wit the solyeing   .   .
Of this questioun, this probleame, and this dout ;
The quhilks lords had al round about,   260
Advysetlie, as weil it sould accord,
Thair language laid upon ane agit Lord.

The quhilk stude up, and richt wyselie did vail
Unto the King, and this began his taill :

The answere to the second questioun.

EXCELLENT, hie, richt mighty Prince and sure !
Ay at your call we ar, under your cure.
And now sen ye have gart us hither cum,
This dout for to declair, baith al and sum,
That is to say, the cause quhairfoir and quhy
Sic worthie Lords war in dayis gane by ;　　270
Sa ful of fredome, worschip, and honour,
Hardie in hart, to stand in everie stour :
And now in us, ye meine ay mair and mair
Into your tyme ye find the hail contrair ?
Sir, this it is the caus, quhairfoir and quhy :
Your Justice are sa ful of sucquedry ;
Sa covetous, and ful of avarice,
That thay your Lords impaires of thair pryce.
Thay dyte your lords, and heryis up your men :
The theif now fra the leillman quha can ken ?　　280
Thay wryte up leill, and fals, baith al and sum ;
And dytes them under ane pardoun.
Thus, be the husbandman never sa leil,
He dytit is, as ane thief is to steil.
Thay luke to nocht bot gif ane man have gude ;
And it I trow man pay the Justice fude :
The theif ful weill he wil himself overby ;
Quhen the leill man into the lack will ly.
The leil man for to compone wil nocht consent,
Because he waits he is ane innocent.　　290
Thus ar the husbands dytit al but dout ;
And heryit quyte away al around about.
Sumtyme, quhen husbandmen went to the weir,
They had ane jack, ane bow, or els ane speir :
And now befoir quhair thay had ane bow,

Ful faine he is on bak to get ane fow.
And, for ane jak, an raggit cloke hes tane;
Ane sword, sweir out, and roustie for the rane.
Quhat sould sic men to gang to ane hoist,
Lyker to beg than enemies to boist?   300
And your Lords, fra thair tennantes be puir,
Of gold in kist na koffer has na cuir.
Fra thay be al puir that ar them under;
Thoch tha be puir your Lords, is na wonder :
For ritch husbands, and tenants of grit micht,
Helps ay thair Lords to hald thair richt.
And quhen your Lords ar puir, thus to conclude,
Thay sel thair sonnes and airs for gold and gude;
Unto ane mokrand carle, for derest pryse,
That wist never yit of honour, nor gentryse.   310
This worship, and honour of linage,
Away it thus weirs for thair disparage.
Thair manheid, and thair mense, this gait they murle ;
In mariage thus unyte with ane churle.
The quhilk wist never of gentrie, na honour,
Of fredome, worship, vassalage, nor valour.
This is the caus dreidles, for withoutin dout,
Fra al your Lords how honour is al out.
And thus my Lords bade me to yow say,
How honour, fredome, and worship, is away.   320
    THAN spak the King, Your conclusion is quaint ;
And thairattour ye mak to us a plaint :
And in your sentence thus ye meine to say
Leil men ar hurt, and theifis gets away.
And thus methink ye meine justice is smuird ;
Your tennants, and your leill husbands, ar puird :
And, quhan that thay ar puird, than ar ye pure.
The quhilk to yow is baith charge and cure ;
That ye for gold baith wed and wage ;
Ye sel your sones and aires in mariage   330

To cairls of kynde ; and, bot for thair riches,
In quhom is na nurture, nor nobilnes,
Fredome, worschip, manheid, nor honour.
The quhilk to us and yow is dishonour.
In same kil this shortly I conclude,
As ye that ar discendand of our blude,
For the quhilk thing I will ye understand,
With God's grace, wee tak it upon hand,
To sef or this as ressoun can rameid ;
In tyme to cum thairof thair be na pleid.   340
With our Justice thair sal pas ane Doctour,
That lufis God, his saul, and our honour.
The quhilk sal be ane Doctour in the Law,
That sal the faith and veritie weil knaw :
And fra hence furth he sal baith heir and se
Baith theif puneist, and liel men live in lie.
For weil I wait thair can be na war thing
Than covetyce, in Justice, or in King,
  Efter this tail in us ye sal not taint ;
Nor yit of our Justice to mak ane plaint.   350
And afterward sa did this King but chessoun ;
On him micht na man plenie of ressoun.
Syne bad his Clark, but onie variance,
Wryte this in his buik of remembrance.

" *To the Clergie.*"

THAN to the Clergie come this nobill king
Of his questioun to heir the absolving.
And thay, as men of wisdome in al wark,
Had laid thair speich upon ane cunning clark.
The quhilk in vane in scule had not tane grie ;
In al science sevin he was an *A per se :*   360
And in termis short, and sentence fair,
The questioun began for to declair.
That is to say quhairfoir and quhy,

In auld times and dayes of ancestry,
Sa monie Bishops war and men of kirk
Sa grit wil had ay gude warkes to wirk ;
And throw thair prayers, maid to God of micht,
The dum men spak ; the blind men gat thair sicht ;
The deif men heiring ; the cruiket gat thair feit ;
Was nane in bail bot weil thay could them beit. 370
And quhairfoir now al that cuir can warie,
Methink ye mene quhairfoir sa may not we ?
And thus it is your quodlibet and dout,
Ye gave to us, to reid, and gif it out.

The answer to the thrid questioun.

THIS is the caus, richt michtie King ! at short,
To your Hienes as we sal thus report.
The lawit folkes this law wald never ceis
But with thair use, quhen Bishops war to cheis
Unto the kirk thay gadred, auld and ying,
With meik hart, fasting and praying ;   380
And prayit God, with words not in waist,
To send them wit doun, be the halie Gaist,
Quhan them amang was onie Bishop deid,
To send to them ane Bishop in his steid.
And yet amang us ar fund wayis thrie
To cheis ane Bishope, after ane uthir die.
That is to say the way of the Halie Gaist,
Quhilk takin is of micht and vertue maist.
The second is, by way of electioun,
Ane Parsone for to cheis of perfectioun,   390
In that cathedral kirk, and in that se,
In place quhair that Bishope suld chosen be :
And gif thair be nane abil thair that can
That office weil steir, quhat sal thay than
Bot to the thrid way to ga forthi ?
Quhilk is callit (via scrutavi)

That is to say, in all the realme and land,
Ane man to get for that office gainand.
Bot thir thrie wayis, withoutin ony pleid,
Ane sould we cheis after ane uther's deid,   400
Bot, Sir, now the contrair wee find,
Quhilk puts al our heavines behind.
Now sal thair nane, of thir wayis thrie,
Be chosen now ane Bishope for to be ;
Bot that your micht and Majestie wil mak
Quhatever he be, to loife or yit to lak ;
Than heyly to fit on the rayne-bow.
Thir Bishops cums in at the north window;
And not in at the dur, nor yit at the yet :
But over waine and quheil in wil he get.   410
And he cummis not in at the dur,
God's pleuch may never hald the fur.
He is na Hird to keip thay sely sheip ;
Nocht bot ane tod in ane lambskin to creip.
How sould he kyth mirakil, and he sa evil ?
Never bot by the dysmel, or the devil.
For, now on dayes, is nouther riche nor pure
Sal get ane kirk, al throw his literature.
For science, for vertew, or for blude,
Gets nane the kirk, bot baith for gold and gude. 420
Thus, greit excellent King! the Halie Gaist
Out of your men of gude away is chaist :
And, war not that doutles I yow declair,
That now as than wald hail baith seik and sair.
Sic wickednes this world is within,
That symonie is countit now na sin.
And thus is the caus, baith al and sum,
Quhy blind men sicht, na heiring gets na dum.
And thus is the caus, the suith to say,
Quhy halines fra kirkmen is away.   430
    Than, quod the King, well understand I yow.

And heir to God I mak ane aith and vow ;
And to my crown, and to my cuntrie to ;
With kirk-gude sal I never have ado,
It to dispone to lytil or to large ;
Kirkmen to kirk sen they have al the charge.
  Than had this nobil King lang tyme and space ;
And in his tyme was mekil luk and grace.
His Lordis honourit him efter thair degrie ;
The husbands peice had and tranquilitie ;   440
The Kirk was frie quhil he was in his lyfe ;
The Burges sones began than for to thryfe.
And eftir long was never king more wyse :
And levit, and deit, and endit in God's servise.
And than spak all that fellowship, but fail,
God and Sanct Martyne quyte yow of your tail.
And than spak Maister Archebald fallis we
Gude tail or evil, quhider that ever it be.
Thus, as I can, I sal it tel but hyre,
To hald my fute out of this felloun fyre.   450

THE SECOND TAILL TALD BE M. ARCHEBALD.

  A KING thair was sumtyme, and eik a Queene,
As monie in the land befoir had bene.
The king was fair in persoun, fresh and fors ;
Ane feirie man on fute, as yit on hors.
And nevertheles feil falts him befell :
Hee luifit over weil yong counsel :
Yong men he luifit to be him neist ;
Yong men to him thay war baith Clark and Priest.
Hee luifit nane was ald, or ful of age ;
Sa did he nane of sad counsel nor sage.   460
To sport and play, quhyle up, and quhylum doun,
To al lichtnes ay was he redie boun.
Sa ouir the sey cummin thair was a clark,
Of greit science, of voyce, word, and wark.

And dressit him, with all his besynes,
Thus with this king to mak his recidens.
Weil saw he with this king micht na man byde,
Bot thay that wald al sadnes set on syde.
With cub, and bel, and partie cote with eiris,
He feinyet him ane fule, fond in his feiris.   470
French, and Dutche, and Italie yit als,
Weil could he speik, and Latine feinye fals.
Unto the kirk he came, befoir the king,
With club, and cote, and monie bel to ring.
Dieu gard, sir King, I bid nocht hald in hiddil ;
I am to yow als sib as seif is to ane riddil.
Betwixt us twa mot be als mekil grace,
As frost and sna fra Yule is unto Pace.
Wait yee how the Frenche man sayis syne,
Nul bon, he sayis, *monsieur sans pyne.*   480
With that he gave ane loud lauchter on loft :
Honour, and eis, sir, quha may have for nocht ?
Cum on thy way, sir king, now for Sanct Jame,
Thow with me, or I with thé, gang hame.
Now be Sanct Katherine, quod the king, and smyld,
" This fule hes monie waverand word, and wyld.
Cum hame with mee : thow sal have drink ynouch."
Grand mercy, quod the fuill agane, and leuch.
Now quod the king, fra al dulnes and dule
Wee may us keip, quhil that wee have this fuil. 490
He feinyet him a fuil in deed and word ;
The wyser man the better can be bourd.
Quhil at the last this fuil was callit alway
Fuill of fuiles, and that ilk man wald say,
Thus was this fuil ay stil with the King,
Quhil he had weil considderit, in al thing,
The conditiouns, use, manner, and the gyse,
And coppyit weil the King on his best wyse.
    Sa fel it on a day this nobil King

Unto ane cietie raid for his sporting :
This fuil persavit weil the King wald pas,
Unto ane uther cietie, as it was,
He tuke his club, and ane table, in his hand,
For to prevene the tyme he was gangand.
Sa be the way ane woundit man fande he ;
And with this fuil war runners, twa or thrie,
Sum of the court, and sum of the kitchene,
And saw ane man, but Leiche or Medycene,
Sa sair woundit micht nouther ga nor steir :
At him this fuil con al the caus speir.   510
He answered, and said, Rever and theif,
Thou hes me hurt, and brocht me in mischeif.
With that his wounds war fillit ful of fleis,
As ever in byke theair biggit onie beis.
Than ane of them, that had pitie, can pray
That he mot skar they felloun fleis away.
Than spak the fuil and said, lat them be now man,
For thay are ful ; the hungry wil cum than.
For thir dois nocht bot sits, as thou may se ;
For thay ar als ful as thay may be :   520
Be thir away it is evil, and na gude,
The hungrie fleis wil cum and souk his blude.
The ofter that thir fleis away be cheist,
The new fleis will mair of his blude waist :
And draw his blude, and souk him sine sa sair ;
Thairfoir lat them alane ; skar them na mair.
The sair man him beheld, and him he demes,
And said he was not sik a fuil as he semes.
   Sone, after that ane lytil, came the King,
With monie man can gladelie sport and sing;   530
Ane cow of birks into his hand had he,
To keip than weil his face fra midge and fle.
For than war monie fleand up and doun,
Throw kynd of yeir, and hait of that regioun.

Sa lukit he ane lytil by the way,
He saw the woundit man, quhair that he lay.
And to him came he rydand, and can fraine,
Quhat ailit him to ly and sairly graine?
The man answered, I have sik sturt,
For beith with theif and rever I am hurt.   540
And yit, suppois I have all the pyne,
The falt is yowris, sir King, and nathing myne.
For, and with yow gude counsal war ay cheif,
Than wald ye stanche weill baith rever and theif.
Have thow with thé, that can weil dance and sing,
Thow taks nocht thocht thi realms weip and wring.
With that the King the bob of birks can wave,
The fleis away out of his woundis to have:
And than began the woundit man to grane,
Do nocht sa, Sir, allace I am slane.   550
How sayis thow, thow tell me quod the King,
Quhy thow sayis sa I ferly of this thing?
And sa said al his men, that stude about,
Thow wald be haill and thay war chasit out.
The sair can say, be him that can us save,
Your fule, sir King, hes mair wit than ye have.
And weil I ken, be his phisnomie,
He hes mair wit nor al your cumpanie.
My tung is sweir, my bodie hes na strenth,
Frane at your fule he can tel yow at lenth;   560
I am but deid, and I may speik na mair,
Adew, sir, for I have said: weil mot ye fair.
  Fra this sair man now cummin is the King,
Havand in mynd great murmour and moving;
And in his hart greit havines and thocht,
Sa wantonly in vane al thing he wrocht;
And how the cuntrie throw him was misfarne,
Throw yong counsel; and wrocht ay as a barne.
And yit, as he was droupand thus in dule,

11

Of al and al he ferleit of his fule :   570
Quhat kynde of man this fuil with him sould be ;
And quhat this sair man be this fuil micht se.
And quhat it is the caus, quhairfoir and quhy,
He was wyser than al his cumpany.
Quhan cummin was the King to that citie,
Full fast than for his fule frainit he.
And quhan the King was set doun to his meit,
Unto his fuil gart mak ane semely seit ;
Ane Roundel with ane cleine claith had he,
Neir quhair the King micht him baith heir and se. 580
Than, quod the King, a lytil wie, and leuch,
Sir fuill, ye ar lordly set aneuch :
Quhan ye ar fuil, quhat cal thay yow and how,
Sa hamely as ye ar with me now ?
Sir to my name thay cal me fule Fictus,
Befoir yow as ye may se me sit thus ;
And of this cuntrie certes am I borne,
With luk, and grace, and fortoun me beforne.
Schir fuill, tell me gif that ye saw this day
Ane woundit man ly granand by the way ?   590
Ye, sir, forsuith sik ane man couth I sie :
And in his wound was monie felloun flie.
Now, quod the King, Sir fuill, to me ye say
Quhy skarrit ye not thay flies al away ?
Thocht ye it was ane deid of charitie,
In seik mans wound for to leife ane flie ?
Sir, trow me weill, full suith it is I say,
Better was stil thay fleis, than skarrit away ;
For gif sa be the fleis away ye skar ;
Than efter them cums hungriar be far.   600
Thairfoir war better let them be, but dout,
For the full fleis halds the hungrie out.
The hungrie flie, that never had been thair,
Scho souks the mans wound sa wonder sair ;

And quhen the flies ar ful than byde thay stil,
And stops the hungrie beis to cum thairtil.
Bot, sir, allace, methink sa do not ye;
Ye ar sa licht and full of vanitie :
And sa weil lufis al new things to persew,
That ilk sessioun ye get ane servant new.   610
Quhat wil the ane now say unto the uther ?
Now steir thy hand myne awin deir brother ;
Win fast be tyme ; and be nocht lidder :
For wit thou weil, Hal binks ar ay slidder.
Thairfoir now, quhither wrang it be or richt,
Now gadder fast, quhil we have tyme and micht.
Sé na man now to the King eirand speik,
Bot gif we get ane bud : or ellis we sal it breik.
And quhan thay ar full of sic wrang win,
Thay get thair leif : and hungryar cums in.   620
Sa sharp ar thay, and narrowlie can gadder,
Thay pluck the puir, as thay war powand hadder.
And taks buds fra men baith neir and far ;
And ay the last ar than the first far war.
Justice, Crounar, Sarjand, and Justice Clark,
Removes the auld, and new men ay thay mark.
Thus fla thay al the puir men belly flaucht ;
And fra the puir taks many felloun fraucht,
And steirs them, and wait the tyde wil gang,
Syne efter that far hungrier cums than.   630
And thus gait ay the puir folk ar at under :
This world to sink for sin quhat is it wonder ?
Thairfoir now, be this exampil we may se,
That ane new servant is lyke ane hungrie fle.
Than, quod the King, quhat say ye to our fule,
Suppois that he had bene ane clark at scule ?
To God now, quod the King, I mak ane vow,
Ye are not sik ane fule as ye set yow.
    Thus wonderit al, the King that sat about,

And of this fule had ferly, dreid, and dout.   640
Thocht he was fule in habit, in al feiris,
Ane wyser speik thay hard never with thair eiris.
Thus ferlyit al thair was, baith he and he,
Quhat maner of ane thing this micht be ;
And lyke to ane was nocht into Rome,
Yit than his word was full of al wisdome.
For he as fule began guckit and gend,
And ay the wyser man neirar the end.
And thus the King, and al his cumpany,
Upon this fuil had wonder and ferly.   650

Of the slaying of the man.

SYNE efter this ane gentleman percace
Had slane ane man, al throw his raklesnes.
And to the court he come, and tald this thing
Unto ane man was inward with the King :
And said, sir, lo I am in the King's grace !
That hes ane man slane in my fault, allace !
And will ye gar the King to that consent,
For it I sal yow pay, and content.
This courteour held on this to the King ;
And tald him al this tail to the ending.   660
And than the King, for his lufe and instance,
Bad bring the man that happened that mischance.
Unto the King his taill quhen he had tald ;
Ful sharplie to this man he could behald :
Ane semelie man of mak sa semit he,
To slay that man he thocht ane greit pitie.
And bad him passe quhair he lykit to gu,
And be gude man and efter sla na ma.
Sone efter that, within half a yair,
Ane uthir man he slew withoutin weir.   670

Of the second slayne man.

THAN to the court he cummin is agane,
Unto this man befoir his gold had tane ;
And said, sir, I have slane, allace !
Aue uther man, throw misfortune and cace.
And wald ye help me, befoir as ye have done,
Ane sowme of silver ye sould have ful sone :
Another sowme I sall give to the King,
Me hartlie to forgive into this thing.
Help me now, for God's owin deid :
Nane uther buit at yow bot I get remeid.   680
This courteour him answered thus agane,
This deid to do I am uncertane.
Quhen that thow slew bot ane, throw raklesnes,
Of that thow micht have gotten forgivenes :
So may it nocht, quhen thow hes slane thus twa,
Notwithstanding I wil for the ga ;
The for to help I sal get sik assay ;
And for the do alsmekil as I may.
Unto the King than come this courteour,
And lukit weil baith to his tyme and hour :   690
He lukit quhan the King was blyth and glad,
And nocht quhen he was heavie nor sad.
Ful lawlie set he doun upon his kne,
Lo, sir, he said, ane thing of greit pitie !
The man that ye forgave, syne halfe ane yeir,
Another man now hes he slane but weir.
Ane certain sowme of gold thus sal ye get,
And ye wald all your crabitnes foryet.
He wepes, and he sichs now sa sair,
That he sik misse will efter do na mair :   700
In all your realme thair is na wichter man ;
Greit pitie is it for to tyne him than.
Ye may him have, and of his gold and geir,

He will stand yow in steid in tyme of weir.
Suppois he hes slane twa, better it is that ye
Have twa men slane, than thus for to sla thric.
Thairfoir heir I beseik yow in this cace
That ye wald tak him in your gudelie grace.
The King bad than bring him to his presence,
And him forgave all fault and offence :   710
And bad him ga, and do sik misse na mair;
Thus tuke this man his leif and hame can fair.
Syne efterward this man that we of reid
The thrid man hes he slane yit indeid.

Of the thride slayne man.

THAN to the court agane maid his repair,
Sik grace to get agane as he did air.
Sa come hee to the courteour to tell,
His fortoun, and his cace how it befell.
This courteour to speik wald not spair,
For yow forsuith, sir, dar I speik na mair :   720
Sa oft and oft ye have done sik mischeif,
I dar not speik it to the King for greif.
Now be my saul, and sa mot I do weill,
Is na remeid, als far as I can feill,
Or quhither that ye sal live the land, allace,
Or put yow yit into the King's grace.
This courteour agane unto the King
Now cummin is, and tald hail this thing ;
And how the man, befoir the twa had slane,
The thrid man thus hes he slane agane.   730
With that the King, quhen that he hard the taill,
In grit greif than wox he wan and pail.
And sweith he said, bring him now heir to me ;
Sal neyther gold nor gude let him to die.
Get he my pitie, than God put me out of mynde ;

And he wald gif me all the Golden Inde.
Syne gart he bring to him the samyn man,
Set doun to judge, to heid or to hang.
This man that was sa cumbred of this cace,
On kneis fel, and askit the Kings grace :   740
The King plainly all grace can him deny ;
And tald to him the caus, and ressoun quhy.
With that upon ane lytil bony stule
Sat Fictus, that was the Kings fule,
And said, now an ye gar not heid or hang
This man, for them that he slew, it war wrang.
The first man, weil I grant, he slew ;
The uther twa in faith them slew yow.
Had thou him puneist, quhan he slew the first,
The uther twa had bene levand I wist :   750
Thairfoir, allace, this tail, sir, is over trew,
For, in gude faith, the last twa men ye slew.
The Psalmes, sayis David, war and wyse ;
Blist mot thay be that keips law and justice :
Thairfoir I wald that ye sould not presume
Na to have count, upon the day of Dome,
For mans body thair to give ane yeild,
Quhome to ye sould be sickar speir, and sheild,
Of all the realme, quhom of ye beir the croun,
Of lawit, and leirit ; riche, pure ; up and doun ;   760
The quhilk, and thay be slane with mans haud,
Ane count thairof ye sall gif I warrand ;
Lesse than it be throw sum grit negligence,
Quhairin his mercy or in his defence.
And on the day of Dome, be Sanct Pauli,
The Bishops mon ay answer for the saull ;
Gif it be lost, for fault of preist or preiching,
Of the richt treuth it haif na chesing ;
In sa far as the saull is forthy
Far worthier is than the blait body ;   770

Many Bishops in ilk realme wee see :
And bot ane King into ane realme to be.
Thus hes the saull mair work and cure
Than the body, that is of na valure.
By this was said, the King sayis, wa is mee !
For I am fule of fules weill I see.
Ise weill I have lytil part of scule,
That thus sould be informit with ane fule :
I se weil be this taill this fule can tel
That I had greatly neid of wyse counsell.   780
To send for all my Lords I consent ;
I desyre this to be in Parliament.
And it be trew my fule hes said me heir,
I sal weil rewaird him withouttin weir :
Aud be it fals, and ful of fantasy,
Ane fule he is, and fule him hald sal I.
And, throw this fule, this man-slayer did get
Unto the Parliament, perfyte respet.
And efter quhan thir Lords al can cum
Unto this Parliament, baith al and sum,   790
Be al the thrie Estaits it was found,
Considerand al the mater, crop and ground,
This Fictus, that was callit the fule,
Was wyse in word, thocht he was clark in scule.
The King bad al the thrie Estaits that thay
Sould sit doun al, and sic a ganand way,
Quhat men in hous war meit with him to dwell,
Of wisdome for to gif him counsel ;
And for to mak, be his Estaits thrie,
Into this realme concordant unitie.   800
And quhen that al this deid was dewlie done,
The King sweir, be his sceptour and his croun,
That he sould never gif mercie to nane,
That slauchter in his realme committit than,
Aganis his will, bot throw his negligence,

Or ellis that it be fund in his defence.
And sik ane rewll made he into his land,
That luck and grace in it was ay growand.
And than this nobill King all lichtnes left;
All bot ane thing that was not fra him reft.　　810
The qubilk for ill toungs long had bene :
Ane still strangenes betwixt him and his Queene.
He beddit nocht right oft, nor lay hir by,
Bot throw lichtnes did lig in lamenry.
　SA happenit throw cace, into the toun,
Into ane burges innis he maid him boun ;
Ane lytill wie before the feist of Yule,
In cumpanie bot fyvesum, and his fule.
This burges had ane dochter to him deir,
Ane bonie wench she was, withoutin weir :　　820
The King on hir he casts his lustie eine,
And with hir faine wald in ane bed haif bene.
Hee wist full weill that nane had hee
That was sa subtill as Fictus was, and slee.
He callit him, and privilie can say,
Sic fantesie hes put me in effray,
I am sa ful of lust and fantesy,
With this madyn, on benk that sits me by,
For gold, for gude ; for wage, or yit for wed ;
This nicht I wald have hir to my bed.　　830
Than, quod the fuill, I understand yow weill ;
I tak on hand to do it everie deill.
Sit still now, Sir, wil ye let me allane ;
Be mee this eirand sall be undertane.
Soon efter, quhan thay war at sport and play,
The fule came to this bonie prettie may ;
And said, Madyn wist ye of the degrie
How plesant it is to God virginitie ?
Tak exampill S. Margaret and Katrine ;
And monie uther sants that are sine :　　840

In Hevins blesse that hes sik joy and grie,
With crown on heid, for thair virginitie.
I wait, for all the gold into this toun,
Of madynheid ye wald not tyne the croun.
Bot ay the King went he had besie bene
Of the mater that was thir twa betwene :
And to the virgine yong thus spak the King,
Quhat my fule sayis a trow be na leving.
Sir, quod sho, his saw was suffisand ;
And as he sayis I sall do God willand.   850
Be that the Kings Stewart cummin is
To have the King to his supper, I wis ;
The King said to his fule in privatie
Of the eirand, Fictus, how sal it be ?
Now hard yow not hirself consent thairto,
That as I said to yow sho hecht to do ?
Bot ane thing have I hecht sickerly
That nane sal cum about hir, Sir, bot I.
The virgine is bot yong, and thinks shame ;
And is full laith to cum in ane ill name.   860
And quhan the Kings supper was at end,
Fictus the fule unto the Queene can wend ;
And to hir said, do my counsel, Madame,
To yow it sall be nouther sin nor shame.
A burges dochter, to her father deir,
This nicht the King thinks to have but weir,
And tald her all the cace, and maner how
Hir for to have he gart the King weil trow ;
Bot that, be God, that with his blude us bocht,
With hir to gar him sin was never my thocht.   870
The King commands to his chief Chalmerlane
Quhan ever I cum with hir I be intane ;
And in his bed sal prively in creip,
Quhil that the King sal cum thair and sleip ;
And privelie thus, be the day agane,

Away with me the madyn sal be tane.
Thairfoir, madame, for God be not agast,
About your heid your cloke clenlie cast:
Quhairfoir sould ye dout or be a-drab?
Is nane bot ye sould bruik the King's bed.   880
The warst may fall, suppose it wittin war,
Methocht he hang yow wil he never skar.
And thus is my counsel, Madame, ye do.
In faith, quod sho, and I consent thairto.
All thus and thus befoir as ye have hard.
The Queene is brocht unto the King's bed;
The quhilk all nicht in uthers arms lay;
Quhat man to tel of al thair sport and play?
The King thocht never nicht to him so short;
Sa lykit he that nichts play and sport.   890
And on the morne, a lytil befoir day,
The fule came in and tuke the Queene away.
And thus, and thus, efter nichts thrie,
With his awin Queene grit gaming had and glie;
And west he wend that it had bene but weir
That with him lay the burges dochter deir;
Quhome throw he had sik joy and sik plesance,
Quhilk maid hym ay the fule for to avance.
Sa was the King sa amorat of his fule,
Besyde himself ay sat upon a stule.   900
Was never yet mair joy and plesance seen
Than the King hes in bed with his awin Queene.
And that was na grit ferly to befal,
For sho was fair, and gude, and yong withal.
And thus the fule, quhen he persaving had
How that the King sa joyful was and glade,
Unto the King he came in privitie,
And said, now, sir, ane thing that ye tel me;
Quhairfoir it is the cace fane wit wald I
Quhy that ye have in yow sik fantasy   910

To ly with wemen, and of law degrie,
Aganis your Queene's wil and majestie?
Considerand weil that sho is fair and gude,
With ilkane uther bewtie to conclude.
Or quhy at hir ye have al this despyte?
And quhy ye find in uthers sik delyte?
Or quhat plesance ye had thir nichts thrie,
With your awin Queene in bed than mair to be?
The King answered, and said, now sickarly
I cannot tel the ressoun, caus, nor quhy,   920
Fictus, my fule, with the na mair to flyte,
Bot wantoulie ay followes my appetyte.
And quhan that my delyte is upon uther,
Than mony foik wil cum, and with me fludder;
And sum wil tel ill tailes of the Queene,
The quhilk be hir war never hard nor sene.
And that I do thay say al weil is done,
Thus fals clatterars puts me out of tone:
And thus, becaus I am licht of feirs,
And heirs evil tailes, and lichtly lendis my eiris. 930
And thus of hir I have na appetyte,
And of al others ay have I grit delyte.
Sir, quod the fule, wil ye not consent
Thir thrie nichts that ye war weil content?
Ye that I grant, be God that is of micht,
Had never nane mair plesance on the nicht.
God, quod the King, send my fortoun had bene
Sen sho I had thir nichts thrie war Queene!
Quhat wil ye gif me, then speiks the fule,
Suppose I be na cunning clark in scule,   940
Within thrie dayes to mak it weil sene,
With God's law for to mak hir your Queene?
And thair to do sal na man say agane;
And do I not my heid sal be the pane.
Than, quod the King, thairto I hald my hand,

Thow sal have gude gold, lordships, and land.
Or cast fra the thy cote, and be thow wyse,
Ane bishoprik sal be thy benefyse.
Than, quod the fule, without feinyeing or fabil,
Hald up your hand to hald this firme and stabiL   950
The King thairto sware oft and oft,
And thair he has his hand haldin on loft.
And now, quod the fule, it fallis to na King
To brek his vow, or yet his oblissing :
And it that I have hecht thus sone sal be ;
Scho is your Queene ye had thir nichts thrie.
That, quod the King, be him that deid on rude,
Sir fule, I trow ye may not mak that gude.
Sir, I pray yow be not evil payit nor wraith,
Efter sa strait ane oblessing and aith.   —   960
And gif that she plesit yow thir nichts thrie,
Fra hyneforth now quhairfoir may not sa be ?
Richt now ye wald have had hir to your wyfe ;
And thairin now with me ye mak ane stryfe.
Quhat, quod the king, be him that was borne in Yule,
Thou art ane auld scollar at the scule.
I farly quhair sik sophine thou hes fund,
That with my awin band thou hes me bund.
Notwithstanding I am hartly content
To my awin Queene I wil hartly consent :   970
And mair attour, I sweir the be the heviu,
I sal hir never displeis for od nor evin.
With thy that she may preif that it was sho,
Thir nichts thrie with quhom I had ado.
And with that word foroutin mair carping,
Unto the Queene's chalmer come the King,
And simply to hir presence can persew,   ·
And tempit hir with tokens gude and trew ;
And sickarly he fand that it was sho
With quhome thay nichts thrie he had ado,   980

Than joyful was he in his hart's splene,
Of the plesance he had with his awin Queene.
Than on his kneis he askit forgivenes
For his licht laytes, and his wantones :
And sho forgave him meiklie this ful tyte
That he had done throw lichtnes of delyte ;
For weil sho saw that al was fantesy
That he usit, and richt greit foly.
And thus the King and Queene, into this cace,
Thankit thair God for thair weilfair and grace.   990
And syne this fule thay thankit of al,
That caused sik concord amang them fal.
And off his coate thay tirlit be the croun,
And on him kest ane syde clarkly goun ;
And quhen this syde goun on him micht be,
Ane cunning clark and wyse than semit he.
Syne efter sone ane Bishop thair was deid,
Ful sone was he maid Bishop in his steid.
And to the King and Queene he was ful leif ;
And of thair inwart counsell ay maist cheif.   1000
And God send sik examples ay wer sene
To ilkane King that luifit nocht his Queene !
God gif us grace and space on eird to spend !
Thus of my tail now cummin is the end.
And than spak all the fallowship thus syne,
Gud quyte yow, sir, your tail, and sant Martyne.
Sir Williame than sayis, now fallis me
To tel ane tail ; thoch I be of yow thrie
The febillest, and leist of literature ;
Yit than, with all my diligence and cure,   1010
Te tell ane taill now sik ane as I have :
Of me methink you sould na uther crave.

THE THRID TAILL, TALD BE MAISTER WILLIAME.

A KING thair is, and ever mair will be,
Thairfoir the KING of kings him call we.
Thus he had a man, as hes mony,
Into this land, als riche as uther ony.
This man, that we of speik, had freinds thrie ;
And lufit them nocht in ane degrie.
The first freind, quhil he wes laid in delf,
He lufit ay far better than himself :   1020
The nixt freind than alsweil lufit he,
An he himself luifit in al degrie :
The thrid freind he luifit this and swa
In na degrie like to the tother twa ;
Suppois he was ane friend to him in name,
To him as freind yit wald he never clame.
The tother twa his freindis war indeid
As he thocht quhen that he had onie neid.
Sa fell it on ane day sone efter than
This [King] he did send about this rich man ;   1030
And sent to him his officer, but weir,
Thus but delay befoir him to compeir.
And with him count and give reckning of all
He had of him al tyme baith grit and smal.
With that this officer past on gude speid,
And summond this riche man we of reid ;
And al the cace to him he can record,
That he in haist sould cum to his awin Lord.
This rich man be he had hard this tail
Ful sad in mynd he wox baith wan and pail.   1040
And to himself he said, sickand ful sair,
Allace how now ! this is ane haisty fair !
And I cum thair, my tail it wil be taggit ;
For I am red that my count be ovir raggit.
Quhat sal I do, now may I say, allace :

A cumbred man I am into this cace.
I have na uther help, nor yit supplie,
Bot I wil pas to my freinds thrie :
Twa of them I luifit ay sa weil,
But ony fault thair freindship wil I feil.   1050
The thrid freind I leit lichtly of ay ;
Quhat may he do to me bot say me nay ?
Now wil I pas to them, and preif them now,
And tel them al the caus, and maner how.

To the first friend.

THVS came he to his freind that he
Lufit better than himself in al degrie.
And said, lo freind ! my hart thow ever had ;
And now, allace, I am ful straitly stad.
The me the King his officer hes send ;
For he wil that my count to him be kend :   1060
And I am laith, allane, to him to ga,
Without with me ane freind thair be, or twa.
Thairfoir I pray yow that ye tel me now to
In this mater quhat is the best ado ?
And thus answered this freind agane, that he
Over al this warld lufit as *A per C*,
The devill of hell, he said, now mot me hing,
And I compeir befoir that crabit King !
He is sa ful of justice, richt, and ressoun,
I lufe him not in ocht that will be chessoun.   1070
He lufis not na riches, be the Rude,
Nor hilenes in hart, nor evil won gude.
Than evil won gude to gar men gif agane
Thair may be na war use now in ane.
Agane him can I get na gude defence ;
Sa just he is, and stark in his conscience.
And al things in this warld that I call richt,

It is nocht worth an eg into his sicht:
And it that is my lyking and my eis
To him alway will neither play nor pleis: 1080
And that to me is baith joy and gloir,
As fantasys judgit him befoir.
And thus he is aganis me ay and ever;
And weill I wait thairfoir he lufit me never.
He hes na lyking lufe, nor lust of me,
Na I to him quhill the day I die.
Quhairto thairof sould mak ony mair?
I cum nocht to the King, I the declair.
Fra tyme that thow art under now areist,
Of the, in faith, I have but lytle feist.   1090
Be me I trow, thow art but lytill meind;
Pas on thy way and seik another freind.
Now is this man sair murnand in his mynde,
Sayand, allace my freind is over unkynde!
Quhome I wend was support and supplie,
And now, allace, the contrair now I sie!
Away he wend, sayand in wordis wylde,
I grant be God that I am all begylde.

The secound friend.

VNTO this tother friend cummin is this man,
That as himselfe befoir he lufit than.   1100
And said, lo freind, the King hes send for me
His officer; and biddis that I be
At him in haist; and cum sone to his call:
And to him mak my count of grit and small,
That I of him in all my dayis had.
And I sie richt I am straitlie stad!
Now, as my freind, I hidder come to the
Quhome as myselfe I lufe in al degre.
For quhen I am in stryfe, or yit in sturt,

12

Into my hart methink thow sould be hurt.   1110
Thairfoir I pray that thow wald underta
With me unto yon king that thow wald ga.
This freind answered, and said to him agane,
I am displeisit, and ill payit of thy pane ;
Bot I am nocht redie, in onie thing,
With thé foir to compeir befoir that King.
Thoch he hes send for the his officer ;
I may not ga with thé : quhat wil thow mair ?
Sa with the I bid nocht for to lane ;
I am ful red that I cum never agane.   1120
Quha sal me mend, and of my bail me beit,
To tak the sower and for to leif the sweit ?
Quhat I have heir daylie in faith I feill ;
And that quhat I sall have I weit not weill.
Thairfoir this tail is trew into al tyde,
Quhair ane feiris the langer sould he byde.
Thairfoir, methink that I sould be to sweir
Befoir yon King with yow for to appeir.
Bot a thing is to say in termes short,
With yow my friend I wil ga to the port :   1130
Trust weil of me na mair of myne ye get,
Fra ye be anis in at the king's yet.
And thus shortly, with yow for to conclude,
Mair nor is said of me ye get na gude.
With that the man that thus charged his freind,
He said, allace I may na longer leind !
Sen I my twa best freinds couth assay :
I can nocht get a freind yit to my pay,
That dar now tak in hand, for onie thing,
With me for to compeir befoir yon king.   1140
Quhasaever vennome or poisoun taist,
That be the hand in quhom thair traist is maist.
Me to begyle quha hes mair craft and gin
Than thay in quhome my traist ay maist is in ?

Quhat ferly now with nane thoch I be meind,
Sen thus falsly now failyes me my freind?
Now weil I se, and that I underta,
Than feinyeit freind better is open fa.
Als suith it is as ships saillis over watters,
And weil I wait al is not gold that glitters.　　1150
Now is over lait to preif my freind indeid,
Quhan that I have sik mister, and sik neid :
Better had bene be tyme I had overtane,
To preif my freind, quhen mister had I nane.
Allace, quhat sal I say? quhat sal I do?
I have na ma friends for to cum to,
Bot ane the quhilk is callit my thrid freind ;
With him I trow I will be lytil meind.
To ga to him I wait bot wind in waist,
For in him I have lytil trouth or traist.　　1160
Becaus to him I was sa oft unkinde ;
And as my freind he was not in my mynde ;
Bot helelie and lichtlie of him leit,
And now to him thus mon I ga and greit,
How sould I mourne, or mak my mane him to?
Befoir with him I had sa lytil ado.
Suppois to me he was ane freind in name,
Yit than as a freind to him wald I never clame,
Of him I had ful lytil joy or feist ;
Of al my freinds in faith I lufit him leist.　　1170
Quhat ferly is I be not with him meind ;
I held him nocht bot for a quarter freind.

To the thrid friend.

NOW cummin the man that we of reid
Unto this thrid freind, quhen he had neid,
And tald him the maner, and the cace,
How on him laid an officer his mace,

And summoned him, and bad he sould compeir
Befoir the King, and gif ane count perqueir;
And to him mak ane sharp count of al
He had into his lyfe, baith grit and smal.   1180
And thus answered his freind to him agane
Of thé in faith, gude freind, I am ful fane.
Of me altyme thow gave but lytil tail;
Na of me wald have dant nor dail.
And thow had to me done one thing,
Nocht was with hart; bot vane gloir, and hething.
With uther freinds thou was sa weill ay wount,
To me thow had ful lytil clame or count.
To thé thow thocht I was not wort ane prene,
And that I am ful rade on the will besene.   1190
And yit the lytil kyndnes that thow
To me hes had weil sal I quyte it now.
For with thé sal I ga unto the King,
And for thé speik, and plie intil al thing.
Quhairever thow ga, with me thow sall be meind,
And ever halden for my tender freind.
The King he lufis me weil, I wait,
Bot ever, allace, to me thow cum ouer lait;
And thow my counsal wrocht had in al thing,
Ful welcum had thou bene ay to that King.   1200
Betwixt us twa wit he of unkyndnes,
Sone wil thow feil he wil the lufe the les:
Wit he betwixt us twa be onie lufe,
He wil be richt weil payit and the apprufe:
And he to me wit thow maid ony falt,
To thé that wil be ful sowre and salt.
And than weil sal thou find, as thou lufit me,
In al maner of way sa sal he thé.
Quhat is thair mair of this mater to meine?
With thé befoir the King I sal be sene.   1210
Quhairever thou ga, withoutin ony blame,

As tender freind to the I sal ay clame;
Without offence to be thy defendar,
And ay trewly to be thy protectour.
Befoir quhat judge thou appeir up or doun,
Thé to defend I sal be reddie boun.
And quhither I cum agane heir ever or never
Fra thé thus sal I never mair dissever.
Thoch he the bind and cast the in a cart,
To heid or hang, fra the I sal nocht part.   1220
Quhat wil thou mair that I may say the til?
I am reddie; cum on quhanever thou wil.
Allace! allace! than sayis this riche man,
Over few I find are in this warld that can
Cheis ay the best of thir friends thrie,
Quhill that the tyme be gane that they sould be.
Thow leifs nocht sin quhill sin hes left the;
And that quhan that thou seis that thow man de:
Than is ouer lait, allace! havand sik let,
Quhan deith's cart will stand befoir thé yet.   1230
Allace, send ilkane man wald be sa kynde
To have this latter freind into his mynde!
And nocht traist in this uther freinds twa,
With him befoir the King that wil nocht ga!

Quha be thir thrie freinds.

GVDE folk, I wald into this warld that ye
Sould understand quhilk ar thir freinds thre;
Quha is the King; quha is this officer;
And quha this riche man is.   I will declair.
The King is God, that is of michts maist,
The Father, Sone, and eik the haly Gaist,   1240
In ane Godheid, and yit in persones thre,
Thairfoir the King of kings him call we.
This officer but dout is callit Deid;

Is nane his power agane may repleid :
Is nane sa wicht, na wyse, na of sic wit,
Agane his summond suithly that may sit.
Suppose they be als wicht as ony wall,
Thow man ga with him to his Lord's hall.
Is na wisdome, riches, na yet science,
Aganis his officer may mak defence :   1150
Is neyther castell, torret, nor yet tour,
May scar him anis the moment of ane hour.
His straik it is sa sharpe it will not stiut,
Is nane in eird that may indure his diut ;
He is sa trew in his office, and lele,
Is na praktik agane him to appele.
Gold, nor gude, corn, cattell, nor yit ky,
This officer with bud may nocht overby.
This riche man is baith thow and he,
And al that in the warld is that mon die.   1260
And als sone as the deid till us will cum,
Then speik we to our friends all and sum.

Quhat is menit be the first freind.

THE first friend is bot gude penny and pelfe,
That mony man lufis better than himselfe.
And quhan to me or the cumis our deid,
Our riches than will stand us in na steid :
To pairt fra it suppose we graine and greit,
It sayis fairweil ! agane we will never meit !
Thus, have we ever sa mekill gold, and gude,
With us nane may we turs, suppose we war wod. 1270
The mair golde and gude that ever we have,
The mair count thairof this King will crave.
And thus the day, and deid, quhan we mon die,
Fra us away full fast all riches.will flie.
Thus hald I man unwyse, I underta,
That halds ane for his friend, and is his fa.

Thir thre ar ay haldin for fais evill,
Our awne flesche, the warld, and the devill.
And thus thy freind, sa mekil of the mais,
Is countit ane of thy maist felloun fais;   1280
And now with thé he will nocht ane fute
Befoir this King, for thé to count or mute,
This may thow sie this warlds wit forthy
Befoir this King is bot great fantasy.

Quha is menit be the secound freind.

THIS secund freind, lat se, quhome will we call
Bot wyfe, and barne, and uther friendis all?
That thus answeres, and sayis in termes schort,
We will nocht ga with thé bot to the port:
That is to say unto the Kingis yet;
With the farder to ga is nocht our det.   1290
Quhilk is the yet, that we call now the port?
Nocht but our graif to pas in, as a mort.
And than with us unto that yet will cum
Baith wyfe, and bairnes, and freinds al and sum:
And thair on me, and thé, lang will thay greit,
Into this world agane or ever we meit.
In at the yet with thé now quha will ga,
That I have tald heir of thy freinds twa?
Riches, nor gude; wyfe, barne, nor freind,
Of thir foirsaid with the will never leind.   1300
And quhan that thow art laid into thy hole,
Thy heid will be na hyer than thy sole.
And than quhair is thy cod, courche or cap,
Baith goun and hude had wont thé for to hap?
Nocht bot ane sheit is on thy body bair;
And as thow hes done heir sa finds thow thair.

Quhat is menit be the thrid freind.

THIS thrid freind quhome will we cal, let sie;

Nocht ellis bot Almos deid and charitie.
The quhilk freind answered with words sweit,
Of me, as freind suppose thou lytle leit,   1310
Yit, for the lytle quantance that we had,
Sen that I se the in strut sa straightly stad,
Quhairever thow ga, in eird or art,
With the, my freind, yet sall I never part.
Quhairever thow ga, suppose a thousand shore thé,
Even I thy Almos deid sall ga befoir the.
For as thow seis watter dois slokkin fyre,
Sa do I Almos deid the Judges ire.
Thairfoir, gude folkes, be exampil we se
That there is nane thus, of thy freinds thre,   1320
To ony man that may do gude, bot ane ;
Almos deid that it be seindle tane.
Into this warld of it we lat lichtly,
Throw fleshely lust fulfillit with folly ;
Quhill all our tyme in fantasy be tint,
And than to mend we may do nocht but minte.
It for to do we have na tyme, nor grace,
Into this eird quhill we have time and space.
Than cumis deid have done ! do fort thy det !
Cum on away the cart is at the yet.   1330
Than will we say, with mony woful wis,
Allace ! allace ! be tyme had wittin this !
I sould have done pennance, fast, and pray ;
And delt my guds in almis deids alway.
Thairfoir my counsall is that we mend,
And lippin nocht all to the latter end.
And syne, to keip us fra the sinnes sevin,
That we may win the hie blys of hevin :
And thus out of this warld that we may win
But shame, or det, or deidly sin.   1340

  And than speiks the tother twa full tyte,
  This gude tale, Sir, I trow God will you quyte.

ANE GODLIE DREAME,

COMPYLIT IN SCOTISH METER.

BE M. M.

ANE GODLIE DREAME, COMPYLIT IN SCOTISH METER, BE M. M. GENTLE-WOMAN IN CULROS, AT THE REQUEIST OF HER FREINDS.

I.

VPON ane day as I did mourne full soir,   [fit,
  With sindrie things quhairwith my saul was grei-
My greif increasit, and grew moir and moir,
My comfort fled, and could not be releifit ;
With heavines my heart was sa mischiefit,
I loathit my lyfe, I could not eit nor drink ;
I micht not speik, nor luik to nane that leifit,
Bot musit alone, and divers things did think.

II.

The wretchit warld did sa molest my mynde,
I thocht upon this fals and iron age ;
And how our harts war sa to vice inclynde,
That Sathan seimit maist feirfullie to rage.
Nathing in earth my sorrow could asswage !
I felt my sin maist stranglie to incres ;
I grefit my Spreit, that wont to be my pledge ;
My saull was drownit into maist deip distres.

III.

All merynes did aggravate my paine,
And earthlie joyes did still incres my wo :
In companie I na wayes could remaine,
Bot fled resort, and so alone did go.

My sillie soull was tossit to and fro
With sindrie thochts, quhilk troublit me full soir;
I preisit to pray, bot sichs overset me so,
I could do nocht bot sich, and say no moir.

IV.

The twinkling teares aboundantlie ran down,
My heart was easit quhen I had mournit my fill;
Than I began my lamentatioun,
And said, "O Lord! how lang is it thy will
That thy puir Sancts sall be afflictit still?
Allace! how lang sall subtill Sathan rage?
Mak haist, O Lord! thy promeis to fulfill;
Mak haist to end our painefull pilgramage.

V.

" Thy sillie Sancts are tossit to and fro,
Awalk, O Lord! quhy sleipest thou sa lang?
We have na strenth agains our cruell fo,·
In sichs and sobbis now changit is our sang:
The warld prevails, our enemies ar strang,
The wickit rage, bot we are puir and waik:
O shaw thy self! with speid revenge our wrang,
Mak short thir days, even for thy chosen's saik.

VI.

" Lord Jesus cum and saif thy awin Elect,
For Sathan seiks our simpill sauls to slay;
The wickit warld dois stranglie us infect,
Most monsterous sinnes increasses day be day:
Our luif grows cauld, our zeill is worne away,
Our faith is faillit, and we ar lyke to fall;
The Lyon roares to catch us as his pray,
Mak haist, O Lord! befoir wee perish all.

VII.

" Thir ar the dayes, that thow sa lang foretald
Sould cum befoir this wretchit warld sould end;
Now vice abounds, and charitie growes cald,
And evin thine owne most stronglie dois offend :
The Devill prevaillis, his forces he dois bend,
Gif it could be, to wraik thy children deir;
Bot we are thine, thairfoir sum succour send,
Resave our saullis, we irk to wander heir.

VIII.

" Quhat can wee do ? wee cloggit ar with sin,
In filthie vyce our sensles saules ar drownit ;
Thocht wee resolve, wee nevir can begin
To mend our lyfes, bot sin dois still abound.
Quhen will thou cum ? quhen sall thy trumpet sound?
Quhen sall wee sie that grit and glorious day ?
O save us, Lord ! out of this pit profound,
And reif us from this loathsum lump of clay !

IX.

" Thou knaws our hearts, thou seis our haill desyre,
Our secret thochts thay ar not hid fra thee ;
Thocht we offend, thou knawis we stranglie tyre
To beir this wecht ; our spreit wald faine be free.
Allace ! O Lord ! quhat plesour can it be
To leif in sinne, that sair dois presse us downe ?
O give us wings, that we aloft may flie,
And end the fecht, that we may weir the crowne !"

X.

Befoir the Lord, quhen I had thus complainit,
My mynde grew calme, my heart was at great rest ;
Thocht I was faint from fuid yet I refrainit,

And went to bed, becaus I thocht it best:
With heavines my spreit was sa apprest
I fell on sleip, and sa againe me thocht
I maid my mone, and than my greif increst,
And from the Lord, with teares, I succour socht.

XI.

" Lord Jesus cum, said I, and end my grief!
My spreit is vexit, the captive wald be frie;
All vice abounds, O send us sum releif!
I loath to live, I wishe desolvit to be:
My spreit dois lang, and thristeth after thee,
As thristie ground requyres ane shoure of raine;
My heart is dry, as fruitles barren tree
I feill my selfe, how can I heir remaine!"

XII.

With sichs and sobs as I did so lament,
Into my Dreame I thocht thair did appeir
Ane sicht maist sweit, qukilk made me weill content,—
Ane Angell bricht, with visage schyning cleir,
With luifing luiks, and with ane smyling cheir:
He askit mee, " Quhy art thou thus sa sad?
Quhy grones thou so? quhat dois thou duyning heir
With cairfull cryes, in this thy bailfull bed?

XIII.

" I heir thy sichs, I sie thy twinkling teares,
Thou seimes to be in sum perplexitie:
Quhat means thy mones? quhat is the thing thou feares?
Quhom wald thou have? in quhat place wald thou be?
Fainte not sa fast in thy adversitie,
Mourne no sa sair, sen mourning may not mend;
Lift up thy heart, declair thy greif to mee,
Perchance thy paine brings pleasure in the end."

XIV.

I sicht againe, and said, " Allace for wo !
My greif is greit, I can it not declair ;
Into this earth I wander to and fro,
Ane pilgrime puir, consumit with siching sair :
My sinnes, allace ! increases mair and mair ;
I loath my lyfe, I irk to wander heir ;
I long for Heaven, my heritage is thair,
I long to live with my Redeimer deir."

XV.

" Is this the cause ? " said he, " ryse up anone,
And follow mee, and I sall be thy gyde ;
And from thy sighes leif off thy heavie mone,
Refraine from teares, and cast thy cair asyde ;
Trust in my strenth, and in my word confyde,
And thou sall have thy heavie heart's desyre :
Ryse up with speid, I may not lang abyde,
Greit diligence this matter dois requyre."

XVI.

My Saull rejoysit to heir his words sa sweit,
I luikit up and saw his face maist fair ;
His countenance revivit my wearie Spreit,
Incontinent I cuist asyde my cair ;
With humbill heart, I prayit him to declair,
" Quhat was his name ? "   He answerit me againe,
" I am thy God for quhom thou sicht sa sair,
I now am cummit ; thy teares ar not in vaine.

XVII.

" I am the way, I am the treuth and lyfe,
I am thy spous that brings thee store of grace ;
I am thy luif quhom thou wald faine embrace ;
I am thy joy, I am thy rest and peace ;

Ryse up, anone, and follow efter mee,
I sall thee leid into thy dwelling place,
The land of rest, thou langs sa sair to sie ;
I am thy Lord, that sone sall end thy race."

XVIII.

With joyfull heart I thankit him againe,
" Reddie am I, said I, and weill content
To follow thee, for heir I leive in paine ;
O wretch unworth ! my dayes ar vainlie spent.
Nocht ane is just, bot all ar fearcelie bent
To rin to vyce, I have na force to stand ;
My sinnes increase, quhilk maks me sair lament,
Mak haist, O Lord ! I lang to sie that land."

XIX.

" Thy haist is greit," he answerit me againe,
Thou thinks thee thair, thou art transportit so ;
That pleasant place must purchaist be with paine,
The way is strait, and thou hes far to go !
Art thou content to wander to an fro,
Throw greit deserts, throw water, and throw fyre ?
Throw thornes, and breirs, and monie dangers mo,
Quhat says thou now ? Thy febill flesh will tyre."

XX.

" Allace ! said I, howbeit my flesh be waik,
My spreit is strang and willing for to flie ;
O leif mee nocht, bot for thy mercies saik,
Performe thy word, or els for duill I die !
I feir no paine, sence I sould walk with thee ;
The way is lang, yit bring me throw at last."
" Thou answeirs weill, I am content, said hee,
To be thy guyde, bot sie thou grip me fast."

XXI.

Than up I rais and maid na mair delay,
My febill arme about his arme I cast :
He went befoir and still did guyde the way,
Thocht I was waik my spreit did follow fast.
Throw mos and myres, throw ditches deip we past,
Throw pricking thornes, throw water and throw fyre ;
Throw dreidfull dennes, quhilk made my heart agast :
Hee buir mee up quhen I begouth to tyre.

XXII.

Sumtyme wee clam on craigie montanes hie,
And sumtymes staid on uglie brayes of sand ;
They war sa stay that wonder was to sie,
Bot quhen I feirit, hee held mee by the hand :
Throw thick and thin, throw sea and eik be land,
Throw greit deserts wee wanderit on our way ;
Quhen I was waik, and had no force to stand,
Yit with ane luik hee did refresh mee ay.

XXIII.

Throw waters greit wee war compellit to wyde,
Quhilk war sa deip that I was lyke to drowne ;
Sumtyme I sank, bot yit my gracious gyde
Did draw me out half deid, and in ane sowne.
In woods maist wyld, and far frae anie towne,
Wee thristit throw, the briers together stak ;
1 was sa waik their strength did ding me downe,
That I was forcit for feir to flie aback.

XXIV.

"Curage," said hee, " thou art mid gait and mair,
Thou may not tyre, nor turne aback againe ;
Hald fast thy grip, on mee cast all thy cair,
Assay thy strength, thou sall not fecht in vaine ;

13

I tauld thee first, that thou sould suffer paine,
The neirer heaven, the harder is the way :
Lift up thy heart, and let thy hope remaine,
Sence I am guyde, thou sall not go astray."

XXV.

Fordwart wee past on narrow brigs of trie
Over waters greit, that hiddeouslie did roir :
Thair lay belaw, that feirfull was to sie,
Maist uglie beists, that gapit to devoir.
My heid grew licht, and troublit wonderous soir,
My heart did feir, my feit began to slyde ;
Bot quhan I cryit, hee heard mee ever moir,
And held mee up, O blissit be my guyde !

XXVI.

Wearie I was, and thocht to sit at rest,
Bot hee said, "Na : thou may not sit nor stand ;
Hald on thy course, and thou sall find it best,
Gif thou desyris to sie that pleasant land."
Thocht I was waik, I rais at his command,
And held him fast ; at lenth he leit me sie
That pleasant place, quhilk semit to be at hand.
" Tak curage now, for thou art neir," said hee.

XXVII.

I luikit up unto that Castell fair,
Glistring lyke gold, and schyning silver bricht :
The staitlie toures did mount above the air,
Thay blindit mee, thay cuist sa greit ane licht.
My heart was glaid to sie that joyfull sicht,
My voyage than I thocht was not in vaine.
I him besocht to guyde me thair aricht,
With manie vowes never to tyre againe.

XXVIII.

" Thocht thou be neir, the way is wonderous hard,
Said hee againe, thairfoir thou mon be stout;
Fainte not for feir, for cowarts ar debard—
That hes na heart to go thair voyage out :
Pluck up thy heart, and grip mee fast about,
Out throw yon trance together we maun go :
The gait is law, remember for to lout,
Gif this war past, wee have not manie mo."

XXIX.

I held him fast as he did gif command,
And throw that trance together than wee went ;
Quhairin the middis grit pricks of iron did stand,
Quhairwith my feit was all betorne and rent.
" Tak curage now," said hee, " and bee content
To suffer this; the pleasour cums at last."
I answerit nocht, bot ran incontinent
Out over them all, and so the paine was past.

XXX.

Quhen this was done, my heart did dance for joy,
I was sa neir, I thocht my voyage endit ;
I ran befoir and socht not his convoy,
Nor speirit the way, becaus I thocht I kend it ;
On staitlie steps maist stoutlie I ascendit,
Without his help, I thocht to enter thair ;
Hee followit fast, and was richt sair offendit,
And haistelie did draw mee down the stair.

XXXI.

" Quhat haist," said he, " quhy ran thou so befoir ?
Without my help, thinks thou to clim so hie ?
Cum down againe, thou yit mon suffer moir,
Gif thou desyres that dwelling place to sie :

This staitlie stair it is not maid for thee,
Hald thou that course, thow sall be thrust aback."
"Allace!" said I, "lang wandering weireit mee,
Quhilk maid me rin, the neirest way to tak."

XXXII.

Than hee began to comfort mee againe,
And said, "My friend, thou mon not enter thair:
Lift up thy heart, thou yit mon suffer paine,
The last assault, perforce, it mon be sair,
This godlie way, althocht it seem sa fair,
It is to hie, thou cannot clim so stay;
Bot luik belaw beneath that staitlie stair,
And thou sall sie ane uther kynde of way."

XXXIII.

I luikit down, and saw ane pit most black,
Most full of smock, and flaming fyre most fell;
That uglie sicht maid mee to flie aback,
I feirit to heir so many shout and yell:
I him besocht that he the treuth wald tell.
"Is this," said I, "the Papists purging place,
Quhair they affirme that sillie saulles do dwell,
To purge thair sin, befoir they rest in peace?"

XXXIV.

"The braine of man maist warlie did invent
That purging place," hee answerit mee againe;
"For gredines, together they consent
To say, that saulles in torment mon remaine,
Till gold and gudes releif them of thair paine:
O spytfull spreits that did the same begin!
O blindit beists! your thochts ar all in vaine,
My blude alone did saif thy saull from sin."

XXXV.

" This Pit is Hell, quhairthrow thou now mon go,
Thair is thy way that leids thee to the land :
Now play the man, thou neids not trimbill so,
For I sall help, and hald thee be the hand."
" Allace ! said I, I have na force to stand,
For feir I faint to sie that uglie sight ;
How can I cum among that bailfull band ?
O help mee now, I have na force nor micht !

XXXVI.

" Oft have I heard, that they that enters thair,
In this greit golfe, sall never cum againe."
" Curage ! " said hee, " have I not bocht thee deir ?
My precious blude it was nocht shed in vaine :
I saw this place, my saull did taist this paine,
Or ever I went into my Father's gloir :
Throw mon thou go, bot thou sall not remaine,
Thow neids not feir, for I sall go befoir."

XXXVII.

" I am content to do thy haill command,"—
Said I againe, and did him fast imbrace :
Then lovinglie he held mee be the hand,
And in wee went into that feirfull place.
" Hald fast thy grip," said hee ; " in anie cace
Let mee not slip, quhat ever thou sall sie :
Dreid not the deith, but stoutlie forwart preis,
For Deith nor Hell sall never vanquish thee."

XXXVIII.

His words sa sweit did cheir my heavie hairt ;
Incontinent I cuist my cair asyde.
" Curage ! " said hee, " play not ane cowart's pairt,
Thocht thou be waik, yet in my strenth confyde."

I thocht me blist to have sa gude ane guyde,
Thocht I was waik, I knew that he was strang:
Under his wings I thocht mee for to hyde,
Gif anie thair sould preis to do me wrang.

XXXIX.

Into that Pit, quhen I did enter in,
I saw ane sicht quhilk maid my heart agast;
Puir damnit saullis, tormentit sair for sin,
In flaming fyre, war frying wonder fast;
And uglie spreits; and as we throcht them past,
My heart grew faint, and I begouth to tyre.
Or I was war, ane gripit mee at last,
And held mee heich above ane flaming fyre:

XL.

The fyre was greit, the heit did peirs me sair,
My faith grew waik, my grip was wonderous small;
I trimbellit fast, my feir grew mair and mair,
My hands did shaik, that I him held withall:
At lenth thay lousit, than thay begouth to fall,
I cryit, "O Lord!" and caucht them fast againe;
"Lord Jesus cum, and red mee out of thrall."
"Curage!" said he, "now thou art past the paine."

XLI.

With this greit feir, I stackerit and awoke,
Crying, "O Lord! Lord Jesus cum againe."
Bot efter this no kynde of rest I tuke,
I preisit to sleip, bot that was all in vaine.
I wald have dreamit of pleasur after paine,
Becaus I knaw, I sall it finde at last:
God grant my guyde may still with mee remaine!
It is to cum that I beleifit was past.

XLII.

This is ane Dreame, and yit I thocht it best
To wryte the same, and keip it still in mynde;
Becaus I knew, thair was na earthlie rest
Preparit for us, that hes our hearts inclynde
To seik the Lord, we mon be purgde and fynde:
Our dros is greit, the fyre mon try us sair;
Bot yit our God is mercifull and kynde,
Hee sall remaine and help us ever mair.

XLIII.

The way to Heaven, I sie is wonderous hard,
My Dreame declairs, that we have far to go;
We mon be stout, for cowards are debarde,
Our flesh on force mon suffer paine and wo.
Thir grivelie gaits, and many dangers mo
Awaits for us, wee can not leive in rest;
Bot let us learne, sence we ar wairnit so,
To cleave to Christ, for he can help us best.

XLIV.

O sillie saullis with paines sa sair opprest,
That love the Lord, and lang for Heaven sa hie;
Chainge not your mynde, for ye have chosen the best,
Prepair your selves, for troublit mon ye be:
Faint not for feir in your adversitie,
Althocht that ye lang luiking be for lyfe;
Suffer ane quhile, and ye sall shortlie sie
The Land of rest, quhen endit is your strife.

XLV.

In wildernes ye mon be tryit a quhile,
Yit fordwart preis, and never flie aback:
Lyke pilgrimes puir, and strangers in exyle,
Throw fair and foull your journey ye mon tak.

The Devill, the Warld, and all that they can mak,
Will send their force to stop you in your way;
Your flesh will faint, and sumtyme will grow slak,
Yit clim to Christ, and hee sall help you ay.

XLVI.

The thornie cairs of this deceitfull lyfe
Will rent your heart, and mak your saull to bleid;
Your flesh and spreit will be at deidlie stryfe,
Your cruel foe will hald yow still in dreid,
And draw you down; yit ryse againe with speid;
And thocht ye fall, yit ly not loytring still;
Bot call on Christ, to help you in your neid,
Quha will nocht faill his promeis to fulfill.

XLVII.

In floudes of wo quhen ye ar lyke to drowne,
Yit clim to Christ, and grip him wonder fast;
And thocht ye sink, and in the deip fall downe,
Yit cry aloud, and hee will heir at last.
Dreid nocht the death, nor be not sair agast,
Thocht all the eirth against yow sould conspyre;
Christ is your guyde, and quhen your paine is past,
Ye sall have joy above your hearts desyre.

XLVIII.

Thocht in this earth ye sall exaltit be,
Feir sall be left to humbill your withall;
For gif ye clim on tops of montaines hie,
The heicher up the nearer is your fall:
Your honie sweit shall mixit be with gall,
Your short delyte sall end with paine and greif;
Yit trust in God, for his assistance call,
And he sall help and send you sum relief.

XLIX.

Thocht waters greit do compas yow about,
Thocht tirannes freat, thocht lyouns rage and roir;
Defy them all, and feir not to win out,
Your guyde is neir to help yow ever moir.
Thocht prick of iron do prick yow wonderous soir,
As noysum lusts that seik your saul to slay;
Yit cry on Christ, and hee sall go befoir,
The neirer Heaven, the harder is the way.

L.

Rin out your race, ye mon not faint nor tyre,
Nor sit, nor stand, nor turne back againe;
Gif ye desyne to have your hearts desyre,
Preis fordwart still, althocht it be with paine:
Na rest for yow sa lang as ye remaine
Ane pilgrim puir, into thy loathsum lyfe:
Fecht on your faucht, it sall nocht be in vaine,
Your riche rewarde is worth ane gritter stryfe.

LI.

Gif efter teires ye leif ane quhyle in joy,
And get ane taist of that Eternal gloir,
Be nocht secure, nor slip nocht your convoy,
For gif ye do ye sall repent it soir:
He knawes the way, and he mon go befoir:
Clim ye alane, ye sall nocht mis ane fall;
Your humblit flesh it mon be troublit moir,
Gif ye forget upon your guyde to call.

LII.

Gif Christ be gaine, althocht ye seime to flie
With golden wings above the firmament;
Come down againe, ye sall nocht better be,
That pride of yours ye sall richt sair repent:

Than hald him fast, with humbill heart aye bent
To follow him, althocht throw Hell and Death;
Hee went befoir, his saull was torne and rent,
For your deserts hee felt his Father's wraith.

LIII.

Thocht in the end ye suffer torments fell,
Clim fast to him, that felt the same befoir;
The way to Heaven mon be throw Death and Hell;
The last assault will troubill yow full soir;
The Lyoun than maist cruellie will roir,
His tyme is short, his forces hee will bend;
The gritter stryfe, the gritter is your gloir,
Your paine is short, your joy sall never end.

LIV.

Rejoyce in God, let nocht your curage fail,
Ye chosin Sancts that ar afflictit heir;
Thocht Sathan rage, hee never sall prevaill,
Fecht to the end, and stoutlie perseveir.
Your God is trew, your bluid is to him deir,
Feir nocht the way, sence Christ is your convoy,
Quhen clouds ar past the weather will grow cleir,
Ye saw in teares, bot ye sall reap in joy.

LV.

Baith Deith and Hell hes lost thair cruell sting,
Your Captaine Christ hes maid them all to yield;
Lift up your hearts, and praises to him sing,
Triumph for joy, your enemies ar keilde:
The Lord of Hostis, that is your strenth and sheild,
The Serpent's heid hes stoutlie trampit downe;
Trust in his strenth, pass fordwart in the feild,
Overcum in fecht, and ye sall weare the Crowne.

LVI.

The King of kings, gif he be on our syde,
Wee neid nocht feir quhat dar agains us stand;
Into the feild may wee nocht baldlie byde,
Quhen hee sall help us, with his michtie hand,
Quha sits abone, and reules baith sea and land,
Quha with his breath doth mak the hilles to shaik?—
The hostes of Heaven ar armit at his command
To fecht the feild, quhen wee appeir maist waik.

LVII.

Pluck up your heart, ye are nocht left alone,
The Lambe of God sall leid yow in the way;
The Lord of Hostes that rings on royall throne,
Against your foes your baner will display.
The Angels bricht sall stand in gude array,
To hald yow up, ye neid not fear to fall;
Your enemies sall flie, and be your pray,
Ye sall triumphe, and they sall perish all.

LVIII.

The joy of Heaven is worth ane moments paine,
Tak curage than, lift up your hearts on hie;
To judge the eirth quhen Christ sall cum againe,
Above the cloudes ye sall exaltit be:
The Throne of joy and trew felicitie
Await for yow, quhen finishit is your fecht;
Suffer ane quhyle, and ye sall shortlie sie
Ane gloir maist grit, and infinite of wecht.

LIX.

Prepair your selfes, be valiant men of weir,
And thrust with force out throw the narrow way;
Hald on thy course and shrink not back for feir,
Chryst is your guyde, ye sall nocht go astray;

The tyme is neare, be sober, watch and pray,
Hee seis your teares, and he hes laid in stoir
Ane rich rewarde, quhilk in that joyfull day
Ye shall resave, and ring for ever moir.

LX.

Now to the King that creat all of nocht,
And Lord of Lords, that reules baith land and sie,
That saifit our saullis, and with his blude us bocht,
And vanquisht Death, triumphant on the trie ;
Unto the grit and glorious Trinitie,
That saifis the puir, and dois his awin defend ;
Be Laud and Gloir, Honour and Majestie,
Power and Praise, Amen, Warld without end.

FINIS.

THE HISTORY OF

A LORD AND HIS THREE SONS,

IN METRE.

A DELECTABLE LITTLE HISTORY, OF A LORD AND HIS THREE SONS, IN METRE.

HEAR Auditors a noble tale,
   This writing shows it wondrous well;
And as mine Author doth record,
Upon a time there was a Lord
Of high renoun, and far more of degree,
Had no bairns but only Sons three.
This noble Lord of high parentage,
Throw cruel sickness he died of age;
At th' end of his life near hand by,
This Lord on death-bed could he ly;   10
This noble Lord withouten mair,
Said, "Fetch to me my Son and Heir."
Who came to him right hastilie,
And hailsit him right reverentlie;
He said, "Dear Father! how do ye?"
"What man of craft thinks thou to be?"
The Child answered his Father till,
"What ye command I shall fulfil;
And here I make a most great vow,
That to your bidding I shall bow."   .20
The Lord answered his Son theretil,
"My broad bennison I leave thee still,
And all my lands after my days."
The Lord unto his Son he says,
With heart and mouth to him did say,
"A rig I will not put away:
Be meek and good, and on the poor do rew,

And to the King see thou be ever true ;
Devout to God, with true humilitie,
And without doubt the great God will defend thee; 30
Keep honour, faith, and thy lawtie,
And my broad bennison I leave thee :
Strive thou thy life for to amend,
God will give thee a blessed end.
Thy mid-most brother thou send to me,
That I may counsel him trulie."
      The mid-most Brother was near hand by,
Came to his Father right speedily,
And hailsit him right reverentlie :
He said, "Father! how now do ye ?"   40
He said, "My Son, as pleases God,—
For here I have not long abode."
"What have ye left me that ye will give ?
How think ye, Father, that I should live ?
I am your Son as well as he,
Ye might have left some part to me."
His Father said, " I'le not permit
Thee of my lands to brook a bit ;
Thy eldest brother shall them brook,
I would he thee in service took :   50
Serve him with all the craft thou can ;
He shall thee hold a gentleman,
Both in horse, cloathing, and in gear."
The Son said, " Not I, here I do swear !
Serve him, Wherefore or ? or yet for Why ?
He is your son and so am I.
I'll not serve him though he were wood ;
Fellow right fain is wondrous good !
At him I think nothing to crave,
My part of land I think to have,   60
And all that will take part with me,
Either in part or privitie."

The Lord answer'd, " Thou ne're was wise,
Thou mayst not come to such a prise ;
Strive not to that thou hast no right,
And to debate thou hast no might ;
Yet Son, I think thee not to tine,
Take thou that Purse, both good and fine,
It hath a vertue I let thee wit,
As oft thou puts thy hand in it,   70
A ducat of gold thou shalt find there,
Take forth and thou shalt spend the mair ;
Then thou may be a man of might."
The young man leugh, and went out right,
And of the purse he was right fain.

When he his brother meets on the plain ;
He says, " Brother ! thou stays too long,
Go thou in time for fear of wrong ;
For I have here into mine hand,
That's worth an Earldom of land.   80
What our Father had far or near,
All is disponed, both land and gear."
The youngest said, " I care not by.
My Father's life rather had I
Nor all the land, and gear alsway,
Betwixt the Heaven and Earth this day."
" Sore sick if he, and wondrous woe,
That thou art thus so far him fro."
" God grant me his bension ere he die."
    He ran to him right hastilie,   90
And hailsit him right reverentlie ;
And said, " Father ! how do ye ? "
" Right sick and feeble, and like to die ;
My death draws near, as thou may see."
He says, " My Son, draw near and hear,
Give me thy heart, my son so dear !
The same blessing I leave to thee
                    14

That Christ left unto mild Marie.
Son! I can leave thee no more here,
All is disponed, both land and gear.—   100
What man of craft thinks thou to be?"
" A clerk to learn till that I die:
I you beseech, my Father, in haste,
My eldest brother you would request
To find me books, and also claise,
That I may learn my God to please."
The Lord answered him right until;
" My eldest son shall that fulfil;
For I perceive well by thy face,
That thou art born to meikle grace.   110
But Son, I think thee not to tyne,
Take thou that Mantle good and fine
It's better to thee than gold or land ;
The vertue none does understand ;
Cast it about thee when ever thou will,
And thir words say the Mantle until,
" God, and my Mantle, and my wish,
If I were in the place, wherever it is ;"
Wherever thou wishes for to be,
Thou shalt be there right speedilie ;   120
Were it a thousand miles and mair,
Into a clap thou shalt be there :
Pass with my blessing, I leave thee it,—
To God I recommend my sp'rit."
    ¶ When he was dead and laid in bear,
Of his Sons guiding you shall hear.
The eldest was a noble Lord,
Keeped his Lands in good concord :
The youngest Son keeped the school :
The mid-most Brother play'd the fool ;   130
The Purse made him so high and nice,
He set his Brother at little price ;

He grew so proud and wanton than,
That he misknew both God and man :
He had more men at his command,
Nor had the Lord that aught the land ;
He was so wanton of gold and treasure,
Defiled women above all measure.
While it fell once upon a day,
In uncouth land he would assay,   140
Fair women for pleasure to fang :
In his countrie he thought so lang.
No stay for him, he made travail,
That he saw ships drest for to sail ;
Syne went to sail with his menzie,
Till he came to a far countrie.
They sail'd the day, they sail'd the night,
Till of a land they got a sight,
The whilk was called fair Portugal ;
There they landed withouten fail,   150
And all his menzie at his back,
Ready him service for to make.
   The King he had a daughter fair,
Had no more bairns, she was his heir ;
He marvell'd who durst be so bold,
That in his countrie enter would,
Withouten seeking any leave !
The whilk thing did the King much grieve :
" I will pass to him, (said he,) " and speir,
Why they are come, I will require :   160
If they be noble men of blood,
They will give me an answer good." .
Yet, at that time he did not pass,
But charged another that readier was,
Bade his Daughter go on her way,
Bring him sure word what ever they say.
She passed quickly thorow the street,

And with the young man could she meet:
He halsit her right reverentlie,
Syne kneeled low down on his knee,   170
And said, " Princess, I you beseek,
As ye are maiden mild and meek,
That ye would grant me and my men
Here to remain nine weeks or ten ;
Mine own goods here onlie to spend,
Till we see farder, ere we wend ;
And afterward you service make
With heart and hand, if you will take."
She says, " Right welcome shall ye be,
Both to my Father and to me :   180
Pass throw the countrie as ye think best,
And spend your goods while they may last."
She called a Squire of great renown,—
" Go, convoy them out throw the town ; "
And swa departed she and he,
Both blyth and glad as they might be,
Swa long as they bade in the town.
When it was time they made them bown,
Spendand and wastand verie fast :
Till so it chanced at the last,   190
The King himself great marvel had,
That coinzie show him if he wad,
Where that he got that kind of gold,
That such like was not on the mold ;
He spended so both late and air
His gold that was pleasant and fair.
Ilk piece thereof he had in hand
Did weigh two duckats, I understand.
The King himself was not so fed,
Nor yet so courtlie-like beclade,   200
As was that man of great renown
While he remained in the town.

And yet I never saw his maik,
"For all his gold was of one straik;
He got none of it, I understand,
Sen he came first into this land;
Where could he get that kind of gold,
That he spends so upon the mold?
Sen he came here what he has spended:
And what he has it is not ended."   210
Right so anone the Lady fair,
Who was the King's daughter and heir,
She trow'd he was some prince or king
Was now come to her in wooing:
He was but a bairnlie young man,
That could not speak his own errand.
She went to him right hastilie,
Requested him right reverentlie,
He would come in her Father's yett,
That better traitment he might get,   220
And in his companie bring not ane;
So blyth he was of that tydane:
He came in haste at her command,
Syne reverentlie he did demand.
    When he came there, within the yett,
The King's daughter then with him met;
He kneeled low down on his knee,
And gave great thanks to the Ladie:
Likeways the Ladie thanks him gave;
Syne asked at him what he would have?   230
" My asking here is not as now,
My mind therefore I will tell you,
Wherefore and why that I came here,
That matter and purpose I shall clear."
" Ask on, Madam, what is your will?
To do your pleasure I shall fulfill,
Saving my honour and my life,

To fight with spear, with sword, or knife,
In credit, wealth, or yet favour,
All shall be whole at your pleasure."   240
When speech was ended, as you may see,
She took him up right reverentlie,
And said to him right secretlie,
" Sir, will you stay a little with me,
Till that you drink, and drink again;
Swa long as we do here remain,
It shall you not at all displease,
Sit down, beside it will you ease:
Where love has its habitation,
Betwixt two it breeds consolation."   250
She cryed for wine, and to him drank;
He said, " Madam, here I you thank."
Caused serve him with dainty cheer,
And said, " Sir, ye are welcome here; "
Then quietlie she to him said,
Whereof himself was no ways glad:
Saying to him, " Me thinks ye be,
Who now is come to this countrie
Me for to woe, or for to geck,
In your own errand cannot speak,   260
For as long here as you have spended,
I marvel, that your gold's not ended."
He says, " Ladie, I am no king,
Nor has great lands in governing;
But if you will grant me my asking,
I will give you a precious thing,
The vertue thereof no man does ken
From this part to the World's end.
Wilt thou my true love for ever be,
And make a vow but to love me,   270
And be my dear while that I live,
Nor yet my person for to grieve,

The vertue of this I shall declare,
Where that I got this gold and mair;
And how that I may daily spend;
And how this gold will never make end."
Quoth she, "Dear welcome mot ye be!
Sua long as your gold lasts trulie
I shall be yours, ye shall be mine,
More dearer than Prince Florentine: 280
I swear to you my plight trulie,
And ever shall till that I die;
Sua that ye bear the like to me,
That I shall do right faithfullie;
And if you keep your privitie,
Your perfect truth plight unto me,
And your intent shall have of me,
Sua ye observe it honestlie."
And so thir two gave other their hand
To this agreement true to stand;   290
Bot faith and truth to her did give,
Syne kissed her with her own leave.
At length the Purse shewed with his hand,
Said to her, "Will you understand,
This samine Purse, I let you wit,
As oft as you put your hand in it
A duckat of gold you shall find there,
Take forth, and ye shall find the mair."
The Ladie perceived that it was swae,
The Purse to her soon can she tae.   300
They kissed other a good space there,
What other pleasures they had mair!
That he chanced upon a sleep,
The Ladie perceived, and had good keep,
And privilie she past away,
Let him ly there till it was day.
    While it was day, and after one,

Wakened belyve and made great moan,
None with him but himself alone,
Right sad in heart, and woe begone;   310
And he left there the Ladie gent,
Then to his lodging soon he went;
While on the morn, in the morning,
Sorrow and care in his sojourning,
He looked about, and astonisht stood,
And marvelled as he were wood,
Saying to himself, " What have I done?
The great God knows that is aboon!"
Sua he perceived the Purse away;
Says, "Woe is me and harmsay!   320
Alas! alas! what shall I do?
Or what art shall I turn me to?
Sent back his boy her to seek,
Beseekand the Ladie, both mild and meek,
To send him his Purse bedeen,
That he left in her chamber yestreen.
Sua soon then as the boy came nie,
He kneeled low down on his knee,
And says, " Ladie, God mot you save,
Of you I must good answer have: 330
My master has sent me you till,
Beseekand you of your good will,
Of your good will and charitie,
A good answer ye grant to me."
" Wherein shall I thee answer give?
Or if thou says ought me to grieve?
Say, what it is thou comes to crave?
Or what is here that thou would have?"
" Send to my Master his Purse bedeen,
That he left in your chamber yestreen.   340
The Lady did start, the Lady lap,
And ilk hand on another did clap:

" Swieth by thee, traitor, out of my sight;
Command thy Master, in all his might,
That he pack out of this countrie,
Or I vow he's be hanged hie :
I had rather hang him on a pin,
Or he come near my chamber within ;—
I shall gar hang him on a knag,
If he speak either of purse or bag."   350
The boy in haste sped him away,
Sped him right soon, made no delay ;
His message from the ladie said,
Whereof his Master was not glad,
Commanded his master for to wend;
Syne charged him, and all his men
To pass in hast of that countrie,
Or else he would be hanged hie ;
And since that he was charged so
Of that his master was full wo.   360
Little spending was left himsell,
Right as the storie doth us tell.
   Thus in a morning forth fure he,
While he came to a far countrie ;
Of his own life began to irk,
For he could neither beg nor work,
On no ways could he beg nor steal,
Though he was poor, he was right leil.
So it fell on a dangerous year,
That meat and drink, and all was dear :   370
He was so hungr'd, and put to pyne,
That he was fain for to keep swyne ;
In all the land, as I heard tell,
There was but very little vittel.
He kept the swine, I leave him still,
And of the youngest speak we will,
Who kept the school, a noble clerk ;

And of him farder we will carp.
   He was a goodly man and wise,
It chanced he did get the prise,   380
The Pope of Rome he hapened to be:
The Cardinals wrote to ilk countrie,
Charging them all on Good-friday,
At mid-night for to watch and pray,
And send to Rome the holiest man,
That the Lord God best may or can;
That God would to the chapter send
On Good-friday or it did end.
Both doors and windows closed fast,
Syne home incontinent they past,   390
And sealed the locks with their own hand,
And gave the keys to the Lord of the land.
The Clerk was blyth when he got wit,
His bony Mantle he hint to it:
Says, " God, and my Mantle and my Wish,
If I were in the place, where ever it is,
In Rome's seat if I were set:"
Soon was he there withouten let,
Into their seat when he came in,
He hint his Mantle then fra him,   400
And syne sat down upon his knee,
And to the great God prayed he.
Soon after meat on Good-friday.
Lords, Barons, came without delay,
And opened the chapter with a gin
Into the seat where he came in;
They said, a Clerk was there sittand,
On both his knees ful fast prayand,
They thanked God both less and mair,
So holy a Clerk who sent them there,   410
Who was sent by the Holy Sp'rit
For to be Pope he was most meet!

Syne with that word they gave him doom,
And crowned him the Pope of Rome ;
And all the bells of Rome they rang,
Priests and Friers all they sang,
So daily ilk ane with a shout,
They bore him all the town about,
And set him down upon his seat :
All men of him had great conceit, 420
Now Pope of Rome we leave him still,
And of the mid-most speak we will.
When that he came within the town,
To enter in he was most bown ;
He told his Brother both less and mair,
Spoiled of all he was most bair,
His Brother was from far countrie,
He marvel'd of him to hear and see,
Into the woods among his faes,
Has left him neither gold nor clais ; 430
The Procession was charged him to meet,
With all solemnities compleat,
With honour great, and good intent,
They were all readie incontinent :
Past throw the whole parts of the street,
The Pope's brother there to meet.
As soon as he his brother saw,
Great pleasure was among them aw ;
Syne took his Brother by the hand,
So did they all at his command : 440
Syne said, " Brother, welcome to me,
Ye shall want neither meet nor fee ;
And a new cloathing ye shall take,
My master household I shall you make ;
And I avow to my ending,
I shall you love attour all thing."
He says, " Dear Brother, God you reward,

Now have you made me lord and laird,
A lord of office ye have me made;
And likeways promist fair lands braid."   450
   He had not been a moneth there,
While he thought on his Ladie fair.
And thought to win the Purse again,
And to the Ladie do no pain,
That his Purse fra him once had tane.
Unto the Pope he said again,
" Now, Brother dear, I you entreat,
Grant me an asking, I think meet."
Then answer'd his Brother right reverentlie,
" Ask on, my Brother, whatever it be."   460
Says " Brother, lend me thy Mantle fine,
I swear to you, I'le not it tyne,
But bring't again after this day,
I no ways shall put it away."
The Pope answer'd, with drearie chear,
" I had rather give you, my brother dear,
A million of gold, alse much of land,
Nor lend my Mantle out of my hand.
Yet, as I have said, it shall be so,
I no ways will it hold thee fro,   470
Now, keep it well, my Brother dear."
With that the Pope made drearie chear,
And frae his brother turn'd his back ;
Syne took his leave, and no more spake.
His Brother had his Mantle in hand,
Cast it about him where he did stand :
Said, " God, and my Mantle, and my wish,
If I were in the place where ever it is,
Wherever she be that Ladie free,
That took that noble Purse from me."   480
. Than be these words came in his thought,
He was into the chamber brought.

She was into her bed sleepand,
And he upon the foot standand:
Laid down his Mantle, and his wish,
Then he began the Ladie to kiss;
First to kiss, and then to clap,
And quietly in the bed he crap.
The Ladie wakened with a cry,
Says, "Who is this that lyes me by?   490
I pray you, tell me the manner,
How came you in?—who brought you here?
Your asking then, what ever it be,
Ye shall have it of me trulie."
He says, "My Mantle and my wish,
If I were in the place, where ever it is,
Where I desire or think to be,
There will I be right hastilie."
She said, "Sweet Sir, for Charitie,
As you would do any thing for me,   500
Now wish me and your Mantle anonc.
Into yon place of Marble stone,
That we may play together there."
And certainly withoutten mair,
Be that same word came in his thought,
They were both in the yle soon brought,
Unto a green place, where they lay;
And unto him there can she say,—
"Lay down your head upon my knee,
That I may look a little wee."   510
He needed no ways more bidding,
But suddenly fell on sleeping;
Upon her knee lay down his head—
Of his Mantle he took no dread.
The Lady well perceived that,—
Quickly she rose, and the mantle gat:
The mantle she took deliverlie,

And wished herself right shortlie,
Into her chamber, and that anone,
And in the yle left him alone,   520
Sleeping there like a drunken sow ;
Both Purse and Mantle wants he now !
But at the last, then wakened he,—
He mist the Mantle and the Ladie ;
Ye may well wit his heart was sair,
When he mourned, and made great care.
" My Purse and Mantle is now both gone,
And in this yland left alone :
No creature is left with me,
Nor none to bear me companie ;   530
Or who will any meat me give?
Alas ! Alas ! how shall I live ? "
Much was the care and dool he made ;
He rave the hair out of his head.
    He stayed not there well days three,
Till he saw ships upon the sea :
They sailed right so near hand by,
While they did hear his voice and cry.
Syne saw him on a craig standand,
A man would fain be at the land,   540
Cryand to them, that they might see,
Help for his sake that died on Tree ;
Said, " It was pitie for to see
A man distrest, whatever he be,
Upon yon craig, mourning full sair,
Right sad in heart, what would you mair ? "
The ship came to the craig near hand,
Their language could he not understand :
He knew them not, nor yet they him,
Yet willingly they took him in.   550
He signed to them, that he would gang,
Showing to them that he thought lang,

He would fain been at Rome again ;
But with them he dought not remain ;
He wanted money, he thought great shame,
He thought he was so long fra hame :
With their cock-boat put him to land,
Where he might see on every hand.
He passed to a part near by,
For meat and drink if he might try,   560
Yeid to a wood, with heart full sair,
Pleasand and wholsome was the air ;
He swouned sorrowfully in that stead,
That he for hunger was almost dead.
He cry'd upon our Ladie dear,
That hunger and thirst strack him so near.
He looked a little near hand by,
A tree of apples he could espy ;
Right blyth and glad he was of that sight,
He took his fill, even as he might,   570
And stepped a space beside the tree,
And said they were good companie.
Syne ate his fill of that fair fruit,
For him to gang it was no buit :
Because the apples that he did eat,
He fand them taking, and right sweet :
A smell they had above measure,
Might pleas'd a king, or emperour :
As well for dame, as mighty queen,
Was never fairer seen with eyne :   580
I may take apples now with me,
For hunger I think not to die :
He pulled the apples, and ate so fast,
And filled himself, till at the last,
He was as lipper as Lazarus,
Or any in the world I wish :
His head ov'r spread with byles black,

That none might ken a word he spak.
Right wisely then perceived he,
And saw fair pears upon a tree :   590
He pull'd the pears, but any baid,
Right gladly ate ere he further gaid :
Sua leper he was, he would have been
For to have gotten medicine :
The pears he eat, the storie does say,
Whilk put the leprosie clean away ;
He was as clean, the storie says this,
As anie into the world I wish.
With him he carried of apples threescore,
Of them surelie he took no more ;   600
And twice as many of the pears he took,
That he took with him, he none forsook ;
And if apples made leperous,
The pears healed most precious :
Of both the sorts with him he had,
All men were welcome, buy who wad.
Thir apples, that the man on fell,
Brought him great good, I shall you tell ;
The apples he carried him about,
A strange vertue they had but doubt :   610
He carried these apples as he did pass,
And took them where the Ladie was.
    Upon a time to the kirk he came,
Where he saw many a Ladie and Dame :
And as he sat in the kirk-yeard
There came about him such a guard,
To buy these apples pleasant and fair :
And manie people he saw there.
Unto the kirk syne could he pass,
Baid still, and saw where the Ladie was,   620
That Purse and Mantle frae him had tane ;
He thought to do the Ladie much pain :

Thus thinking there as he could gang,
To bring the Ladie into such thrang;
Saying unto himself alone,
But kind of fair words spake he none.
He wist not to whom his moan to make,
He went to church door a seat to take;
And at the kirk door he sat down,
Where the Ladie went readie bown :   630
He knew right well she would be there,
Where that she used to make repair.
The apples were seemlie to be seen,
Men did not see such with their een ;
There gathered about him a great meinzie,
They wondred meikle the apples to see :
" How sell ye the apples?" they bad him tell,
" For ten ducats the piece I sell.
Please you to buy I will take money ;
Stand by if ye will not buy any,   640
Do not stand here my market to spill :
I bid none buy but these that will."
In the mean time the Ladie was command,
Unto the kirk with maidens in a band :
She strangely marvelled at the repair she saw,
And hither-ward then she began to draw :
A maiden answered, " It I shall you tell,
A daft fellow it is has apples to sell ;
They are verie fair and comelie to see,
Ten ducats the piece for them seeks he."   650
The people answered, call'd him daft man,
As for an apple to seek that price, than,
It cannot be but they have a vertue,
The apples right pleasant have a fair shew.
Then forward to the market the Ladie can gang,
To see the apples she thought great lang ;
Some of them bought she, it was her pleasure,

15

To look and to view she took great leasure.
None of them she priev'd till morn afternoon,
And for that cause she sped her home soon,   660
And when she came into her Father's hall,
Syne after her maidens shortly did call,—
"Bring hither the apples ye bought to me,
For they are fair and seemly to see."
She ate of them three, and thought them right dulce,
Till she was as leper as Lazarus ;
Her head overspread with byles black, ·
That none might hear a word she spake :
Syne looked in a glass and saw her self so,
Out of her right wits she was like to go,   670
Waryand the hour that ever she was born,
She saw her self so, "Alas ! I'm forlorn."
Be that her Father came in right at noon,
And call'd for his Daughter to come to him soon,
Then a maiden answered meekly and spake,
"Your daughter is vexed with uglie byles black ;
I cannot tell you how it fell the case : "
Be that the blood shot into his face.
Her Father came soon without any baid,
Received his daughter into his arms braid ;   680
Right sore he grat for his daughter's skaith ;
For she to him comfort and joy brought baith,
He now does say, "Alas ! full woe is me,
Upon my daughter this sad sight to see."
She said to her Father, "My heart is full wo.
Now what shall I do ? or where shall I go ? "
The King then said, " Good Lords of grace,
Cause shortlie to proclaim in everie place,
If any there be that her heal might,
My daughter shall him marrie outright."   690
Then to this counsel the Lords came in hy,
Both great and small, and that hastilie.

Throw all Portugal both up and down,
Proclaimed through land eik borrowstown.
The gentleman could well the matter speir,
Right blyth he was these tydings for to hear ;
Yet he thought again the Ladie to beguile,
Both Purse and Mantle to get with a wyle.
Prepared cloths right seemlie to be seen,
Syne call'd himself Doctor of medicine :			700
This Lord he rode unto the borrowstoun,
At the best lodging there he lighted down,
After the hostage incontinent speirit,
Both horse and man after him then requirit,
" Spare not for cost, although no Lord I be,
What ever my count is shall be pay'd surelie,"—
They were right glad the tidings that he spake,
Yea, man and horse did both him service make,
So past his time compleat three days there.
The hostage said to him, " Sir, what will ye ? "		710
" A Doctor of medicine I'm ready at command,
There's none in Christendom I say this day livand,
Can heal diseases that I will take in hand,
And thereon I will lay my life in paund."
The hostage said, " Of Leprosie have ye skill ? "
" Yes, I can heal it, and that right wonder well ;"
Then was he right blyth of that certaintie ;
So was there one past from his companie,
And that anone, they went and told the King,
That such a man in his bounds was living—		720
A fine doctor, the best in all this land,—
No finer is as we now understand."
The King was glad, and his daughter also,
Commands the Porter unto him for to go,
Who made no stay, but came incontinent.
" Let me see now where is the Patient,
That I should heal, and also take the cure,

That shall I do by God's grace, be ye sure,
Take ye no fear, since I have tane in hand,
God be my guide, he is my sure warrand :   730
Let no dreadure enter into your heart,
I shall her heal before I do depart,   .
Or lose my life, before that I do go,
What I have said, if that it be not so."
When that he came, he saw the Ladie stand,
" This lipperness will I now take in hand,
Mend her sickness, in truth I take no fear ;
Because I know the form and the manner,
To heal her person both without and in,
And likeways als what fashion to begin,   740
If ye will keep your promise unto me."
" What I have said in faith and truth to be ;
What I have sworn I will keep very well,
What I have said shall testifie my seal :
Nor shall deny the thing that I have said."
Whereof the doctor was both blyth and glad.
The company rejoyced all about,
The King's daughter maid hail without doubt :
Fra she heard that, rejoyced greatumly,
Before them came and hails'd the company.   750
Then she before her Father lighted down,
And unto God made her devotion.
That same command she vowed to fulfill,
Without faining of deceit thereintil ;
" Get up right soon, and rise up off your knee,
Make true confession both to God and me,
And if that you make your confession leil,
I promise here to make you sound and well."
So she shew forth, and her confession made :
The Purse and Mantle no ways she opened,   760
And so these two she keeped still in mind ;
Reveal'd them not : but kept herself in pine,

Caus'd her grow worse into her leprosie.
She said, " Alas! alas! and wo is me,
Now I am worse than ever I was before,
Full wo is me, and wo is me therefore."
The Doctor answer'd, saying, " I have no might
To help you now, you have not told the right,
I am right sure some things ye have forget,
Hid in your heart, to tell you will not set;   770
Out of the world far better I had been,
To kyth my craft, and ye no ways made clean."
The King said, " Daughter, likes thou to be hail?
I thee request make thy confession leal,
And here, I pray thee by the great God abone,
Without dissimulance make thy confession :
A lipper woman again shall never be,
Nor ever vext with such infirmitie.
When I am dead he's be King after me.
Please thou him wed, and married on him be,   780
If thou desires, it lyes into thy heart,
That he and thou in love be afterwart :
He to be King, and thou the Queen also,
From bail to bliss ye may together go."
The Daughter said, " Remain, and now bide still,
And my confession I shall declare you till :
Now, Lord of Heav'n, thou knows I did receive
A Purse and Mantle, that wrongously I have,
Whilk I took fra a young man sickerlie,
Who was then once familiar with me;   790
In marble yle I left him mourning sore,
Pennance for him I dree'd the same therefore;
This is the cause that I do wish for him,
Health to my body, both without and within."
The Doctor says, " Thir twa ye cast you fra;
And see that ye forsake the same alswa,
And beseek God while ye are on your knee:

The Purse and Mantle ye render unto me."
She said, " Sir, I beseek with all my will,
The Purse and Mantle you freely take you till." 800
The gentleman was blyth, I understand,
Receiv'd them both, and took them in his hand,
Then past aside a little the Ladie him fra,
And said these words before he past away :
"Now God and my Mantle and my wish,
If·I were in the place where ever it is."
Be this was said, incontinent he was there,
And left the Ladie into great dool and care,
Waryand the time that she was ever born,
Into this wretched life, thus for to be forlorn.   810
" Thus leave I now the lady sick and sair,
And to return to Rome I now will fare,
And shew my brother of my great craft and skill,
The truth to see, and als to know my will :
How I have done, and what way I have wrought,
The Purse and Mantle how I again have brought :
Of my coming he will be wondrous blyth,
And als be glad, I pray God make me thrive."
He would not bide, but went to him right soon,
He said, " Brother, ye're welcome here to Rome!" 820
" I have gotten my Purse and Mantle again,
Brother, (he said,) of that I am right fain.
She that deceived me, both meek and mild,
Is lipper sick, and I have her beguil'd."
" Fy, now," he says, " that will our conscience grieve,
Keep God's command, and help her for to live :
If thow has any skill, throw help of God and man,
Help thou the Ladie with all the craft thou can.
Be not unkind, but help with all thy might,
Do her the good thou can, both day and night : 830
If she were whole, and seemly to be seen,
Great commendation bears thow where she has been,

Right shortly go and help her out of pain ;
Shew love to her who can thee love again :
Do not deny, but grant when thou art here,
And for her sake see that thou to me swear,
Thou shalt do right, and not thy conscience grieve,
But trulie help, and I will thee believe ;
Thou's be her husband, syne wed her with a ring,
And after that unto thy bed her bring :   840
Syne as a Prince live at thy own liking,
It may befal thereafter thow be King !"
To that effect grant writ most hastily,
And for to pray the King especiallie,
Sayand, " My brother is a worthy gentleman,
Of medicine full well the craft he can ;
All sorts of sickness we hear that he can heal ;
He leprosie can cure withoutten fail :
We hear ye have a daughter wise and fair,
No moe ye have, we know she is thy heir :   850
I am inform'd for my brother she is meet,
Betwixt them both would ye with band compleat,
Great pitie is that ought should now her ail,
I would she were relieved and made hail.
If that ye please, he wed her with a ring,
And after that in Portugal be King."
The letters then to Portugal went right soon :
If this matter betwixt them might be done,
And so conclude, amongst them make a bond,
The cause and why, how the matter should stand; 860
With their consents and yours, that it might be,
'Twixt Pope and King this was made sickerlie.
Syne send his brother with letters of parchment,
That written was within to stand content.
So at that time the letters to him gave,
Saying to him, " My blessing mot ye have :
Go on the way, thou take thir men with thee,

Forsooth, they are a goodlie companie,
With thee to fare, in ship as ye may sail,
Till that thou come to land in Portugal.   870
I give thee here a million for to spend,
Although thou sail'd unto the world's end.
When thou art come into the King's palace,
Show my commission, and thanks unto his Grace,
Syne come again to Rome, and show to me
With thy message, what the King said to thee.
If his daughter thou heal of her disease,
The samine done, my self it shall well please."
    Sua the Lady was brought from care to bliss,
And after that she ay remained his: 880
Syne married her with joy and comforting,
So he gave her rich rubies in a ring;
In midst of it a great jewel there was,
Shined more bright than glittering was the glass;
The price of it I heard men right tell,
Was worth half the kingdom of Portugal:
Rich was the jewel, if richer there might be,
The like I hear was not in no countrie,
For preciousness and vertue that it had,
It was so fine, that she thereof was glad.   890
Content she was to all his bidding,
And him obey'd and pleased in all thing;
With earls, lords, knights, barons comforting;
What wisht she more, she had much rejoycing.
The nobles all that dwelt in her countrie,
Were all obedient to her Majestie,
Ready to do her service and pleasure,
What she would have of gold and rich treasure;
Brought to her Grace abundance of plentie,
Of rich jewels and wonders for to see.   900
They gave her one that was most worthy all,
The light of it shined on every wall.

For why, it was a thing most precious,
Shining within like rubies radious,
And so without, as many one might see,
A vertue had, all marvelled what it could be,
In such a jewel that all men marvel had,
Of what sickness it healed, lass or lad.
   So to be short, in this my tale I tell,
The samine was, the book shows wondrous leil,   910
Thir two were married, lived in joy and bliss,
In earthly pleasure, no farder could they wish.
They had delights and pleasures manifold,
In earthly things with pleasures as they would.
Of children I hear none was them between,
They wanted not that might them intertain ;
At length deceast, no farder can I tell,
But I hope that they in Heaven do dwell.

FINIS.

THE RING

OF THE ROY ROBERT, KING

OF SCOTLAND.

THE RING OF THE ROY ROBERT.

IN to the ring of the roy Robert,
   The first King of the gud Stewart;
Hary of Ingland the ferd King
In Scotland send, and askit this thing
At King Robert, quhy he nocht maid
Him seruice for his landis braid?
And quhy he causit to be spilt
Ffell Cristiane blude throw his gilt?
He said, he aucht of heretage,
In Loundoun for to mak homage,   10
Eftir the richt of Brutus King,
Quhilk had all Ingland in gouerning!—
   Ffra that King Robert, wyse and wicht,
Had hard and sein this wryt be sicht;
Sa he grew in matelent,
On till his barounis, tauld his intent;
[He called a Council to Striviling town,
And there came Lords of great renown;]
And at thame all he askit it
That he micht ansueir be his awin wit.   20
Thay war richt joyfull of that thing,
Referrit thame to thair nobill King.
Than, without counsall of ony man,
To dyt and wryt our King began:
[This was the effect of his writeing,
All is sooth, and na liesing.]
   WE ROBERT, throw Godis micht,
King of Scotland and Ylis richt,

That inebbis in the Occeane see,
That to this day was euir free,   30
To thé Henrie of Longcastell,
Thy epistill we considder weill :
Duik of that Ilk thow suld be cald,—
It is thy richtest style of auld ;
And I admit thé nocht as King,
Ffor certane poyntis of degrading :
Thairfoir, ane King I call nocht thé,
Ffor hurt of Kingis Maiesté ;
[For I will take nae heeding
Of thy unrighteous invading,   40
For what was right, as is well knawin,
Ye all defould within your awin :]
Wit thow that we haue understand
Ffor to declayre anent Scotland :
Thy wryt be wourd we haue sene,
Ffra first to last at thow can mein ;
Quhairthrow that thow sall answer haue,
Of my awin self, accept the laif.
And in the First, thow schawis ws till
Na Cristiane blude that thow wald spill,   50
On to the quhilk, we witnes beir,
Na blude for ws beis spilt in weir,
Bot gif it be in our defence,
Throw thy corruptit violence.
    And quhair thow wrytis and schawis till ws,
Sen borne was sonnis of auld Brutus,
That our succesouris aucht to be
Servandis till youris, gré be gré ;
Thou leyd thairof ! it is weill knawin,
We war euir fré within our awin !   60
Thocht Johne Balzoun maid ane band,
Contrair the richt of fayr Scotland ;
Thair he was mainsworne that we defend :

On till ws all, it is weill kend,
Anent the barnis of auld Brutus,
That kyndnes hes bene kepit till ws :
Scotland euir yit hes bene fré,
Sen Scota of Egipt tuik the see !
Bot ye are thirlit and our harlit,
The grit refuse of all the warld,   70
Ffor nichtbure tressoun amangis your sell
Ffor tymes, as the Cronicle will tell,
Ye haue halelie conqueist bene :
Ten thousand pvndis of gold so schene
To Julius Cesar payit ye
Off tribute, thus ye war nocht free.
Be Saxounis als ye war ouer thrawin
Be tua borne chiftanis of your awin,
And Germaneis in cumpany,
All borne Saraȝenis vtterlie,   80
At come with Horsus and Ingest,
And maid your auld blude richt waist ;
And slew the gentillis of Ingland
At Salisberrie, I vnderstande ;
And till ane takin the hingand stanis,
Ambrosius set vp for the naneis ;
In till ane lestand memoriall,
At Saxounis had ourset yow all.
Vndir the hewin is no kinryk
Off sorrow hes bein to yow lyk   90
Ye war put syn in subiectioun
At we, nor yit nane vnder croun,
Was never in sic necessitie
As hapnit your aduersatie !
Then Henslot, sone of Denmark king
The thrid tyme rais o're yow to ring ;
The quhilk, of Ingland maid conquest,
And left amangis yow at the last

Ane Dane in ilk ane hous, was knawin,
Yow to defoull with in your awin;   100
That occupiit bayth gude and wyff;
Thus in bondage ye leid your lyff!
    Quhen this was done, and all bypast,
The ferd conquest approchit fast,
Off the Bastarde of Normandie,
Quhilk conqueist Ingland halelie;
Quhilk yit amangis yow ringis thair blude,
And meikill vther that is nocht gude:
And gif ye trow this nocht south be,
Reid the Registar, and ye may see,   110
And the croniclis of braid Bartane,
Quhairout of our authoris ar tane;
That this is suth thow may nocht lane,
Ffrance and Bartane kennis in plane
Thow art nocht richtuous for to ring,
Ffor all realmis knawis this thing;
In Londoun thow swoir in Parliament,
Ingland ten yeiris [thou should absent,—
Then wast thou manifestlie mansworne
Or cuir three yearis] and ane half was worne; 120
Thou rais tressonablie for to ring,
And hes vndone Richart thy king.
Gif you knawis nocht thy meikle mis
The suth in proverb spokin is:
Flyt with thy nichtburis, and thai will tell
All the mischeif that the befell.
Bot for our Realme, I dar weill say
Was never none hyn to this day,
Brocht Scotland in subiectioun!
Bot ane was mansworne of your croun,
The quhilk of Langschankis, hecht Edwarde,   130
Tuik on him to declayr the parte,
Betuix the Brus and Johnne Balioun;

Than throw your fals illusioun,
Johne Balʒoun, quhair he had no richt,
Tuik tressonablie to hald with slicht,
Strenthis and castellis of our Cuntré,
Ye gat throw your subtilitie.
Than Williame Wallace, wicht and wyse,
Wichtlie reskewit ws thrys;   140
And Robert the Bruce rakleslie
Ffirst tynt, syn wan ws wichtlie;
And with him James the gud Douglas
Quhilk preivit weill in everie place;
Erle Thomas Randell, wyse and wicht,
As than was neuer ane hardyar knycht;
Thir exilit all your fals barnageis,
And fred our realme of all thirlageis.
And gif thow trowis this nocht suth is,
Off sextie thousand, we thocht no miss,   150
At Bannokeburne discomfist was;
Als your fals king away culd pas,
Throw an inborne tratour at was kend
Quhilk fré in Ingland he him send;
Or ellis we had tane your king,
And Ingland had in gouering.
   Quhen all this was cuming and gane,
Than Edward of Carnauerane
Discumfist he was at Biland
Be my Father, I tak on hand;   160
Walter Stewart that in hy
Chaissit him all opinlie,
Ane hundreth myle on King Edward,
Quhill that he was reskewit be parte,
Till Scaribur castell, and thair him lest;
Syn till his ost returnit Est;
Be than your clergy of Ingland
Renewit agane with stalwart hand

16

At Myltoun, as it is weill knawin,
Thair haistellie ye war ourthrawin   170
Be the gud Douglas, the suth to say,
And Thomas the gud erle of Murray;
Quhair twentie hundred war dungin to deid,
Withoutin succour, or remeid
Off preistis, that beir schawin croun,
That hardie men war of renoun.
  Eftir this, Robert the Bruce
Tuik stait, and halelie culd reduce
Northummerland, all till him sell,—
Ye may nocht say nor this befell !—   180
Syn ye war fane, or ye wald ces,
To proffer mariage for peice,
And askit the Prince of Bruce, Dauid
Till dame Jonet Touris till ally.
Ye maid that euidentis, and that band,
Vnder the grit seill of Ingland,
The quhilk ye call your goldin Chartour
In Ingland hes maid mony martyr !
Quhilk we haue plainlie for to schaw
The verité, quha will it knaw;   190
And falslie brokin is in yow,
All tyme befoir als weill as now;
And throw your fals suppleying
Quhen Edwarde Balȝoun rais to ring !
This is suth, I profer me
To preif on sextie agane sextie,
Or fourtie agane fourtie, gif ye lyk,
Or xx agane xx of our kinryk,
Gif tho be pacient and tholumdie
And wald nocht spill na Cristane blude   200
And gif thou thinkis it best sa
Let ws dereinȝe it betuix ws tua;
I proffer me to preif on thĕ

At we and Scotland yit art fré,—
And of the Paip nothing we hald,
Bot of the Kirk our fayth of auld,—
At we ar bunding of det to do,
At all Cristiane pepill aucht to do.
    ¶ This wryt to Londoun he hes send,
And quhen the Barounis had it kend,
And had considderit it in plane,—
Yit na said ansuer come agane.   210

FFINIS THE RING OF THE ROY ROBERT
MAID BE DENE DAUID STEILL.

KING ESTMERE.

KING ESTMERE.

HEARKEN to me, gentlemen,
 Come and you shall heare;
Ile tell you of two of the boldest brethèr,
 That ever born y-were.
The tone of them was Adler yonge,
 The tother was Kyng Estmere;
The were as bolde men in their deedes,
 As any were farr and neare.
As they were drinking ale and wine
 Within his brother's halle: 10
When will ye marry a wyfe, brother,
 A wyfe to gladd us all?
Then bespake him Kyng Estmere,
 And answered him hartilye:
I knowe not that ladye in any lande,
 That is able to marrye with mee.
Kyng Adland hath a daughter, brother,
 Men call her bright and sheene;
If I were kyng here in your stead,
 That ladye sholde be queene.   20
Sayes, Reade me, reade me, deare brother,
 Throughout merrye Englànd,
Where we might find a messenger
 Betweene us two to sende.
Sayes, You shall ryde yourselfe, brothèr,
 I'le beare you companye;
Many a man throughe fals messengers is deceived,
 And I feare lest soe shold wee.
Thus they renisht them to ryde
 Of twoe good renisht steedes,   30

And when they came to Kyng Adlands halle,
  Of red golde shone their weedes.
And whan they came to Kyng Adlands halle
  Before the goòdlye yate,
Ther they found good Kyng Adlànd,
  Rearing himselfe theratt.
Nowe Christ thee save, good Kyng Adlànd;
  Now Christ thee save and see.
Sayd, You be welcome, Kyng Estmere,
  Right hartilye unto mee.   40
You have a daughter, sayd Adler yonge,
  Men call her bright and sheene,
My brother wold marrye her to his wyffe,
  Of Englande to be queene.
Yesterdaye was at my deare daughtèr
  The King his sonne of Spayne;
And then she nicked him of naye,
  And I doubt shee'le do you the same.
The Kyng of Spayne is a foule paynìm,
  And 'leeveth on Mahound;   50
And pitye it were that fayré ladyé
  Shold marrye a heathen hound.
But grant to me, sayes Kyng Estmere,
  For my love I you praye;
That I may see your daughter deare
  Before I goe hence awaye.
Althoughe itt is seven yeare and more
  Syth my daughter was in halle,
She shall come once downe for your sake
  To glad my guestès alle.   60
Downe then came that mayden fayre,
  With ladyes lacede in pall,
And halfe a hondred of bolde knightes,
  To bring her from bowre to hall;
And as manye gentle squieres,

To waite upon them all.
The talents of golde, were on her head sette,
  Hanged lowe downe to her knee;
And everye rynge to her smalle fingèr,
  Shone of the chrystall free. 70
Sayes, Christ you save, my deare madàme;
  Sayes, Christ you save and see.
Sayes, You be welcome, Kyng Estmere,
  Right welcome unto mee.
And iff you love me, as you saye,
  So well and hartilee,
All that ever you are comen about
  Soon sped now itt may bee.
Then bespake her father deare:
  My daughter, I saye naye; 80
Remember well the King of Spayne,
  What he sayd yesterdaye.
He wold pull downe my halles and castles,
  And reave me of my lyfe:
I cannot blame him if he doe,
  Iff I reave him of his wyfe.
Your castles and your towres, father,
  Are stronglye built aboute;
And therefore of the King his sonne of Spaine
  Wee need not stande in doubt. 90
Plyght me your troth, nowe, Kyng Estmère,
  By heaven and your righte hand,
That you will marrye me to your wyfe,
  And make me queene of your land.
Then Kyng Estmere he plight his troth
  By heaven and his righte hand,
That he wolde marrye her to his wyfe,
  And make her queene of his land.
And he tooke leave of that ladye fayre,
  To goe to his owne countree, 100

To fetche him dukes and lordes and knightes,
  That marryed they might bee.
They had not ridden scant a myle,
  A myle forthe of the towne,
But in did come the Kyng of Spayne,
  With kempès many a one.
But in did come the Kyng of Spayne,
  With many a bolde baròne,
Tone daye to marrye Kyng Adlands daughter,
  Tother daye to carryc her home.   110
Shee sent one after Kyng Estmère
  In all the spede might bee,
That he must either turne againe and fighte,
  Or goe home and lose his ladye.
One whyle then the page he went,
  Another while he ranne ;
Till he had oretaken Kyng Estmere !
  I wis, he never blanne.
Tydinges, tydinges, King Estmere :
  What tydinges nowe, my boye ?   120
O tydinges I can tell to you,
  That will you sore annoye.
You had not ridden scant a mile,
  A myle out of the towne,
But in did come the Kyng of Spayne
  With kempès many a one :
But in did come the Kyng of Spayne
  With manye a bolde baròne,
Tone daye to marrye King Adlands daughter,
  Tother daye to carrye her home.   130
My ladye fayre she greetes you well,
  And ever-more well by mee :
You must either turne againe and fighte,
  Or goe home and lose your ladye.
Sayes, Reade me, reade me, deare brother,

My reade shall ryse at thee,
Whether it is better to turne and fighte,
  Or goe home and lose my ladye.
Now hearken to me, sayes Adler yonge,
  And your reade must rise at me,   140
I quicklye will devise a waye
  To sette thy ladye free.
My mother was a westerne woman,
  And learned in gramarye,
And when I learned at the schole,
  Something shee taught itt mee.
There growes an hearbe within this fielde,
  And iff it were but knowne,
His color, which is whyte and redd,
  It will make blacke and browne: 150
His color, which is browne and blacke,
  Itt will make redd and whyte;
That sworde is not in all Englande,
  Upon his coate will byte.
And you shal be a harper, brother,
  Out of the North countrye;
And I'le be your boye, so faine of fighte,
  And beare your harpe by your knee.
And you shall be the best harpèr,
  That ever tooke harp in hand;   160
And I will be the best singèr,
  That ever sung in this land.
Itt shal be written in our foreheads
  All and in grammarye,
That we towe are the boldest men,
  That are in all Christentye.
And thus they renisht them to ryde,
  On towe good renish steedes;
And when they came to King Adlands hall,   170
  Of redd gold shone their weedes.

And whan they came to Kyng Adlands hall
  Untile the fayre hall yate,
There they found a proud portér
  Rearing himselfe theratt.
Sayes, Christ thee save, thou proud portér;
  Sayes, Christ thee save and see.
Nowe you be welcome, sayd the portér,
  Of what land soever ye bee.
We been harpers, said Adler yonge,
  Come out of the Northe countrée;   180
We beene come hither untill this place,
  This proud weddinge for to see.
Sayd, and your color were white and redd,
  As it is blacke and browne,
I would saye King Estmere and his brother
  Were comen untill this towne.
Then they pulled out a ryng of gold,
  Layd itt on the porters arme :
And ever we will thee, proud portér,
  Thou wilt saye us no harme.   190
Sore he looked on Kyng Estmère,
  And sore he handled the ryng,
Then opened to them the fayre hall yates,
  He lett for no kind of thyng.
Kyng Estmere he stabled his steede
  Soe fayre att the hall board ;
The frothe, that came from his brydle bitte,
  Light on Kyng Bremors beard.
Sayes, Stable thy steede, thou proud harpèr,
  Sayes, Stable him in the stalle ;   200
Itt doth not beseeme a proud harpèr
  To stable his steede in a kyngs halle.
My ladd he is so lither, he sayd,
  He will do nought that's meete ;
And aye that I cold but find the man,

Were able him to beate.
Thou speakst proud words, sayes the Kyng of Spayne,
  Thou harper here to mee;
There is a man within this halle,
  That will beate thy ladd and thee.   210
O lett that man come downe, he sayd,
  A sight of him wold I see;
And whan hee hath beaten well my ladd,
  Then he shall beate of mee.
Downe then came the kemperye man,
  And looked him in the eare;
For all the gold, that was under heaven,
  He durst not neigh him neare.
And how nowe, kempe, sayd the Kyng of Spayne,
  And how what aileth thee?   220
He sayes, Itt is written in his forhead
  All and in gramarye,
That for all the gold that is under heaven,
  I dare not neigh him nye.
Then Kyng Estmere pulled forth his harpe,
  And playd a pretty thinge:
The ladye upstarte from the boarde,
  And wold have gone from the King.
Stay thy harpe, thou proud harpèr
  For God's love I pray thee;
For and thou playes as thou beginns,
  Thou'lt till my bryde from mee.
He stroake upon his harpe againe,
  And playd a pretty thinge;
The ladye lough a loud laughter,
  As shee sate by the king.
Saies, sell me thy harpe, thou proud harper,
  And thy stringès all,
For as many gold nobles " thou shalt have,"
  As heere be ringes in the hall.   240

What wold ye doe with my harpe, " he sayd,"
   If I did sell itt ye?
To play my wiffe and me a FITT,
   When abed together wee bee.
Now sell me, quoth hee, thy bryde soe gay,
   As shee sitts by thy knee,
And as many gold nobles I will give,
   As leaves been on a tree.
And what wold ye doe with my bryde soe gay,
   Iff I did sell her thee ?   250
More semelye it is for her fayre bodye
   To lye by mee than thee.
Hee played agayne both loud and shrille,
   And Adler he did syng,
" Oh ladye, this is thy owne true love ;
   " Noe harper, but a kyng.
" O ladye, this is thy owne true love ;
   " As playnlye thou mayest see ;
" And I'le rid thee of that foule paynim,
   " Who partes thy love and thee."   260
The ladye looked, the ladye blushte,
   And blushte and lookt agayne,
While Adler he hath drawne his brande,
   And hath the Sowdan slayne.
Up then rose the kempeye men,
   And loud they gan to crye:
Ah! traytors, yee have slayne our kyng,
   And therefore yee shall dye.
Kyng Estmere threwe the harpe asyde,
   And swift he drew his brand ;   270
And Estmere, and Adler yonge
   Right stiffe in stour can stand.
And aye their swordes soe sore can fyte,
   Through help of gramarye
That soone they have slayne the kempery men,

Or forst them forth to flee.
King Estmere tooke that fayre ladye,
  And marryed her to his wiffe,
And brought her home to merry England
  With her to leade his life.   280

FINIS.

THE BATTLE OF HARLAW.

17

THE BATTLE OF HARLAW, FOUGHTEN UPON FRIDAY, JULY 24, 1411, AGAINST DONALD OF THE ISLES.

I.

FRAE Dunideir as I cam throuch,
   Doun by the hill of Banochie,
Allangst the lands of Garioch ;
   Grit pitie was to heir and sé
   The noys and dulesum hermonie,
That evir that dreiry day did daw ;
   Cryand the Corynoch on hie,
Alas! alas! for the HARLAW.

II.

I marvlit quhat the matter meint,
   All folks war in a fiery fairy :
I wist nocht quha was fae or freind ;
   Yit quietly I did me carrie.
   But sen the days of auld King Hairy,
Sic slauchter was not hard nor sene,
   And thair I had nae tyme to tairy,
For bissiness in Aberdene.

III.

Thus as I walkit on the way,
   To Inverury as I went,
I met a man, and bad him stay,
   Requeisting him to mak me quaint
   Of the beginning and the event,
That happenit thair at the Harlaw ;

Then he entreited me tak tent,
And he the truth sould to me schaw.

IV.

Grit Donald of the Yles did claim
  Unto the lands of Ross sum richt,
And to the Governour he came,
  Them for to haif, gif that he micht:
  Quha saw his interest was but slicht;
And thairfore answerit with disdain;
  He hastit hame baith day and nicht,
And sent nae bodward back again.

V.

But Donald richt impatient
  Of that answer Duke Robert gaif,
He vowd to God Omnipotent,
  All the hale lands of Ross to haif,
  Or ells be graithed in his graif.
He wald not quat his richt for nocht,
  Nor be abusit lyk a slaif,
That bargin sould be deirly bocht.

VI.

Then haistylie he did command,
  That all his weir-men should convene,
Ilk an well harnisit frae hand,
  To meit and heir quhat he did mein;
  He waxit wrath, and vowit tein,
Sweirand he wald surpryse the North,
  Subdew the brugh of Aberdene,
Mearns, Angus, and all Fyfe, to Forth.

VII.

Thus with the weir-men of the Yles,
  Quha war ay at his bidding bown,

With money maid, with forss and wyls,
　　Richt far and neir baith up and doun:
Throw mount and muir, frae town to town,
Allangst the land of Ross he roars,
　　And all obey'd at his bandown,
Evin frae the North to Suthren shoars.

VIII.

Then all the Countrie men did yield;
　　For nae resistans durst they mak,
Nor offer battill in the feild,
　　Be forss of arms to beir him bak;
　　Syne they resolvit all and spak,
That best it was for thair behoif,
　　They sould him for thair chiftain tak,
Believing weil he did them luve.

IX.

Then he a proclamation maid,
　　All men to meet at Inverness,
Throw Murray Land to mak a raid,
　　Frae Arthursyre unto Spey-ness.
　　And further mair, he sent express,
To schaw his collours and ensenȝie,
　　To all and sindry, mair and less,
Throchout the boundies of Boyn and Enȝie.

X.

And then throw fair Strathbogie land,
　　His purpose was for to pursew,
And quhasoevir durst gainstand,
　　That race they should full sairly rew.
　　Then he bad all his men be trew,
And him defend by forss and slicht,
　　And promist them rewardis anew,
And mak them men of mekle micht.

XI.

Without resistans, as he said,
  Throw all these parts he stoutly past,
Quhair sum war wae, and sum war glaid,
  But Garioch was all agast.
  Throw all these feilds he sped him fast,
For sic a sicht was never sene ;
  And then, forsuith, he langd at last
To sé the Bruch of Aberdene.

XII.

To hinder this prowd enterprise,
  The stout and michty Erle of Marr,
With all his men in arms did ryse,
  Even frae Curgarf to Craigyvar ;
  And down the syde of Don richt far ;
Angus and Mearns did all convene
  To fecht, or Donald came sae nar
The ryall bruch of Aberdene.

XIII.

And thus the martial Erle of Marr,
  Marcht with his men in richt array,
Befoir the enemie was aware,
  His banner bauldly did display.
  For weil enewch they kend the way,
And all their semblence weil they saw,
  Without all dangir, or delay,
Came hastily to the HARLAW.

XIV.

With him the braif Lord Ogilvy,
  Of Angus Sherriff principall,
The constabill of gude Dundè,
  The vanguard led before them all.

Suppose in number they war small,
Thay first richt bauldie did pursew,
  And maid thair faes befoir them fall,
Quha then that race did sairly rew.

XV.

And then the worthy Lord Salton,
  The strong undoubted Laird of Drum,
The stalwart Laird of Lawristone,
  With ilk thair forces all and sum.
  Panmuir with all his men did cum,
The Provost of braif Aberdene,
  With trumpets and with tuick of Drum,
Came schortly in thair armour schene.

XVI.

These with the Erle of Marr came on,
  In the reir-ward richt orderlie,
Thair enemies to sett upon ;
  In awfull manner hardilie,
  Togither vowit to live and die,
Since they had marchit mony mylis
  For to suppress the tyrannie .
Of douted Donald of the Yles.

XVII.

But he in number ten to ane,
  Richt subtilie alang did ryde,
With Malcomtosch and fell Maclean,
  With all their power at their syde,
  Presumeand on thair strenth and pryde,
Without all feir or ony aw,
  Richt bauldie battill did abyde,
Hard by the town of fair HARLAW.

XVIII.

The armies met, the trumpet sounds,
  The dandring drums alloud did touk,
Baith armies byding on the bounds,
  Till ane of them the feild sould bruik.
  Nae help was thairfor, nane wald jouk,
Ferss was the fecht on ilka syde,
  And on the ground lay mony a bouk
Of them that thair did battill byd.

XIX.

With doutsum victorie they dealt,
  The bludy battil lastit lang,
Each man his nibours forss thair felt;
  The weakest aft-tymes gat the wrang.
  Thair was nae mowis thair them amang,
Naithing was hard but heavy knocks,
  That eccho maid a dulefull sang,
Thairto resounding frae the rocks.

XX.

But Donald's men at last gaif back;
  For they war all out of array.
The Earl of MARRIS men throw them brak,
  Pursewing shairply in thair way,
  Thair enemy to tak or slay,
Be dynt of forss to gar them yield,
  Quha war richt blyth to win away,
And sae for feirdness tint the feild.

XXI.

Then Donald fled, and that full fast,
  To mountains hich for all his micht;
For he and his war all agast,
  And ran till they war out of sicht:

And sae of Ross he lost his richt,
Thocht mony men with him he brocht,
   Towards the Yles fled day and nicht,
And all he wan was deirlie bocht.

XXII.

This is, (quod he,) the richt report
   Of all that I did heir and knaw,
Thocht my discourse be sumthing schort,
   Tak this to be a richt suthe saw.
   Contrairie God and the King's law,
Thair was spilt mekle Christian blude,
   Into the battil of HARLAW;
This is the sum, sae I conclude.

XXIII.

But yit a bony quhyle abyde,
   And I sall mak thé cleirly ken
Quhat slauchter was on ilkay syde,
   Of Lowland and of Highland men,
   Quha for thair awin haif evir bene.
These lazie lowns micht weil be spaird,
   Chessit lyke deirs into thair dens,
And gat thair waiges for rewaird.

XXIV.

Malcomtosh of the clan heid chief,
   Macklean with his grit hauchty heid,
With all thair succour and relief,
   War dulefully dung to the deid.
   And now we are freid of thair feid,
They will not lang to cum again;
   Thousands with them without remeid,
On Donald's syd that day war slain.

XXV.

And on the uther syde war lost,
 Into the feild that dismal day,
Chief men of worth, (of mekle cost,)
 To be lamentit sair for ay.
The Lord Saltoun and Rothemay,
A man of micht and mekle main ;
 Grit dolour was for his decay,
That sae unhappylie was slain.

XXVI.

Of the best men amang them was,
 The gracious gude Lord Ogilvy,
The Sheriff-Principal of Angus ;
 Renownit for truth and equitie,
 For faith and magnanimitie.
He had few fallows in the feild,
 Yit fell by fatall destinie,
For he nae ways wad grant to yield.

XXVII.

Sir James Scrimgeor of Duddap, Knicht,
 Grit constabill of fair Dundé,
Unto the dulefull deith was dicht,
 The Kingis chief banner-man was he,
 A valziant man of chevalrie,
Quhais predecessors wan that place
 At Spey, with gude King William frie,
Gainst Murray and Macduncan's race.

XXVIII.

Gude Sir Allexander Irvine,
 The much renownit Laird of Drum,
Nane in his days was bettir sene,
 Quhen they war semblit all and sum,

To praise him we sould not be dumm,
For valour, witt, and worthyness,
　To end his days he ther did cum,
Quhois ransom is remeidyless.

XXIX.

And thair the Knicht of Lawriston
　Was slain into his armour schene;
And gude Sir Robert Davidson,
　Quha Provest was of Aberdene;
　The Knicht of Panmure, as was sene,
A martiall man in armour bricht;
　Sir Thomas Murray stout and kene,
Left to the warld that last gude nicht.

XXX.

Thair was not, sen King Keneth's days,
　Sic strange intestine crewel stryf
In Scotland sene, as ilk man says,
　Quhair mony liklie lost thair lyfe;
　Quhilk maid divorce twene man and wyfe,
And mony children fatherless,
　Quhilk in this realme has bene full ryfe;
Lord help these lands, our wrangs redress.

XXXI.

In July, on Saint James his even,
　That four and twenty dismall day,
Twelve hundred, ten score and eleven
　Of yeirs sen Chryst, the suthe to say:
　Men will remember as they may,
Quhen thus the veritie they knaw,
　And mony a ane may murn for ay,
The brim battil of the HARLAW.

FINIS.

LICHTOUN'S DREME.

LICHTOUN'S DREME.

QUHA douttis Dremis ar bot phantasye?—
  My spreit was reft, and had in extasye,
My heid lay laich into this Dreme, but dout;
At my foirtop my five wittis flew out,
I murnit, and I maid a felloun mane:
Me thocht the King of Farye had me tane,
And band me in ane presoun, fute and hand,
Withoutin rewth, in ane lang raip of sand:
To perss the presoun wall it was nocht eith,
For it was mingit, and maid with mussill teith;   10
And in the middis of it ane myne of flynt;
I sank thairin, quhill I was neir hand tynt,
And quhen I saw thair was none uthair remeid,
I flychterit up with ane feddrem of leid;
For that I thocht me ferys of my youth,
I tuke my lytill tae into my mouth,
And kest my self rycht with ane mychtie bend
Out thruch the volt, and percit nocht the pend;
And thus, I thocht into my dullie Dreme,
I brak my heid upoun ane know of reme;   20
That I suld hurt my self, I had dispyte,
And, in all tene, I turnit up full tyte,
Drank of ane well that wes gane drye sevin yeir,
Syne lap thre lowpis, and I was haill and feir.—
  Syne eftir that I had eschapit this cace,
Me thocht I wes in monye divers place,
Quhilk wer to lang to have in perfyte mynd;
In Egipt, Ireland, Arragone, and Ynd;
In Burgonye, Burdeaux, and in Bethleem,
In Jurye land, and in Jerusalem;   30

In France, in Freisland, and in Cowpland fellis,
Quhair clokkis clekkis crawburdis in cokkill schellis;
In Poill, Pertik, Peblis, and Portjafe,
And thair I schippit into ane barge of drafe;
We pullit up sailis, and culd our ankeris wey,
And suddanelye out thruch the throsin sey
We sailit in storme, but steir, gyde, or glass
To Paradice, the place quhair Adame was.
Be we approchit into that port, in hye
We ware weill ware of Enoch and Elye,   40
Sittand, on Yule evin, in ane fresch grene schaw,
Rostand straberries at ane fyre of snaw;
I thocht I wald nocht skar them in that place,
Quhill thai had drawin the burd, and said the grace:
Than suddanelie I wolk, out throw the plane
To see mae farleis, that I mycht tell agane.
    Me thocht I happinnit on ane montane sone,
I' wanderit up, and was wer of the Mone,
And had nocht bene I lowtit in the steid,
I had strukkin aue lump out of my heid   50
Quhen I was weill, me thocht I culd nocht leif,
Bot than I tuke the Sone beme in my neif,
And wald haif clumin, bot at was in ane clipss;
Schortlie I slaid, and fell upoun my hipss
Doun in ane medow, besyde ane busk of mynt;
I socht my self, and I was sevin yeir tynt,
Yit in ane mist I fand me on the morne.
I hard ane Pundler blaw ane elrich horne;
And syne besyde me, in ane medow grene,
I saw thrè quhyte quhailis, semelie to be sene: 60
Thair Tedderis wes of grene gershopperis hair,
Off mige schankis baith clene, quhyte, and fair;
Thair tedderis wer maid weill grit to graip
With silkin schakillis, and sowlis of quhyte saip.
This Pundler ran fast, faynaud for to find

Thir quhailis thré upoun his gerss to pind;
He had ane cloik weill maid, and wounder meit,
Off ganand graith, of gude gray girdill feit;
Ane cleirly coit maid, in courtly wyiss
Of Emmot skynis, with mony sketh and plyiss.   70
Ane pair of hoiss maid of ane auld myll hopper,
Ane pair of courtly schone, of gude reid copper,
Ane heklit hud maid of the wyld wode sege:
Trest weill this Pundlar thocht him no manis pege!
He bure ane club, made mony ane carle coy,
Maid of ane auld burd of the ark of Noy;
He draif thir thré quhailis unto ane lie,
Ane him swelleit, and bair him to the sie,
And thair he levit on lempettis in hir wame,
Quhill harvist tyme, that hirdis draif them hame.   80
Be this wes done, the tuder twa returnit
To suallow me, grit dule I maid, and murnit:
Me thocht I fled, and throcht a park cowd pass
And walknit syne, quhair trow ye that I was?
Doun in ane henslaik, and gat ane fellon fall,
And lay betuix ane picher and the wall!
  As wyffis commandis, this DREME I will conclude,
God and the Rude mot turn it all to gud!
Gar fill the cop, for thir auld Carlingis clames
That gentill Aill is oft the causs of Dremes.   90

EXPLICIT
QUOD LICHTOUN MONICUS.

18

THE MURNING MAIDIN.

THE MURNING MAIDIN.

I.

STILL undir the levis greene,
   This hindir day, I went alone :
I hard ane May sair mwrne and meyne,
To the King of·Luif scho maid hir mone.
   Scho sychit sely soir ;
   Said, " Lord, I luif thi lore ;
Mair wo dreit nevir woman one !
O langsum lyfe, and thow war gone,
   Than suld I mwrne no moir ! "

II.

As rid gold-wyir schynit hir hair ;
And all in greene the May scho glaid.
Ane bent bow in hir hand scho bair ;
Undir hir belt war arrowis braid.
   I followit on that fre,
   That semelie wes to se :
With still mwrning hir mone scho maid.
That bird undir a bank scho baid,
   And lenit to ane tre.

III.

" Wanweird," scho said, " Quhat have I wrocht,
That on me kytht hes all this cair ?
Trew luif so deir I have thé bocht !
Certis so sall I do na mair :
   Sen that I go begyld
   With ane that faythe has syld :
That gars me oftsyis sich full sair ;
And walk amang the holtis hair
   Within the woddis wyld.

IV.

"This grit disese for luif I dre—
Thair is no toung can tell the wo !—
I lufe the luif, that lufes not me ;
I may not mend—but murning mo.
  Quhill God send sum remeid,
  Throw destany, or deid :
I am his freind—and he my fo.
My sueit, alace ! quhy dois he so ?
  I wrocht him nevir na feid !

V.

"Withoutin feyn I wes his freynd,
In word, and wark, grit God it wait !
Quhair he wes placit, thair list I leynd,
Doand him service ayr and late.
  He kepand eftir syne
  Till his honour and myne :
Bot now he gais ane uthir gait ;
And hes no é to my estait ;
  Quhilk dois me all this pyne.

VI.

" It dois me pyne that I may prufe,
That makis me thus murning mo :
My luif he lufes ane uther lufe—
Alas, sweithart ! Quhy does he so ?
  Quhy sould he me forsaik ?
  Have mercie on his maik !—
Thairfoir my hart will birst in two.
And thus, walking with da and ro,
  My leif now heir I taik."

VII.

Than wepit scho, lustie in weyd,
And on hir wayis can scho went.
In hy eftir that heynd I zeyd,
And in my armis culd hir hent;
   And said, " Fayr lady at this tyde,
   With leif ye man abyde;
And tell me quho yow hidder sent ?
Or quhy ye beir your bow so bent
   To sla our deir of pryde ?

VIII.

" In wraithman weid sen I yow find
In this wod, walkand your alone,
Your mylk-quhyte handis we sall bind
Quhill that the blude birst fra the bone.
   Chairgeand yow to preisoun,
   To the king's deip dungeoun.
Thai may ken be your fedderit flane
Ye have bene mony beistis bane,
   Upon thir bentis broun."

IX.

That fré answerd with fayr afeir,
And said, " Schir, mercie for your mycht !
Thus man I bow and arrowis beir,
Becaus I am ane baneist wycht:
   So will I be full lang.
   For God's luif lat me gang;
And heir to yow my treuth I plycht,
That I sall, nowdir day nor nycht,
   No wyld beist wait with wrang !

X.

"Thoch I walk in this forest fré,
With bow, and eik with fedderit flane,
It is weill mair than dayis thre,
And meit or drink yit saw I nane.
   Thoch I had nevir sic neid
   My selfe to wyn my breid,
Your deir may walk, schir, thair alane.
Yit wes I nevir na beistis bane.
   I may not sé thame bleid.

XI.

"Sen that I nevir did yow ill,
It wer no skill ye did me skayth.
Your deir may walk quhairevir thai will :
I wyn my meit with na sic waithe.
   I do bot litil wrang,
   Bot gif I flouris fang.
Gif that ye trow not in my aythe,
Tak heir my bow and arrowis baythe
   And lat my awin selfe gang."

XII.

"I say your bow and arrowis bricht !
I bid not have thame, be Sanct Bryd.
Bot ye man rest with me all nycht,
All nakit sleipand be my syd."
   "I will not do that syn !
   Leif yow this warld to wyn !."
"Ye ar so haill, of hew and hyd,
Luif hes me fangit in this tyd :
   I may not fra yow twyn."

XIII.

Than lukit scho to me, and leuch ;
And said, " Sic luf I rid yow layne;
Albeid ye mak it nevir sa teuch,
To me your labour is in vane :
   Wer I out of your sycht,
   The space of halfe a nycht,
Suppois ye saw me nevir agane—
Luif hes yow streinyeit with little paine
   Thairto my treuth I plycht."

XIV.

I said, " My sueit, forsuythe I sall
For ever luif yow, and no mo ;
Thoch uthers luif, and leif, with all :
Maist certainlie I do not so.
   I do yow trew luif hecht,
   Be all thi bewis bricht !
Ye ar so fair, be not my fo !
Ye sall have syn and ye me slo
   Thus throw ane suddan sycht."

XV.

" That I yow sla, that God forscheild !
Quhat have I done, or said, yow till ?
I wes not wont wapyns to weild ;
Bot am ane woman—gif ye will,
   That suirlie feiris yow,
   And ye not me, I trow.
Thairfor, gude schir, tak in none ill :
Sall never berne gar breif the bill
   At bidding me to bow.

XVI.

" Into this wode ay walk I shall,
Ledand my lyf as woful wycht ;—
Heir I forsaik bayth bour and hall,
And all thir bygings that are brycht !
    My bed is maid full cauld,
    With beistis bryme and bauld.—
That gars me say, bayth day and nicht,
Alace that ever the toung sould hecht
    That hart thocht not to hauld !"

XVII.

Thir words out throw my hart so went
That neir I wepit for hir wo.
But thairto wald I not consent ;
And said that it sould not be so ;
    Into my armis swythe
    Embrasit I that blythe.
Sayand, " Sweit hart, of harmis ho !
Found sall I never this forest fro,
    Quhill ye me comfort kyth."

XVIII.

Than knelit I befoir that cleir ;
And meiklie could hir mercie craif ;
That semelie than, with sobir cheir
Me of her gudlines forgaif.
    It wes no neid, I wys,
    To bid us uther kys ;
Thair mycht no hairts mair joy resaif,
Nor ather culd of uther haif :
    Thus brocht wer we to blys.

FINIS.

THE EPISTILL

OF THE HERMEIT OF ALAREIT

TO THE GRAY FREIRS.

ANE EPISTILL DIRECTED FRA THE HAILIE HERMEIT OF ALAREIT, TO HIS BRETHREN THE GRAY FREIRS.

I THOMAS, hermeit in Lareit,
  Sanct Francis brother do hartilie greit;
Beseikand you, with gud intent,
To be wakryif and diligent.
Thir Lutheranis, rissen of new,
Our Ordour daylie dois persew:
They smaikis dois set their haill intent,
To reid the Inglische New Testament;
And sayis we have thame clein decevit,
Thairfore in haist they mon be stoppit.   10
Our Stait hypocrisie they prysse,
And us blasphemis on this wyse:
Sayand, That we ar heretyckis,
And false loud lying mastis tykes;
Cumerars and quellars of Christis kirk,
Sweir swyngeours that will not wirk,
But idillie our leving wynnis,
Devoiring woilfis into scheipis skynnis;
Huirkland with huidis into our neck,
With Judas mynd to jouk and beck;   20
Seikand Christis pepill to devoir,
The doun-thringers of Christis gloir;
Professours of hypocrisie,
And Doctouris in idolatrie;
Stout fischeiris with the Feindis net,
The upclosers of Hevins yet;
Cankcart corruptors of the creid,
Humlock sawers among gud seid;

To trow in trators, that men do tyist;
The hie way kennand them fra Christ;   30
Monsters with the Beistis mark,
Dogges that nevir stintis to bark;
Kirkmen that ar to Christ unkend,
A sect that Satanis self hes send;
Lourkand in hoils, lyik trator toddis,
Mainteiners of idollis and fals goddis;
Fantastik fuillis, and fenzeit fleicheors,
To turn fra treuth the verray teichers:
For to declair thair haill sentence,
Wald mekill cumber your conscience.   40
To say your fayth it is sa stark,
Your cord and lousie cote and sark
Ye lippin may bring you to salvatioun,
And quyte excludis Chrystis passioun,—
I dreid this doctrine, and it last,
Sall outher gar us wirk or fast:
Thairfoir with speid we mene provyde,
And not our profite overslyde.
I schaip myself, within schort quhill,
To curs our Ladie in Argylle,   50
And thair on craftie wayis to wirk,
Till that we biggit have ane Kirk;
Syne miracles mak be your advyce.
The Ketterells, thocht thai had bot lyce,
The twa parte to us they will bring.
Bot ordourlie to dress this thing,
A Gaist I purpois to gar gang,
Be counsaill of frier Walter Lang;
Quhilk sall mak certane demonstratiounis
To help us in our procuratiounis,   60
Your halie ordour to decoir:
That practick he provit anis befoir,
Betwix Kirkaldie and Kinghorne;

Bot lymmaris maid thereat sick scorne,
And to his fame maid sic degressioun,
Sensyne he hard not the Kingis confessioun.
Thoicht at that time he come no speid,
I pray yow tak gude will as deid;
And him amongst your selfe ressave,
As ane worth many of the lave.   `70
Quhat I obtein may, throw his airt,
Ressone wald ye had your parte;
Your Ordour handillis no money,
Bot for uther casualitie,
As beif, meill, butter, and cheiss,
Or quhat we have, that ye pleis,
Send your brethren, *et habete.*
As now nocht ellis, bot *valete*,
   Be THOMAS your brother at comand,
   A Culrun kythit throw mony a land.   80

THE HISTORY OF
ROSWALL AND LILLIAN.

THE HISTORY OF ROSWALL
AND LILLIAN.

NOW will ye list a little space,
   And I shall send you to solace,—
You to solace, and to be blyth,
Hearken, and ye shall hear belyve
A tale that is of veritie,
If ye will hearken unto me.
  In Naples lived a worthy King,
Had all the lands in governing;
He had a Lady, fair and young,
Whose name was called Lillian :   10
This Lady, pleasant was and fair,
Bare him a Son, which was his heir,
Whose name was called Roswall ;
Of fairer heard I never tell ;
Princes to him could not compare,
Wight Hannibal, nor Gaudifere,
Nor Diomeid, nor Troyalus,
Nor yet his father Priamus ;
Nor the gentle Clariadus,
Nor fair Philmox, nor Achilles,   20
Nor Florentine of Almanie,
Was never half so fair as he ;
Nor knight Sir Launcelot du Lake,
In fairness to him was no make :
The Knight that kept the Parent well,
Was not so fair as Roswall.
  There lived into that Countrie,
Of noble worth Lords three,
That to the King had done treason,

Therefore he put them in prison ;   30
And there he held them many a day,
Till they were aged quite away,
Aged and quite o'ergrown with hair,
While of their lives they did despair,
That they knew of no remedie,
But looked after death daily.
So it befell upon a day
As the young Prince went forth to play,
Him for to play, and to solace,
And so it happened in that case,   40
Toward the prison he is gone,
And heard thir Lords making their moan.
He sate down and a little staid,
To hearken what thir Lords said :
They said, "Dear God, have mind of us,
Even for the sake of dear Jesus
Who bought us with his precious blood,
And for us dyed on the Rood;
In this great danger without doubt
We know no way how to win out,   50
Now help us, if thy will it be,
And of this prison make us free."
    The young Prince heard right wondrous well,
All this their carping every deal,
Right sad in heart, all wo begone,
Straight to his chamber he is gone,
He sate down and did foresee,
How best thir Lords might helped be;
And so he thought upon a wyle
The King how he might best beguile :   60
A custome then had the jaylors,
Who keeped ay the prisoners,
After the doors all locked were,
Unto the King the keyes to bear;

The King used them for to lay
Under his bed-head privily.
The young Prince soon perceiving had,
Where the King the keyes laid;
And on a night he watch did keep
Till that the King was fallen asleep: ·   70
He took the keyes full privilie,
And to the prison gone is he,
Who did deliver thir Lords three,
Bade them passe home to their Countrie;—
They thanked him right reverentlie,'   ·
And to their country went in hy;
They answered him " By sweet Jesus,
If ever ye mister help of us
We shall you help, and you supply
So long as we are living three."   80
He to his Chamber passed with speed
Right blyth that he had done this deed,
And to his bed went quietly
And sleeped while the day did see.
   The King rose up, and eke the Queen,
The Prince, and all the Lords bedeen;
They went to messe, and then to dyne,
The Jaylors all did come in syne,
And asked from the King the keyes,
Which to deliver did him please.   90
Then to the prison they went in fear,
To give the Lords their dinnèr.
But when they came all were away!
They wist not what to do nor say:
The prisoners away were gone,
How, or what way knowen to none.
The King was then so dollorous,
That the three Lords were scaped thus:
He sayes, " O Lord, how may this be

That thir prisoners hath been made free ?   100
Under my bed-head lay the keyes,
None knew thereof, as God me ease !—
And here I make a solemn vow,
Before you all my Lords now,
Who ere he be hath done the deed,
He shall be hang'd without remeed ;
Or else, so soon as I him see,
My own two hands his bane shall be."
   It was reported through the town,
That the young Prince the deed had done ;   110
The word out through the pallace ran,
Which made the King a grieved man,
When he the vow considered,
And that his Son had done the deed.
The most worthy king Priamus
In heart was not so dolorous,
When stout Hector, his son, was slain,
He suffered not so meikle pain ;
Nor, in his heart was so woe
When that his men had gone him fro,   120
As was the noble worthy King,
For Roswall, that most princely thing :—
And far more grieved was the Queen ;
She mourn'd, and weeped with her een,
And quickly to the King went she,
And, kneeling down upon her knee,
Thus said, " For Him that sits on hie,
Let your Son's fault forgiven be."
   " That may not be, Madam ! (he said,)

L. 103-107.   In one of the modern copies are as follows :

    The King he swore by God's dead,
    Who has the keys tane from my head.
    Although he be my son Roswall
    He's hang, or by my hand die shall.

For I a faithful vow have made,   130
That as soon as I do him see,
My own two hands his bane shall be ;
Therefore, I pray you, day and night,
To keep him well out of my sight,
Till I send him to a far Countrie,
Where he may safely keeped be."
    And then, in haste, down sate the King,
Wrote letters without tarrying,
To send his Son to the King of Bealm,
For to remain there in that Realm :   140
Still to continue with the King,
Till he sent for his home-coming.
Letters in haste then soon wrote he,
Desiring the King especiallie,
For to receive his own dear Son,
Which for most trust was sent to him.
His furnishing was made ready,
And he got gold in great plenty.
    The King's Stewart, a stalward knight,
Was made to keep him day and night ;   150
And so his servant for to be,
To keep him well in that Countrie ;
The Queen did look to the Steward,
And said, " My love, my joy, my heart,
Sir Steward, now I do thee pray,
To keep my Son, both night and day,
And serve him both by foot and hand,
And thou shalt have both gold and land,

L. 156 to 186. In one of the modern copies these lines are thus ackwardly abridged ;

> " Along the road as they did trot,
> False Stewart he did lay a plot ;
> And so just at a river's brink,
> The Prince lay down on's wame to drink ;

Or yet, of any other thing,
That thou'lt seek from me, or the King.   160
He said, Madam, "That may not be
But I will serve him tenderlie." ·
She sayes, "My only Son Roswall,
Hearken what I to thee will tell,
When thou dost come in that Country,
Carry thy self right honestly,
Be courteous, gentle, kind and free,
And use aye in good companie :
And if thou needest ought to spend,
Send word to me, I shall thee send."   170
He took his leave then of the Queen,
And of her Ladies all bedeen :
Great mourning and great care they made
When that out of the Town they rade,
The gracious God mot be his guide.
   So on a time as they did ride,
Side for side, hand for hand rode they,
None other saw they in the way,
Only they two in companie,
Came to a river, fair to see :   180

> The villain took him by the feet,
> And vow'd to throw him in the deep,
> Unless the gold and letters both
> He did resign to him by oath.
> He gave him all his life to save,
> The man turn'd master, master knave."

The Prince then said unto the Knight,
My counsell is that here we light ;
For in this place, I thirst so sore,
That further can I ride no more,
Till of this water I get my fill ;
Wot ye how I may win theretill?
The Knight leapt down deliverlie,

And drank the water hastilie :
He bade him light, and drink also
His fill, ere he should further go :   190
And on his belly, as he lay down
To drink the water ready bown,
The false Knight took him by the feet,
And vow'd to throw him in the deep,
Unlesse that he should swear an oath,
That he the gold and letters both
Should unto him resign gladly,
And his servant become truly.
To serve him well, both day and night,
This oath he made to the false Knight ;   200
He the Master, and he the Knave ;
He gave to him what he would crave ;
And then anone, withoutten stay,
They mounted both and went their way ;
While they came to the land of Bealm,
And had past much of that Realm.
The King's pallace when they came near,
Roswall made but sorry chear ;
For the Knight did him forbid,
Further with him for to ride ;   210
Hee would find service in the town,
Abundance of all fashion.
Away he rode then with his gold,
Leaving poor Roswall on the mold,
With not a penny in his companie
To buy his dinner, though he should die !
So to the town in hy he rode,
And in the King's pallace abode ;
In his heart was great rejoycing,
And shewed his letters to the King.   220
He read his letters hastily,
And said, " Sir, welcome mot ye be ;

Ye shall to me be love and dear,
So long as ye will tary here."
Now in the Court we let him dwell,
And we will speak of fair Roswall.
　　Roswall was mourning on the mold,
Wanting his letters and his gold;
He sayes, " Alace! and woe is me,
For lack of food, I'm like to die;　　　　　230
O! that my Mother knew my skaith,
My Father and my Mother baith;
For now I wot not what to do,
Nor what hand to turn me to;
Neither know I how to call me,—
I'm Dissawar whate'er befall me."
As then he making was his moan,
Beside none but himself alone,
He lookt a little, and did espy
A little house, none else hard by;　　　　　240
To himself he sayes quietly,
To yonder house I will me hy,
And ask some vittals for this night,
And harbour while the day be light.
He stepped forth right sturdily,
And to the little house went he;
He knockt a little at the door,
And then went in upon the floor;
He found no creature was therein,
Neither to make a noise nor din,　　　　　250
But a silly and aged wife,
In honesty had led her life :
He sayes, " Dame, for Saint July,
This night let me have harbery,
And als some vittals till the morn,
For him that was in Bethlehem born."
She sayes, " To such meat as I have

Ye are welcome, part thereof receive."
She set him down, and gave him meat,
Even of the best that she could get, 260
And prayed him to make good cheer,—
"For you are very welcome here :
I know you are of a far Countrie,
For ye are seemly for to see;
Tell me your name in charitie,
And do not it deny to me."
He sayes, "Dissawar they call me,
So was I call'd in my Countrie."
She sayes, " Dissawar, wo is me !
That is a poor name verilie ; 270
Yet Dissawar you shall not be,
For good help you shall have of me :
I have a son, no children mo,
Who each day to the school doth go ;
If ye will here bide still with me,
To him full welcome will ye be ;
And daily you and he together
May go to school, and learn each other."
He sayes, " Good Dame, God you foryield,
For here I get of you good bield." 280
    As he and she was thus talkand,
In comes her son even at her hand :
"Good Dame, (he sayes,) my Mother dear,
Who's this that ye have gotten here."
"This is a Clark of far Countrie,
Would fain go to the school with thee."
He sayes, " Dear welcome mot he be,
For I have got good companie."
And then they past to their supper,
For his sake had the better chear. 290
Then Dissawar, fairest of face,
After supper said the grace ;

And quickly to their beds went they,
And sleeped till it was near day.
And in the morn right airly rose,
And put upon them all their cloaths;
They went to school right hastilie,
By that time they could day-light see.
Into the school the Master came,
And asked at Dissawar his name?   300
He sayes, " Dissawar they call me,
So was I call'd in my Countrie."
The Master said, " Now Dissawar,
Thou shalt want neither meat nor laire :
When even thou needest, come to me,
And I shall make you good supplie."
Great skill of learning before he had
Into the country where he was bred.
He had not been a moneth there,
Into the school, even little maire,   310
But the steward of that land's King,
Of Dissawar, had perceiving :
He did set well his courtesie,
His nature, and his great beautie;
Into his heart he greatly thought
In service to have him, if he mought.
The Steward to the wife is gone,
And sayes, " God save you, far Madam,
Where got ye this child so fair,
That to this lodging makes repair."   320
" Sir, they do call him Dissawar,
And ay hes done since he came here ;
He is my joy, he is my heart,
For he and I shall never part."
Hes sayes, " Madam, that may not be,
He must go to the Court with me."
She sayes, " Sir, it's against my will

I'd rather here he would stay still."
   The Steward took Dissawar, fair of face,
And brought him to the King's grace ;   330
He had not been a moneth there
Into service, or little mair,
But he was lov'd of old and young,
As he had been a Prince or King.
   The King he had a daughter fair,
And no moe bairns, she was his heir ;
She was by name call'd Lillian,
One fairer, forsooth, I read of nane ;
No, not the fair noble French Queen,
Nor yet the lady Pellan,   340
Nor yet Helen, that fair ladie,
Nor yet the true Philledy,
Nor yet the lady Christian
Was not so fair as Lillian.
This lusty lady Lillian
Choos'd him to be her Chamberlane,
Of which the Steward was full wo,
That he so soon should part him fro ;
Yet would not say nay to Lillian :
Of which the Lady was right fain ;   350
And entered him in her service,
For he was both leill, true and wise ;
He brake her bread, and made good chear,
Filled the cup, the wine the beer :
She took such comfort then of him,
She lov'd him better nor all her kin.
  Aside she call'd him on a day,
And thus unto him she did say,
" Now tell me, Dissawar, for charitie,
Into what country born was ye ? "   360
He said, " I am of a far countrie,
My father's a man of low degree."

" I cannot trust, (said she,) by the Rood,
But you are come of noble blood ;
For I know by your courtesie,
And by your wonder fair bodie,
That ye are come of noble blood,—
This is my reason, by the Rood."
" Madam, by that ye may well ken,
That I am come of sober men."   370
" Dissawar, my little flower,
I wish thou were my paramour ;
God, sen I had thee to be King,
That I might wed you with a ring."
In her arms she did him embrace,
And kist him thrice into that place ;
He kneeled down upon his knee,
And thanked that Lady heartilie :
He said, " Lady, God you foreyeeld,
That ye should love so poor a child ;   380
And I vow, Lady, while I die,
To love you again most heartilie."
Within his heart he was right glad
And he did think mair then he said.
Soon after that this Lady fair,
Said anone to Dissawar :—
" Dissawar, I do you pray,
Cast that name from you away ;
Call you Hector or Oliver,
Ye are so fair without compare ;   390
Call your self Sir Porteous,
Or else the worthy Emedus ;
Call you the noble Predicase,
Who was of fair and comely face ;
Because that I love you so well,
Let your name be Sir Lyeadale ;
Or great Florent of Albanie,

My heart, if you bear love to me!
Or call you Lancelot du Lake,
For your dearest true-love's sake;　　　　400
Call you the knight of arms green,
For the love of your lady sheen."
He sayes, "Dissawar they must call me,
While afterward I more do see."
"If ye will have no other name,
Call you a Squire to the King,
Or to his daughter Chamberlan,
For love of his daughter Lillian."
She laugh'd, and once or twice him kist,
And to her ladies then she past,　　　　410
And Dissawar was very glad,
For the joy he of the Lady had.
So it befell upon a day,
His Father to his Mother did say,—
"I think right long for to hear tell
Of my fair son, my dear Roswall;
I think so long, I cannot sleep."
With that the Queen began to weep,
Who said, "Good Sir, for charitie,
Let some be sent him for to see;　　　　420
It is long since he from us went,
Perchance his gold is now all spent."
As the King his Father was to send,
There came messengers even at hand
With letters from that noble King,
Which made him glad in every thing;
But they beguiled were both, so
That none of them the case did know.
The King had written on this manner,
Desiring his Son to his daughter.　　　　430
The King his father was right glad,
That such a marriage should be made;

Therefore, he every way consented,
Even as the King by writ had sent it ;
An answer to him he did send,
When he the wedding would intend,
That he might send Lords of that countrie,
To bear witnesse to that marriage free.
The messengers went home again,
And told their King what they had done ;   440
And then anone, without delay,
Appointed was the Marriage day :
Who sent word to the noble King,
And he without more tarrying,
Sent to solemnize that day,
An Earle and lusty Lords tway.
With them went the lusty knight,
And many a gallant Squire bright.

  The King of Bealm caus'd make a cry,
Three dayes before the Marriage day,   450
To come and just a course of wier,
Before him and his Queen full dear,
To see who best will undertake,
To just then for his ladies sake.
But when to Lillian it was told,
Wit ye well her heart was cold ;
For she lov'd none but Dissawar ;
Who, went and told him lesse and mair,
Said, " At yon justing you must be,
For to just for your ladie ;   460
And if you will not just for me,
Just for your love wherever she be."
He saith, " Lady, by my good fay,
I ne'er was bred with such a play,
For I had rather be at hunting,
Then singing, dancing, or at justing :
Yet I shall stand by you Lady,

To see who bears away the gree."
And so they parted on that night.
    And, on the morn when it was light,   470
Dissawar got up his way,
Went to the forrest be it was day;
His hounds leading into his hand,
Full well tripping at his command;
And when he came to the forrest,
He looked East, and looked West,
He looked over the bents brown,
Where he saw neither house nor town;
The Myrle and Mavese shouted shrill,
The Sun blinked on every hill;   480
In his heart he had great rejoycing
Of the birds full sweet singing;
He looked down upon the spray,
When it was nine hours of the day,
And saw a little space him fra,
A Knight coming, with him no mae;
Riding on a milk-white steed,
And all milk-white was his weed.
To Dissawar he came ridand,
And lighted down even at his hand,   490
And said, anone, "My full sweet thing,
I must be drest in your cloathing:
Take you my armour and my steed,
And dresse you all into my weed;
And to yon justing you must faire,
To win you praise and honour mair:
When ye have done come ye to me,
Of vennisoun ye shall have plentie."
Then Dissawar armed him quickly,
The Knight him helped that stood by;   500
He stoutly lap upon his steed,
And ran alane through the mied,
20

Till he came to the justing place ;
He saw his Mistres face to face,
And he saw many ladies gay,
And many lords in rich array,
And he saw many a lustie knight,
Justing before him in his sight ;
He rade unto the justing place,
Where knights encountered face to face,   510
And many a saddle toom'd he there,
Both of knights, and many a squyer :
All men wondred what he was,
That of justing had such praise ;
The ladies heart was wonder sair
And said, " Alace, for Dissawar !
Why would he not tarry with me,
This noble justing for to see ? "
And when the justing was near done,
Then he beheld the Steward soon ;   520
His heels turn upward there he made ;
All that him saw were sore afraid :
Then he unto the forrest ran,
As light as ever did a man.
The King cry'd with voice on hie,
" Go, take yon Knight, bring him to me,
And who so brings him to my hand,
Shall have an earldome of land."
But all for nought, it was in vain,
For to the woods he rode again,   530
Delivered his armour and his steed,
And drest himself in his own weed.
The Lord had taken him vennisoun,
And homeward with him made he bown ;
As for help desired none he,
Presented them to his ladie.
She says, " Now, wherefore Dissawar

Beguil'd ye me in this manner?"
He answered, "My Lady dear,
Why say ye that unto me here?   540
Wherefore shall I come to justing?
I have no skill of such a thing."
She says, "A Knight with a white steed,
And all milk-white was his weed,
He hath born away the gree,
Of him is spoken great plentie;
And if ye bide the morn with me,
Ye peradventure shall him see."
"I shall do so, (said he,) Madam
The morn I will not pass from home."   550
Then Lillian to her ladies went,
Past to their supper incontinent,
And on the morn, right timously,
He did rise up be he might see;
And forth unto the forrest went,
After the night was fully spent.
   When that he came to those woods green,
The place where he before had been;
Under the shadow of a tree
He laid him down right privatlie;   560
The birds did sing with pleasant voice,
He thought himself in Paradice;
To bear a part, for joy sang he
Even for the love of his ladie,
How she lov'd him her paramour,
And she of all the world the flower.
For pleasure of the weather fair,
So clear and pleasant was the air,
His heart was light on leaf on tree,
When that he thought on his lady.   570
He looked then over an hill,
And saw a Knight coming him till,

Having a red shield and a spear,
And all red shined his gear.
To Dissawar he came full soon,
And at his hand he lighted down,
And said, " Sir, take this horse of mine,
And all my armour good and fine ;
To the justing in haste ride ye,
The gracious God your guide be."   580
And soon to him he reacht a spear
Which he did take withoutten fear.
He then did ride forth merrilie,
And soon his Lady can he see,
And she was cloathed all in white,
To look on her was great delight :
He made the Lady full gay halsing,
And then he went to the justing ;
And if he justed well before,
Better that day by fifteen score.   590
He hunted the knights here and there,
Even as the hound doth hunt the hare,
And many a knight he bare to ground,
And some of them got their deed's wound.
Of the Steward he got a sight,
And off his horse he made him light,
And then unto the forrest ran,
As light as ever did a man.
The King cryed with voice on hie,
" Go, take yon Knight, bring him to me,   600
And whoso brings him to my hand
Shall have an earldome of land."
But all for nought, it was in vain,
For to the woods he rade again.
When he came there the Knight he leugh,
" Have I not vennisonn enough ?
Ye have been at the field all day,

And I at hunting, and at play."
Then Dissawar gave him his steed,
His shield, his armour, and his weed ;　610
His steed was all of apple-gray,
None better was, I dare well say.
Then Dissawar went home quickly,
With a white hind to his Lady,
When he came home, as I heard tell,
She greatly did at him marvell
That he came not to the justing :
"Lady, grieve not at such a thing."
She sayes, "A Knight with a gray steed,
And all red shined his weed,　620
This day hath born away the gree,
Of him is spoken great plentie ;
And I have ever in my thought
That it was you the deed hath wrought."
"I pray, Madam, trust no such thing,
For I no skill have of justing."
She says, "The morn go not away,
Because it is the hindmost day."

But Dissawar full soon the morn
Got up and blew his hunting horn,　630
And went into the forrest soon
With hounds and ratches of renown,
And there he had great comforting
Of all the birds full sweet singing ;
And then he looked up full swyth,
He saw a sight which made him blyth,
A Knight upon a stalwart steed,
And glittring gold was all his weed ;
His shield was red, his armour green,
Ov'r all the land it might be seen.　640
To Dissawar he came full soon,
And at his hand he lighted down,

And said, " Sir, take this horse of mine,
And all my armour good and fine ;
To the justing in haste ride ye,
And may good fortune your guide be."
And even so soon as he came there,
He saw his Lady that was so fair ;
And all the weed that she did wear,
In glitt'ring red gold did appear.   650
He at his Lady did cast a ring.
Then past he on to the justing ;
He rade among them with such force,
That he dang down both man and horse ;
Out through the field where that he ran,
At each stroak he dang down a man ;
Sir Roland and Sir Oliver
In their justing made no such steir :
When he beheld the Steward than
He dang him down both horse and man ;   660
Both horse and man on the ground lay,
And of his ribs were broken tway.
Then to the forrest he rade full soon,
When that the justing was all done ;
As swift as Falcon of his flight
Upon a bird when he doth light.
The King cryed with voice full shrill
" Go, take yon Knight, bring him me till ;
And whoso brings him to me here,
Shall have my land, and daughter dear."   670
But all for nought, it was in vain,
For to the woods he rade again,
Delivered his armour and his steed,
And drest himself in his own weed.
     He thanked him right reverently,
Then came the other two Knights in hy.
The same two Knights we spake of aire,

Who said, " O blessed Master dear,
From prison you delivered us,
Wherefore mot thank you sweet Jesus;   680
And this is also most certain,
We promised to you again,
If ever you help of us did need,
We should perform the same with speed.
The morn the Marriage should be
Of the Steward who beguiled thee ;
But therefore do thou nothing fear,
The Bride's bed he shall not come near."
They took their leave withoutten mair,
And he went to his Lady fair.   690
   And when that they were coming home
From the justing every one,
He went unto his Lady gent,
Saluting her incontinent.
" Are ye, Dissawar, welcome to me,
That so oft hath beguiled me ;
But yet I must forgive you soon
Of all that ever you have done ! "
She sayes, " A Knight, with a stalwart steed,
And glittering gold was all his weed,   700
This day hath born away the gree
Of all the justing dayes three.
If to my father the truth ye tell,
That it was you justed so well,
Then dare I surely take in hand,
He'll give you me, and all the land.
The morn the marriage should be
Betwixt yon young Prince and me ;
But here I make a solemn vow,
I never shall have man but you :   710
Therefore, I heartily do you pray,
The morn that ye go not away."

"I shall do that, my Lady bright,
I shall not go out of your sight."
 Then she the morn right airly rose,
And put upon her all her cloaths,
Unto the King then is she gone,
Who kneeled on her knees full soon.
Then said he, " Lillian, what would ye ?
Declare your mind now unto me ;   720
If it be lawfull ye require,
I shall it grant at your desire."
" Grant me my asking for Christ's sake,
That is a Prince to be my maik."
" Ask on," he sayes, " How that may be ?
I have devised one for thee."
She sayes, " They call him Dissawar,
I ask no more at you, Father."
" That asking I to tell thee plain,
Is not befitting for thy train ;   730
For he is but a batcheller,
For aught that I do know or hear ;
We know of none he is become,
But this man is a great King's son ;
Therefore, ye shall let such things be,
For it becomes not you nor me,
That we the King's son should forbear,
And match you with a batcheller :
To me it were a great defame,
And also to you a very shame ;   740
Therefore, I counsell you forbear,
And wed yon Prince withoutten peer."
 And then she past the kirk untill,
And married him sore against her will ;
And when the marriage was done,
She past unto her chamber soon,
And mourned there till dinner time,

That she was brought to hall to dine.
The King was set, and eke the Queen,
The said Prince, and Lillian sheen ;   750
Then every lord and gentle knight
Marched with a lady bright ;
The courses came abundantlie,
With bread and wine, in great plenty.
   At mid'st of dinner as they sat,
In came the three Lords at the gate ;
They did salute the King and Queen,
And the fair Lady Lillian sheen ;
But the Bride-groom that sate near by,
To him they made no courtesie.   760
The King thereat great marvell had,
That they to him no reverence made ;
And said, " Why do you not resign
Homage to your Prince and King ? "
They said, " By Him that us dear bought,
Into the hall we see him nought."
Then all the hall they looked round,
At last him in a chamber found ;
And then they kneeled down in hy,
Saluting him right reverently,   770
And by the hand they have him tane.
Then marvelled in hall ilk ane ;
The King wondered, and eke the Queen,
But blyth was Lady Lillian !
They did enquire how it befell,
So he the manner did them tell,
" How that he thought him for to drown,
And in the river cast him down ;
And how his gold from him took he,
And letters to let him go free ;   780
How he made him an oath to take,
Which will turn to his shame and lack,

That I a servant so should be
To him my Father sent with me."
The which he could not well deny,
But granted all right hastily.
Then Roswall told unto the King
All the manner of the justing,
And shewed to him, That it was he
Who won the justing dayes three.   790
And then they took the Steward soon,
And hanged him high afternoon.
　　Then to the kirk they passed there,
And married him and Lillian fair.
There is no tongue on earth can tell
The joy that then had Roswall;
And wit ye well if he was fain,
Fainer was Lady Lillian,
For blyther was not Meledas,
When as she married Claudias;   800
Nor Belsant, that most pleasant flower,
When she got Ronald to paramour,
As was this Lady Lillian:
In heart she was right wonder fain.
They ate the spice, and drank the wine,
And past unto their dancing syne:
The King danced with the Queen,
Then Roswall and Lillian sheen;
Every lord and gentle knight
Danced with a lady bright;   810
They danced till supper time,
So past unto their supper syne;
There was no knight, the truth to tell,
But at his supper fure right well.
When that the supper ended was,
A bishop rose, and said the grace,
And syne they past to the dancing,

The Minstrel's play'd with pleasant spring;
Roswall danced with the Queen,
The King himself with Lillian;   820
Then every lord and gentle knight
Danced with a lady bright,
The Minstrels played with good will,
Till they had danced all their filll:
They ate the spice, they drank the wine,
Unto their beds they passed syne.
Roswall and Lillian glad
First are they gone unto their bed:
But what they did I cannot say,
I wot they sleeped not till day.   830
    The Bridal lasted twenty dayes,
With dancing, carols, and many playes,
With justing and with tornament.
Then for the old wife he sent,
And to the King the manner told,
How she did in her house him hold,
And sent him to school with her son,
And how the master treated him;
How the Steward did him perceive,
And how the wife did him receive,   840
Who loved him even as his son,
In service to remain with him.
The King did marvell much again
To hear thir tidings so certain.
Then Roswall he rewarded soon
All that ever him good had done:
First he gave to the old wife
Gold that lasted all her life,
And then without delay anone
He made a bishop of her son: 850
The master that did him instruct
His own chapland he did him make.

And every one that did him good
He made them rich, for to conclude
To servants he gave good rewarding
And Minstrells also for their playing.
   When all those things were past and done
Roswall past to his Mother soon;
His Father long time before was dead,
But his Mother of him was glad.   860
Roswall and Lillian free
Had five bairns sickerlie,
Three sons, and two daughters dear,
Right fair they were, withoutten peer.
The eldest son was King of Bealm;
The second son of Naples realm,
For he thereof was made the King
Right after his Father's days ending;
The third son was made Pope of Rome;
And then anone when this was done,   870
The eldest daughter, it was her chance,
Married the great Daulphin of France,
The second married the Prince of Pole.
I pray heartily that death may thole,
To bring us to his lasting glore,
Which shall endure for evermore.

FINIS.

POEM BY GLASSINBERRY.

POEM BY GLASSINBERRY.

I.

THIS is Goddis awne complaint,
   Fro man to man that he has boucht,
And thus he sais, to thame in taynt,
Myne awne pepill, quhat have I wroucht
To thé, that is to me so faynt,
And I thi lufe, so deir has soucht?
In thyne ansuer no thing that paynt
To me, becaus I knaw thi thoucht!
Have I nocht done all that I oucht?
Have I left ony thing behynd?
Quhy wrethis thou me? I greif thé nocht:
Quhy arttow to thi freind unkynd?

II.

I socht thi lufe, and that wes sene,
Quhen that I maid thé like till me;
In erd my werk, baith quyk and grene,
I pat undir thin awne pousté;
And fra Pharo, that wes sa kene,
Of Egip I deliverit thé,
And drownit him and his men bedene;
The Red sey twinit I thé to fle;
I bad all dry that it suld bee,
I cessit baith wattir and wynd,
And brocht thé oure, and maid thé free;
Quhy arttow to thi freind unkynd?

III.

And fourti yheir in wildernes,
With angele fude syne I thé fed,

And til a land of grete richess,
To wyn thi lufe, syne I thé led :
And yhit, to schaw thé mair kyndnes,
To tak thi kynd na thing I dreid ;
I left my micht, and tuke mekenes,
Myne awne hert blude for thé I bled :
To by thi saule my blude I sched,
And band my self thé til unbynd ;
Thus, with my wo, thi neid I sped,
Quhy arttow to thi freind unkynd ?

IV.

[In] my wyne yhard I plauntit thé
Full of gude saver and swetnes ;
And nobil seid of all degré,
Bettir in erd nevir sawin wes :
Quhy suld thou thus gat fra me flé,
And turne all in to bittirnes ?
The croce, for my reward, to me
Thou grathit and gaif, this is no leis,
Yhit had I evir to thé grete hers,
Resistand thame that to thé rynd
And puttand thé of mony a pres ;
Quhy arttow to thi friend unkynd ?

v.

For thé I ordanit Paradise,
Fré will wes thi infeftment ;
How mycht thou me mair disples,
Na brek my awn commaundiment ?
And syne, in vij maner of wiis,
Til myn enemy thou has consent ;
I put thé downe, thou mycht nocht ryse
Thi mycht, thi wit away wes went ;
Baith pure, nakit, schamit and schent

Of friendschip mycht thou no thing fynd,
Till that I on the Rude wes rent;
Quhy arttow to thi friend unkynd?

VI.

Man! I lu fe é, quhom luffis thou?
I am thi friend, quhy lest thé wayn?
I forgaif thé that thou me slew,
Quha has partit oure lufe in twane?
Turne to me, and unite think thou,
Thou has gane mys, yhit turne agane,
And thou salbe als welcum now,
As sum with syn that nevir did nane:
Think how did Mary Magdalane,
And quhat said I, Thomas of Ynd,
I graunt thé blis; quhy lest thé pane?
Quhy arttow to thi friend unkynd?

VII.

O a friend the best preif
Is lufe with dreid, and nocht disples,
Was nevir thing to me mair leif,
Na man that na thing may appes,
I sufferit for thi synis repreif,
And dulfull deid thi saul to es;
Hangit and drawin as a theif,
Thou did the deid, I haf dishes;
Now can thow nother thank no ples,
No do gude deid, no have in mynd,
I am thi leich, to thi males;
Quhy arttow to thi friend unkind?

VIII.

Man unite, think thé quhat thou art?
Fra quhom thou come? quhar arttow bowu?

All thocht thou be to day in quart,
To morn I can cum put thé down:
Let mynd and meiknes mele in hart,
And rew of my compasioun,
Apon my woundis, hert and smert,
Of skourgis, nalis, spere, and crowne;
Let dreid and gude discretioun,
With lufe thi hert wp to me wynd,
Thus has v. wittis and resoun,
And gif thou will, thou may be kind!

IX.

Lord! with thé we will nocht plete,
Bot as thou sais, It is and wes;
We have deserwit hell heit
Now we ws held unto thi gres;
We sal aby, and thou sal beit
And chasty ws for oure trespes;
Let mercy so for ws entret,
That nevir the feynd our saulis ches.
And Mary mild! fairest of faice,
Helps ws, or we be fer behynd,
Or wepand, we mon say, Allace!
That we bene till our freind unkynd!

EXPLICIT QUOD GLASSINBERRY.

SIR JOHN BARLEYCORN.

SIR JOHN BARLEYCORN.

THERE came three merry men from the east,
   and three merry men were they,
And they did swear a solemn oath,
   that Sir John Barleycorn they would slay.

They took a plough and plough'd him down,
   and laid clods upon his head ;
And then they swore a solemn oath,
   that Sir John Barleycorn was dead :

But the Spring-time it came on amain,
   and rain towards the earth did fall :   10
John Barleycorn sprung up again,
   and so surpriz'd them all.

The Summer heat on him did beat,
   and John grew pale and wan ;
John Barleycorn he got a beard,
   and so became a man.

They took a scythe that was full sharp,
   and cut him down at the knee ;
And they tied him in a cart,
   like a rogue for perjury.   20

They took two sticks that were full hard
   and sore they thresh'd his bones;
The Miller serv'd him worst of all,
   for he crushed him 'twixt two stones.

The Brewster-wife we'll not forget,
   she well her tale can tell,

She has ta'en the sap out of his bodie,
and made of it good ale.

And they have filled it in a cup,
and drank it round and round ;   30
And aye the more they drank of it
the more did joy abound.

Sir John Barleycorn is the wichtest man
that ever throve in the land,
He will do more than many merry men,
by the turning of his hand.

Put Brandy in a brimming glass,
put Rum into a can,
Put Sir John Barleycorn in a stout brown mug,
He'll prove the stoutest man.   40

He'll change a boy into a man,
a man into an ass ;
He'll change your gold into silver,
and your silver into brass.

He'll make the huntsman shoot his dog,
and never blow his horn ;
He'll make a maid stark naked dance,
my pretty little Barleycorn.

And if you'll to yon village go
you need not fear no scorn,   50
I swear he will make you twice as strong,
before this time the morn.

THE END.

Printed by Alexander Gardner, Paisley.

NEW BOOKS AND NEW EDITIONS.

NOCTES AMBROSIANÆ. By PROFESSOR JOHN WILSON ("Christopher North"). Popular Edition. Post 8vo. Price 4s. 6d.

In issuing a POPULAR edition of this remarkable work, the editor has omitted those portions which were of interest ONLY at the time of original publication, such as matters of merely passing interest, questions of politics and science, and other affairs that have now passed out from that stage from which they were viewed fifty years ago. But there are other matters, the interest surrounding which is as great as ever—these the editor has been careful to retain. Especial care has also been taken with regard to the amusing element, with which these pages will be found laden.

THE EARLY PROSE AND POETICAL WORKS OF JOHN TAYLOR, The Water Poet, 1580-1653. Post 8vo. Price 5s.

A most remarkable man. His writings are highly descriptive of the manners and customs of the period. In 1618 he travelled on foot from London to the Wilds of Braemar, and published an account of the journey, entitled "The Penniless Pilgrimage." In the Scottish Highlands he became the guest of the Earl of Mar at a hunting encampment among the hills, all of which he saw and describes.

THE LAIRD OF LOGAN: Being Anecdotes and Tales illustrative of the wit and humour of Scotland. Post 8vo. Price 3s. 6d.

A complete, very handsome, and the only large type edition of the famous "Laird of Logan." This work was compiled by three very distinguished literary Scotchmen, namely, John Donald Carrick, William Motherwell, and Andrew Henderson, all of them authors of works relating to Scotland. This is the only unadulterated edition, and is here given to the public as it came direct from the hands of the editors.

THE WILD SPORTS AND NATURAL HISTORY OF THE SCOTTISH HIGHLANDS. By CHARLES ST. JOHN. Post 8vo. Popular Edition. Price 4s. 6d.

One of the most interesting works published on Scottish field sports. Its pages are devoted to the author's experience in deer-stalking, otter-hunting, salmon-fishing, grouse-shooting, as well as with all the representatives of animal life to be found in the Highlands, such as the eagle, wild cat, black game, owl, hawk, wild duck, wild geese, wild swan, seal, fox, etc., etc.

THE HISTORICAL TALES AND LEGENDS OF AYRSHIRE. By WILLIAM ROBERTSON. Post 8vo. Price 5s.

The County of Ayr is especially rich in story and tradition. In the centuries when feudal strife was rampant, the great county families maintained ceaseless activity in their warrings with one another. And the result of their plots, raids, enmities, machinations, and contests are to be seen in the existing social life in Ayrshire. The volume presents a series of historical tales and legends illustrative of the feudal and early social history of the shire. In every instance the author deals with facts of an intensely interesting nature.

EARLY SCOTTISH METRICAL TALES. Edited by DAVID LAING, LL.D. Post 8vo. Price 6s.

Extremely interesting early metrical tales in the original spelling, with valuable notes by the distinguished antiquary who collected the tales and issued the first edition of the book. The tales are thirteen in number, and comprise such as "The History of Sir Gray Steill," "The Tales of the Priests of Peblis," "The History of a Lord and his Three Sons," etc., etc.

BRITISH TRADE; or, CERTAIN CONDITIONS OF OUR NATIONAL PROSPERITY. By PROFESSOR JOHN KIRK. Crown 8vo. Price 4s. 6d

A companion volume to "Social Politics," by the same author, and now out of print. Regarding the latter volume, Ruskin says: "I had no notion myself, till the other day, what the facts were in this matter. Get if you can, Professor Kirk's 'Social Politics;' and read for a beginning his 21st Chapter on Land and Liquor, and then as you have leisure all the book carefully."—FORS CLAVIGERA, March, 1873.

SPORTING ANECDOTES. Being Anecdotal Annals, Descriptions, and Incidents relating to Sport and Gambling. Edited by "ELLANGOWAN." Post 8vo. Price 5s.

An entirely new and most interesting collection of anecdotes, relating to all sections of sporting life and character, such as horse-racing, boxing, golfing, jockeys, cover-shooting, gambling, betting, cock-fighting, pedestrianism, flat-racing, coursing, fox-hunting, angling, card-playing, billiards, etc., etc.

THE LIFE OF JOHN KNOX. By THOMAS M'CRIE, D.D. Demy 8vo. Stiff Paper Boards. Price 1s. 6d.

A cheap edition of this important work. The life of Knox comprises a history of Scotland at one of the most critical periods, namely that of the Reformation.

HUMOROUS READINGS FOR HOME AND HALL. Edited by CHARLES B. NEVILLE. FIRST SERIES. Price 1s.

Humorous and amusing Readings for large or small audiences, and for the fireside. This series (the first) contains thirteen pieces, such as "Old Dick Fogrum Getting Settled in Life," "The Bachelor Feeling his Way," "Mr. Gingerly's Delicate Attentions," etc., etc.

HUMOROUS READINGS FOR HOME AND HALL. Edited by CHARLES B. NEVILLE. SECOND SERIES. Price 1s.

A sequel to the above. The second series contains fourteen readings, such as "Dick Doleful's Disinterested Motives," "Ferney Fidget, Esq., in London Lodgings," "A Philosopher Getting Married," etc., etc.

HUMOROUS READINGS FOR HOME AND HALL. Edited by CHARLES B. NEVILLE. THIRD SERIES. Price 1s.

The concluding series of Mr. Neville's readings. This issue contains fourteen pieces, all of a highly humorous nature, such as "Dandy Nat's Hopes and Fears," "How Billy Muggins was brought to Terms," "Cousin Jones's Valuable Legacy," etc., etc.

HUMOROUS READINGS FOR HOME AND HALL. Edited by CHARLES B. NEVILLE. Post 8vo. Price 3s. 6d.

The three aforementioned series bound in one thick handsome volume, cloth gilt.

THE SCOTTISH BOOK OF FAMILY AND PRIVATE DEVOTION. By TWENTY SCOTTISH CLERGYMEN. Crown 8vo. Price 5s.

Morning and evening prayers for family and private use for quarter-a-year. Week day and sunday. Also prayers for the sick, forms of invocation of the Divine blessing at table, etc.

ANGLING REMINISCENCES OF THE RIVERS AND LOCHS OF SCOTLAND. By THOMAS TOD STODDART. Post 8vo. Price 3s. 6d.

If not the most useful, this is at least the most interesting of all Stoddart's angling works, of which there are three in number. The above is not to be confounded with "The Scottish Angler" on the one hand, or "The Angler's Companion" on the other, though from the same pen. The present work is colloquial throughout, and teeming with the richest humour from beginning to end.

4

r4 NEW BOOKS

HUMOROUS AND AMUSING SCOTCH READINGS.
For the Platform, the Social Circle, and the Fireside.
By ALEXANDER G. MURDOCH. First Series. Paper Covers. Price 1s.

Humorous and amusing Scotch readings, fifteen in number, and illustrative of the social life and character of the Scottish people, than which the author believes no more interesting subject can be found. Among other readings may be mentioned, "Mrs. Macfarlane's Rabbit Dinner," "The Washin'-Hoose Key," "Jock Broon's Patent Umbrella," "Willie Weedrap's Domestic Astronomy," etc., etc.

HUMOROUS AND AMUSING SCOTCH READINGS. For the Platform, the Social Circle, and the Fireside. By ALEXANDER G. MURDOCH. SECOND SERIES. Paper Cover. Price 1s.

A sequel to the foregoing, contains fourteen readings, comprising "Johnny Gowdy's Funny Ploy," "Jock Turnip's Mither in-Law," "Lodgings in Arran," "Robin Rigg and the Minister," etc., etc.

HUMOROUS AND AMUSING SCOTCH READINGS. For the Platform, the Social Circle, and the Fireside. By ALEXANDER G. MURDOCH. THIRD SERIES. Paper Covers. Price 1s

The third and concluding series of Mr. Murdoch's popular and highly amusing Scotch readings. This issue contains "Jean Tamson's Love Hopes and Fears," "The Amateur Phrenologist," "Peter Paterson the Poet," "Coming Home Fou'," etc., etc.

HUMOROUS AND AMUSING SCOTCH READINGS. For the Platform, the Social Circle, and the Fireside. By ALEXANDER G. MURDOCH. Thick Post 8vo. Cloth. Price 3s. 6d.

The three aforementioned series, bound in one thick handsome volume, cloth gilt.

THE COURT OF SESSION GARLAND. Edited by JAMES MAIDMENT, Advocate. New edition, including all the Supplements. Demy 8vo. Price 7s. 6d.

A collection of most interesting anecdotes and facetiae connected with the Court of Session. Even to those not initiated in the mysteries of legal procedure, much of the volume will be found highly attractive, for no genuine votary of Momus can be insensible to the fun of the Justiciary Opera, as illustrated by the drollery of the "Diamond Beetle Case," and many others of an amusing nature, such as "The Poor Client's Complaint," "The Parody on Hellvellyn," "The King's Speech," "Lord Bannatyne's Lion," "The Beauties of Overgrogy," etc., etc.

ST. KILDA AND THE ST. KILDIANS. By ROBERT CONNELL. Crown 8vo. Price 2s. 6d.

"*A capital book. It contains everything worth knowing about the famous islet and its people.*"—THE BAILIE.

"*Interesting and amusing. It includes a lively description of the daily life of the inhabitants, the native industries of fishing, bird catching, and the rearing of sickly sheep and cattle, and gives a vivid picture of the Sabbatarian despotism of the Free Church minister who rules the small population.*"—SATURDAY REVIEW.

THE PRAISE OF FOLLY. By ERASMUS. With Numerous Illustrations by Holbein. Post 8vo. Price 4s. 6d.

An English translation of the "Encomium Moriae" which has always held a foremost place among the more popular of the writings of the great scholar. This work is probably the most satirical production of any age. It is intensely humorous throughout, and is entirely unique in character. This edition also contains Holbein's illustrations, attaching to which there is very considerable interest.

ANECDOTES OF FISH AND FISHING. By THOMAS BOOSEY. Post 8vo. Price 3s. 6d.

An interesting collection of anecdotes and incidents connected with fish and fishing, arranged and classified into sections. It deals with all varieties of British fish, their habits, different modes of catching them, interesting incidents in connection with their capture, and an infinite amount of angling gossip relating to each. Considerable space is also devoted to the subject of fishing as practised in different parts of the world.

TALES OF A SCOTTISH PARISH. By JACOB RUDDIMAN, M.A. Post 8vo. Paper Covers. Price 1s.

The deceased author was a person of singular beauty and originality of mind, and may well be ranked alongside of Wilson, Hogg, Bethune, Pollok, and other such standard writers of Scottish tales. The tales are nineteen in all, and comprise such as "The Sexton," "The Unfortunate Farmer," "The Lonely Widow," "The Foreboding," etc., etc.

SCOTTISH LEGENDS. By ANDREW GLASS. Post 8vo. Paper Covers. Price 1s.

Four legends, relating chiefly to the west and south of Scotland, entitled, "A Legend of Rothesay Castle," "The Laird of Auchinleck's Gift," "The Cruives of Cree," "The Grey Stones of Garlaffin."

A BANQUET OF JESTS AND MERRY TALES.
By ARCHIE ARMSTRONG, Court Jester to King James I. and King Charles I., 1611-1637.

An extremely amusing work, reprinted in the original quaint spelling of the period. In addition to the immense fund of amusement to be found in its pages, the work is highly valuable as throwing much light on the social customs and ideas of the period. The author experienced life in connection with all ranks and sections of society, from his own peasant home in the north, to that of the Court of his Sovereign.

AMUSING IRISH TALES. By WILLIAM CARLETON.
Post 8vo.　Price 2s. 6d.

A collection of amusing and humorous tales descriptive of Irish life and character. The distinguished author has been designated the Sir Walter Scott of Ireland. The tales are fifteen in number, such as " The Country Dancing Master," " The Irish Match-Maker," " The Irish Smuggler," " The Irish Senachie," " The Country Fiddler," etc., etc. All of them are overflowing with the richest wit and humour.

THE WHOLE FAMILIAR COLLOQUIES OF ERASMUS. Translated by NATHAN BAILEY.
Demy 8vo.　Price 4s. 6d.

A complete and inexpensive edition of the great book of amusement of the sixteenth century. Probably no other work so truly and intensely depicts the life and notions of our forefathers 350 years ago, as does this inimical production of the great Erasmus.

There are 62 dialogues in all, and an immense variety of subjects are dealt with, such as " Benefice-Hunting," " The Soldier and the Carthusian," " The Franciscans," " The Apparition," " The Beggar's Dialogue," " The Religious Pilgrimage," " The Sermon," " The Parliament of Women," etc., etc. The whole work is richly characteristic, and is full of the richest humour and satire.

AMUSING PROSE CHAP BOOKS, CHIEFLY OF LAST CENTURY. Edited by ROBERT HAYS CUNNINGHAM. Post 8vo.　Price 4s. 6d.

A collection of interesting prose chap books of former times, forming a good representative of the people's earliest popular literature, such as " The Comical History of the King and the Cobbler," " The Merry Tales of the Wise Men of Gotham," " The Merry Conceits of Tom Long, the Carrier," " The Pleasant History of Poor Robin, the Merry Saddler of Walden," etc., etc.

THE DANCE OF DEATH: Illustrated in Forty-Eight Plates. By JOHN HOLBEIN. Demy 8vo. Price 5s.

A handsome and inexpensive edition of the great Holbein's most popular production. It contains the whole forty-eight plates, with letterpress description of each plate, the plate and the description in each case being on separate pages, facing each other. The first edition was issued in 1530, and since then innumerable impressions have been issued, but mostly in an expensive form, and unattainable by the general public.

THE LITERARY HISTORY OF GLASGOW. By W. J. DUNCAN. Quarto. Price 12s. 6d. net. *Printed for Subscribers and Private Circulation.*

This volume forms one of the volumes issued by the Maitland Club, and was originally published in 1831. This edition is a verbatim et literatim reprint, and is limited to 350 copies, with an appendix additional containing extra matter of considerable importance, not in the original work.

The book is chiefly devoted to giving an account of the greatest of Scottish printers, namely, the Foulises, and furnishes a list of the books they printed, as likewise of the sculptures and paintings which they so largely produced.

GOLFIANA MISCELLANEA. Being a Collection of Interesting Monographs on the Royal and Ancient Game of Golf. Edited by JAMES LINDSAY STEWART. Post 8vo. Price 4s. 6d.

A collection of interesting productions, prose and verse, on or relating to, the game of golf, by various authors both old and recent. Nothing has been allowed into the collection except works of merit and real interest. Many of the works are now extremely scarce and, in a separate form, command very high prices. It contains twenty-three separate productions of a great variety of character—historical, descriptive, practical, poetical, humorous, biographical, etc.

THE BARDS OF THE BIBLE. By GEORGE GILFILLAN. Seventh Edition. Post 8vo. Price 5s.

The most popular of the writings of the late Rev. Dr. Gilfillan. The author, in his preface, states that the object of the book was chiefly a prose poem or hymn in honour of the poetry and the poets of the Bible. It deals with the poetical side of the inspired word, and takes up the separate portions in chronological order.

ONE HUNDRED ROMANCES OF REAL LIFE. By
  LEIGH HUNT. Post 8vo. Price 3s. 6d.

*A handsome edition of Leigh Hunt's famous collection of
romances of real life, now scarce in a complete form. The
present issue is complete, containing as it does the entire hundred
as issued by the author. All being incidents from real life, the
interest attaching to the volume is not of an ordinary character.
The romances relate to all grades of society, and are entirely
various in circumstance, each one being separate and distinct in
itself.*

*UNIQUE TRADITIONS CHIEFLY OF THE WEST
  AND SOUTH OF SCOTLAND.* By JOHN GORDON
  BARBOUR. Post 8vo. Price 4s. 6d.

*A collection of interesting local and popular traditions
gathered orally by the author in his wanderings over the
West and South of Scotland. The author narrates in this
volume, thirty-five separate incidental traditions in narrative
form, connected with places or individuals, all of a nature to
interest the general Scottish reader, such as " The Red Comyn's
Castle," " The Coves of Barholm," " The Rafters of Kirk
Alloway," " Cumstone Castle," " The Origin of Loch Catrine,"
etc., etc.*

*MODERN ANECDOTES: A Treasury of Wise and
  Witty Sayings of the last Hundred Years.* Edited,
  with Notes, by W. DAVENPORT ADAMS. Crown 8vo.
  Price 3s. 6d.

*The Anecdotes are all authenticated and are classed into
Sections—I. Men of Society. II. Lawyers and the Law. III.
Men of Letters. IV. Plays and Players. V. Statesmen and
Politicians. VI. The Church and Clergy. VII. People in
General.*

*In compiling a work like this, Mr. Adams has steadily kept
in view the necessity of ministering to the requirements of those
who will not read anecdotes unless they have reason to know
that they are really good. On this principle the entire editorial
work has been executed. The book is also a particularly
handsome one as regards printing, paper, and binding.*

*THE LITURGY OF JOHN KNOX: As received by
  the Church of Scotland in* 1564. Crown 8vo. Price 5s.

*A beautifully printed edition of the Book of Common Order,
more popularly known as the Liturgy of John Knox. This is
the only modern edition in which the original quaint spelling is
retained. In this and other respects the old style is strictly
reproduced, so that the work remains exactly as used by our
forefathers three hundred years ago.*

THE GABERLUNZIE'S WALLET. By JAMES
    BALLANTINE. Third edition. Cr. 8vo. Price 2s. 6d.

*A most interesting historical tale of the period of the Pre-
tenders, and containing a very large number of favourite songs
and ballads, illustrative of the tastes and life of the people at
that time. Also containing numerous facetious illustrations by
Alexander A. Ritchie.*

THE WOLFE OF BADENOCH. A Historical Romance
    of the Fourteenth Century. By SIR THOMAS DICK
    LAUDER. Complete unabridged edition. Thick Crown
    8vo. Price 6s.

*This most interesting romance has been frequently described as
equal in interest to any of Sir Walter Scott's historical tales. This
is a complete unabridged edition, and is uniform with "Highland
Legends" and "Tales of the Highlands," by the same author. As
several abridged editions of the work have been published, especial
attention is drawn to the fact that the above edition is complete.*

THE LIVES OF THE PLAYERS. By JOHN GALT, Esq.
    Post 8vo. Price 5s.

*Interesting accounts of the lives of distinguished actors, such as
Betterton, Cibber, Farquhar, Garrick, Foote, Macklin, Murphy,
Kemble, Siddons, &c., &c. After the style of Johnson's "Lives of
the Poets."*

KAY'S EDINBURGH PORTRAITS. A Series of Anec-
    dotal Biographies, chiefly of Scotchmen. Mostly written
    by JAMES PATERSON. And edited by JAMES MAIDMENT,
    Esq. Popular Edition. 2 Vols., Post 8vo. Price 12s.

*A popular edition of this famous work, which, from its exceedingly
high price, has hitherto been out of the reach of the general public.
This edition contains all the reading matter that is of general interest;
it also contains eighty illustrations.*

THE RELIGIOUS ANECDOTES OF SCOTLAND.
    Edited by WILLIAM ADAMSON, D.D. Thick Post 8vo.
    Price 5s.

*A voluminous collection of purely religious anecdotes relating to
Scotland and Scotchmen, and illustrative of the more serious side of
the life of the people. The anecdotes are chiefly in connection with
distinguished Scottish clergymen and laymen, such as Rutherford,
Macleod, Guthrie, Shirra, Leighton, the Erskines, Knox, Beattie,
M'Crie, Eadie, Brown, Irving, Chalmers, Lawson, Milne, M'Cheyne,
&c., &c. The anecdotes are serious and religious purely, and not
at all of the ordinary witty description.*

DAYS OF DEER STALKING in the Scottish High lands, including an account of the Nature and Habits of the Red Deer, a description of the Scottish Forests, and Historical Notes on the earlier Field Sports of Scotland. With Highland Legends, Superstitions, Folk-Lore, and Tales of Poachers and Freebooters. By WILLIAM SCROPE. Illustrated by Sir Edwin and Charles Landseer. Demy 8vo. Price 12s. 6d.

" *The best book of sporting adventures with which we are acquainted.*"—ATHENÆUM.

" *Of this noble diversion we owe the first satisfactory description to the pen of an English gentleman of high birth and extensive fortune, whose many amiable and elegant personal qualities have been commemorated in the diary of Sir Walter Scott.*"— LONDON QUARTERLY REVIEW.

DAYS AND NIGHTS OF SALMON FISHING in the River Tweed. By WILLIAM SCROPE. Illustrated by Sir David Wilkie, Sir Edwin Landseer, Charles Landseer, William Simson, and Edward Cooke. Demy 8vo. Price 12s. 6d.

" *Mr. Scrope's book has done for salmon fishing what its predecessor performed for deer stalking.*"—LONDON QUARTERLY REVIEW.

" *Mr. Scrope conveys to us in an agreeable and lively manner the results of his more than twenty years' experience in our great Border river. . . . The work is enlivened by the narration of numerous angling adventures, which bring out with force and spirit the essential character of the sport in question. . . . Mr. Scrope is a skilful author as well as an experienced angler. It does not fall to the lot of all men to handle with equal dexterity, the brush, the pen, and the rod, to say nothing of the rifle, still less of the leister under cloud of night.*"—BLACKWOOD'S MAGAZINE.

THE FIELD SPORTS OF THE NORTH OF EUROPE. A Narrative of Angling, Hunting, and Shooting in Sweden and Norway. By CAPTAIN L. LLOYD. New edition. Enlarged and revised. Demy 8vo. Price 9s.

" *The chase seems for years to have been his ruling passion, and to have made him a perfect model of perpetual motion. We admire Mr. Lloyd. He is a sportsman far above the common run.*"—BLACKWOOD'S MAGAZINE.

" *This is a very entertaining work and written, moreover, in an agreeable and modest spirit. We strongly recommend it as containing much instruction and more amusement.*—ATHENÆUM.

PUBLIC AND PRIVATE LIBRARIES OF GLAS-GOW. A Bibliographical Study. By THOMAS MASON. Demy 8vo. Price 12s. 6d. net.

A strictly Bibliographical work dealing with the subject of rare and interesting works, and in that respect describing three of the public and thirteen of the private libraries of Glasgow. All of especial interest.

THE LIFE OF SIR WILLIAM WALLACE. BY JOHN D. CARRICK. Fourth and cheaper edition. Royal 8vo. Price 2s. 6d.

The best life of the great Scottish hero. Contains much valuable and interesting matter regarding the history of that historically important period.

THE HISTORY OF THE PROVINCE OF MORAY. By LACHLAN SHAW. New and Enlarged Edition, 3 Vols., Demy 8vo. Price 30s.

The Standard History of the old geographical division termed the Province of Moray, comprising the Counties of Elgin and Nairn, the greater part of the County of Inverness, and a portion of the County of Banff. Cosmo Innes pronounced this to be the best local history of any part of Scotland.

HIGHLAND LEGENDS. By SIR THOMAS DICK LAUDER. Crown 8vo. Price 6s.

Historical Legends descriptive of Clan and Highland Life and Incident in former times.

TALES OF THE HIGHLANDS. By SIR THOMAS DICK LAUDER. Crown 8vo. Price 6s.

Uniform with and similar in character to the preceding, though entirely different tales. The two are companion volumes.

AN ACCOUNT OF THE GREAT MORAY FLOODS IN 1829. By SIR THOMAS DICK LAUDER. Demy 8vo., with 64 Plates and Portrait. Fourth Edition. Price 8s. 6d.

A most interesting work, containing numerous etchings by the Author. In addition to the main feature of the book, it contains much historical and legendary matter relating to the districts through which the River Spey runs.

OLD SCOTTISH CUSTOMS: Local and General. By E. J. GUTHRIE. Crown 8vo. Price 3s. 6d.

Gives an interesting account of old local and general Scottish customs, now rapidly being lost sight of.

A HISTORICAL ACCOUNT OF THE BELIEF IN WITCHCRAFT IN SCOTLAND. By CHARLES KIRKPATRICK SHARPE. Crown 8vo. Price 4s. 6d.

Gives a chronological account of Witchcraft incidents in Scotland from the earliest period, in a racy, attractive style. And likewise contains an interesting Bibliography of Scottish books on Witchcraft.

"Sharpe was well qualified to gossip about these topics."—SATURDAY REVIEW.

"Mr. Sharpe has arranged all the striking and important phenomena associated with the belief in Apparitions and Witchcraft. An extensive appendix, with a list of books on Witchcraft in Scotland, and a useful index, render this edition of Mr. Sharpe's work all the more valuable."—GLASGOW HERALD.

TALES OF THE SCOTTISH PEASANTRY. By ALEXANDER and JOHN BETHUNE. With Biography of the Authors by JOHN INGRAM, F.S.A.Scot. Post 8vo. Price 3s. 6d.

"It is the perfect propriety of taste, no less than the thorough intimacy with the subjects he treats of, that gives Mr. Bethune's book a great charm in our eyes."—ATHENÆUM.

"The pictures of rural life and character appear to us remarkably true, as well as pleasing."—CHAMBERS'S JOURNAL.

The Tales are quite out of the ordinary routine of such literature, and are universally held in peculiarly high esteem. The following may be given as a specimen of the Contents:—" The Deformed," "The Fate of the Fairest," "The Stranger," "The Drunkard," "The Illegitimate," "The Cousins," &c., &c.

A JOURNEY TO THE WESTERN ISLANDS OF SCOTLAND IN 1773. By SAMUEL JOHNSON, LL.D. Crown 8vo. Price 3s.

Written by Johnson himself, and not to be confounded with Boswell's account of the same tour. Johnson said that some of his best writing is in this work.

THE HISTORY OF BURKE AND HARE AND OF THE RESURRECTIONIST TIMES. A Fragment from the Criminal Annals of Scotland. By GEORGE MAC GREGOR, F.S.A.Scot. With Seven Illustrations, Demy 8vo. Price 7s. 6d.

" *Mr. MacGregor has produced a book which is eminently readable.*"—JOURNAL OF JURISPRUDENCE.

" *The book contains a great deal of curious information.*"— SCOTSMAN.

" *He who takes up this book of an evening must be prepared to sup full of horrors, yet the banquet is served with much of literary grace, and garnished with a deftness and taste which render it palatable to a degree.*"—GLASGOW HERALD.

THE HISTORY OF GLASGOW: From the Earliest Period to the Present Time. By GEORGE MAC GRE-GOR, F.S.A.Scot. Containing 36 Illustrations. Demy 8vo. Price 12s. 6d.

An entirely new as well as the fullest and most complete history of this prosperous city. In addition it is the first written in chronological order. Comprising a large handsome volume in Sixty Chapters, and extensive Appendix and Index, and illustrated throughout with many interesting engravings and drawings.

THE COLLECTED WRITINGS OF DOUGAL GRAHAM, "Skellat," Bellman of Glasgow. Edited with Notes, together with a Biographical and Biblio-graphical Introduction, and a Sketch of the Chap Literature of Scotland, by GEORGE MAC GREGOR, F.S.A.Scot. Impression limited to 250 copies. 2 Vols., Demy 8vo. Price 21s.

With very trifling exceptions Graham was the only writer of purely Scottish chap-books of a secular description, almost all the others circulated being reprints of English productions. His writings are exceedingly facetious and highly illustrative of the social life of the period.

SCOTTISH PROVERBS. By ANDREW HENDERSON. Crown 8vo. Cheaper edition. Price 2s. 6d.

A cheap edition of a book that has long held a high place in Scottish Literature.

THE BOOK OF SCOTTISH ANECDOTE: Humorous, Social, Legendary, and Historical. Edited by ALEXANDER HISLOP. Crown 8vo., pp. 768. Cheaper edition. Price 5s.

The most comprehensive collection of Scottish Anecdotes, containing about 3,000 in number.

THE BOOK OF SCOTTISH STORY: Historical, Traditional, Legendary, Imaginative, and Humorous. Crown 8vo., pp. 768. Cheaper edition. Price 5s.

A most interesting and varied collection by Leading Scottish Authors.

THE BOOK OF SCOTTISH POEMS: Ancient and Modern. Edited by J. Ross. Crown 8vo., pp. 768. Cheaper edition. Price 5s.

Comprising a History of Scottish Poetry and Poets from the earliest times. With lives of the Poets and Selections from their Writings.

*** These three works are uniform.

A DESCRIPTION OF THE WESTERN ISLES OF SCOTLAND, CALLED HYBRIDES. With the Genealogies of the Chief Clans of the Isles. By SIR DONALD MONRO, High Dean of the Isles, who travelled through most of them in the year 1549. Impression limited to 250 copies. Demy 8vo. Price 5s.

This is the earliest written description of the Western Islands, and is exceedingly quaint and interesting. In this edition all the old curious spellings are strictly retained.

A DESCRIPTION OF THE WESTERN ISLANDS OF SCOTLAND CIRCA 1695. By MARTIN MARTIN. Impression limited to 250 copies. Demy 8vo. Price 12s. 6d.

With the exception of Dean Monro's smaller work 150 years previous, it is the earliest description of the Western Islands we have, and is the only lengthy work on the subject before the era of modern innovations. Martin very interestingly describes the people and their ways as he found them about 200 years ago.

THE SCOTTISH POETS, RECENT AND LIVING.
By ALEXANDER G. MURDOCH. With Portraits, Post
8vo. Price 6s.

*A most interesting resumé of Scottish Poetry in recent times.
Contains a biographical sketch, choice pieces, and portraits of
the recent and living Scottish Poets.*

THE HUMOROUS CHAP-BOOKS OF SCOTLAND.
By JOHN FRASER. 2 Vols., Thin Crown 8vo (all
published). Price 5s.

*An interesting and racy description of the chap-book literature
of Scotland, and biographical sketches of the writers.*

THE HISTORY OF STIRLINGSHIRE. By WILLIAM
NIMMO. 2 Vols., Demy 8vo. 3rd Edition. Price 25s.

*A new edition of this standard county history, handsomely
printed, and with detailed map giving the parish boundaries
and other matters of interest.*

*This county has been termed the battlefield of Scotland, and
in addition to the many and important military engagements
that have taken place in this district, of all which a full account
is given,—this part of Scotland is of especial moment in many
other notable respects,—among which particular reference may
be made to the Roman Wall, the greater part of this most
interesting object being situated within the boundaries of the
county.*

---

*A POPULAR SKETCH OF THE HISTORY OF
GLASGOW:* From the Earliest Period to the Present
Time. By ANDREW WALLACE. Crown 8vo. Price 3s. 6d.

*The only attempt to write a History of Glasgow suitable for
popular use.*

---

*THE HISTORY OF THE WESTERN HIGHLANDS
AND ISLES OF SCOTLAND,* from A.D. 1493 to
A.D. 1625. With a brief introductory sketch from
A.D. 80 to A.D. 1493. By DONALD GREGORY. Demy
8vo. Price 12s. 6d.

*Incomparably the best history of the Scottish Highlands, and
written purely from original investigation. Also contains particularly full and lengthened Contents and Index, respectively at
beginning and end of the volume.*

THE HISTORY OF AYRSHIRE. By JAMES PATERSON. 5 Vols., Crown 8vo. Price 28s. net.

The most recent and the fullest history of this exceedingly interesting county. The work is particularly rich in the department of Family History.

MARTYRLAND: a Historical Tale of the Covenanters. By the Rev. ROBERT SIMPSON, D.D. Crown 8vo. Cheaper Edition. Price 2s. 6d.

A tale illustrative of the history of the Covenanters in the South of Scotland.

TALES OF THE COVENANTERS. By E. J. GUTHRIE. Crown 8vo. Cheaper Edition. Price 2s. 6d.

A number of tales illustrative of leading incidents and characters connected with the Covenanters.

PERSONAL AND FAMILY NAMES. A Popular Monograph on the Origin and History of the Nomenclature of the Present and Former Times. By HARRY ALFRED LONG. Demy 8vo. Price 5s.

Interesting investigations as to the origin, history, and meaning of about 9,000 personal and family names.

THE SCOTTISH GALLOVIDIAN ENCYCLOPÆDIA of the Original, Antiquated, and Natural Curiosities of the South of Scotland. By JOHN MACTAGGART. Demy 8vo. Price raised to 25s. Impression limited to 250 copies.

Contains a large amount of extremely interesting and curious matter relating to the South of Scotland.

THE COMPLETE TALES OF THE ETTRICK SHEPHERD (JAMES HOGG). 2 vols., Demy 8vo.

An entirely new and complete edition of the tales of this popular Scottish writer.

GLASGOW: THOMAS D. MORISON.
LONDON: HAMILTON, ADAMS & CO.

www.ingramcontent.com/pod-product-compliance
Lightning Source LLC
Chambersburg PA
CBHW020941030726

47496CB00005B/1298